SWELL

Ioanna Karystiani

SWELL

Translated from the Modern Greek
by Konstantine Matsoukas

Europa
editions

Europa Editions
116 East 16th Street
New York, N.Y. 10003
www.europaeditions.com
info@europaeditions.com

Copyright © 2006 by Ioanna Karystiani, Kastaniotis Editions S.A., Athens
First publication 2010 by Europa Editions

Translation by Konstantine Matsoukas
Original title: Σουελ
Translation copyright © 2010 by Europa Editions

Library of Congress Cataloging in Publication Data is available
ISBN 978-1-933372-98-3

Karystiani, Ioanna
Swell

Book design by Emanuele Ragnisco
www.mekkanografici.com

Cover photograph © Matthias Kulka/Zefa/Corbis

Prepress by Plan.ed – Rome

Printed in Canada

SWELL

At five in the morning, with Port Pirie's lights strewn on the hillside three miles back, the white cat, as always in the last four years, balanced dancingly along the rail, pink paws pointed, tail vibrating like a rope walker's pole in the air, went slowly around the ship, all eight hundred and ninety feet of it, stopped on the stern and bowed before the two men standing with legs spread wide and hands clasped behind their backs.

–Maritsa, intoned the second mate Cleanthis Birbilis.

Before this here Maritsa, the same choreography was performed for three years by Maritsa his mom, before the mom there was grandpa Maritsa, before that, great grandma Maritsa and still further back was the original and unsurpassable master, the elegant tom with the feminine élan and the cha-cha dance steps, himself a member of the clan and a Maritsa to boot. Cats, the lot of them, that had lived onboard.

–The Spaniards in Cuba court-martialed a native cat because she savaged a parrot of theirs, and sent her off to the firing squad, the forty-odd-year-old second mate told Maritsa, the cat's daily performance regularly bringing up historic trivia from their inexhaustible fund of feline lore.

The cucumbers were all we had time to enjoy, the garden still had a long time to go, rejoined just after daybreak by Dimitris Avgoustis, the captain, Mitsos to his crew, Mimis to his wife Flora, of average height, freshly laundered, with white shoulder-length hair and a silver beard waving down to the chest, both proclaiming his seventy five years and his passion for shampoo and cologne.

Cucumbers and garden, borrowed words, his father's, referring to the small vegetable garden of Atzanos, at the beginning of September 1922.

Triantafilos Avgoustis, then a fisherman in his thirties, had tied his three-year-old daughter Pelagia with a rope to the waist of his wife, who held in her arms little Dimitrakis, barely forty days old, lifted the family up onto the boss's thirty foot long, red and blue *Garifalos*, helped the families of neighbors also squeeze in any old way and in successive trips, along with the men from another three fishing boats and dinghies, picked up the entire village of Atzanos and set it down across the way. And there they sat, afterwards, staring at the plumes of smoke. Smyrna et cetera, all too familiar. Next morning the *Garifalos* was nowhere to be seen, along with Triantafilos. Nor the morning after that.

The curly haired fisherman with the brown eyes that, when brimming with tears, gave out an aroma like fresh-made coffee, was fit to bust for having forgotten his cat on Asia Minor. One month before the evacuation, Maritsa, pregnant, with a viper wrapped twice around her belly crawled half-dead onto the pier and stood across from the *Garifalos*, mewling pathetically.

Two men mending their trammels and sardine nets, broke apart a wooden fish crate, split the wooden planks between them and pounded the snake till they turned its head to pulp.

Triantafilos Avgoustis went back across, alone, to look for Maritsa and her three kittens.

Seven days later, by which time his wife was mourning him, and his boss was mourning both his workman and his boat, dozens of Atzanotians stood silent and dark purple, like dusk upon the rocky shores of Lesbos, watching the return of their twin pride and joy, *Garifalos* and Triantafilos and listening to a

cacophony of mewling. The boat sailed in hugging the shore-
line, carrying the last installment of migrants, the twenty-seven
cats of Atzanos, as many as the fisherman was able to lure away
during his cautious escapade to the ghost town.

He distributed them to their owners, the Yiatzoglous got
back Chanoum, Yiovanakis got his Kiki, the Chirimperis their
Athena, Eleni her Eleni and Sotiris his Sotiris, but none of
them got a word, not then and not ever, from the daredevil Triantafilos about what he saw back home. Ask the cat for its tale,
he would answer and move off.

As of 1922, he never again raised his gaze to the starry sky.
He was afflicted with a nervous listlessness and he turned
instead to cats, fattening them up with plenty of fish bones and
tasty morsels, even letting the inaugural and all the subsequent
Maritsas nestle in the gill nets and the trammels and, taking
advantage of his soft spot, tear them up with their claws and
extravagant prancing.

The eyes, at all events, of Triantafilos Avgoustis, that brimmed
with increasing frequency, still remained fragrant and set his
wife Eleftheria on fire, the free syrupy treats that flowed between the two of them, the only pleasure left during those
deprived years when people kept leaving, kept suffering losses.

Yet, another child didn't come to be, the finely-spun Mersina,
lost at age seven to pneumonia leaving the couple with just the
only son, the spoiled, blue-eyed boy of the Settlement, a tiddler
fish bobbing up and down in the endless fields of yellow
daisies. In Greece now. The waves of flight having deposited
people here there and everywhere, their lot was the poverty of
Elefsina.

Astern the carrier ship ATHOS III, that son, now a captain,
caressing Maritsa of the half-eaten ears, recalled the story without repeating it and the second mate remembered it without the
retelling, familiar as it all was, the phrase about the cucumbers
bringing to mind all the rest, which summed up the tragedy.

–Good morning.

Stamatis Vekrelis, the plump steward, brought the tray, gave the cat the bowl of milk, offered the customary spoonful of tequila for the rheumatism and the double coffee, no sugar, to Avgoustis, then the frappe latte to the other and, after the first few sips, left them again to themselves, strolling in fine spirits down memory lane, like a remarried couple, towards January 1997 and *The Woman in Red*.

By mistake, the Wallport pack contained the same movies as the previous six months, all of them old. *Jay and Silent Bob Strike Back*, *Naked Gun*, *Highway Thunder,* an all-American cornucopia of punching, kicking, blowing up and away in every conceivable size and shape, especially the nude scenes in *The Woman*, the only ones that the crew of twenty hadn't had enough of through all the festivities of the Christmas period and which some might well pore over again in the coming days as they crunched up the sea miles, scuttling through shoreless seas and then past Java, Sumatra and Singapore in that order to arrive, yet again, at good old immovable Thailand, unload their cargo at Bangkok and pick up another.

High midsummer, January 3. The sea was thirsty. A sudden, two-minute storm smashed like panes of glass on the deck of ATHOS III and straight afterwards, Avgoustis and Birbilis became eye witnesses to a lethal sunrise that burst like a bomb and set the place on fire. In those latitudes, that is how the day got started.

Silent, with the sea brine in his nostrils, with his sea blue eyes reflecting the steely light and his eyelashes quivering and echoing the swell after the rain, Avgoustis passed the empty cup to the second mate, passed the aluminum comb through his St. Nicholas beard and mane and, with Maritsa in tow, headed for the chartroom to check on their course.

–Right on time. Midshipman Miltos Lavdas held out to him the cell phone. The Company wants a word with you.

Avgoustis took out a cigarette and asked for a light, Lavdas offered him one, placed the phone in his free hand and left him to his call.

–Good morning, this is Chadzimanolis. What's the time over there? Six in the morning? Seven?

Six o'clock, Friday, January 3, the beginning of a new year and new plans on the part of Shipping Maritime Company.

The Company's number one was recalling Avgoustis back to Greece. This wasn't the first time but, now, there was a bait as well. At the beginning of this February, the Association of Greek Shipowners was scheduling a grand reception in his honor, with a gold plated plaque and a bonus of 3,000,000 drachmas for being the longest serving captain on the merchant marine, fifty-eight years at sea.

–They can eat shit, his reply.

–Government officials will be there in your honor, and television channels.

–There's plenty of shit to go around.

–Your family hasn't seen you in years.

–You be in charge of your own.

Pissed off, Chadzimanolis, putting on his boss's voice nurtured by power and money, stated dryly and coldly that, this time, the game was over, they have already arranged for a replacement and he'll be there waiting at the next port of call.

–I'll smother him.

–Captain Avgoustis, when I gave a solemn oath to my father to respect you, I hadn't counted on it being for so long. The merchant marine has changed, you haven't. You delay me and you set me back.

–Find me a cargo for Japan.

–There is nothing going.

–Then I'm going empty.

–No can do. You've got to come home, already.

–Listen. The teapot's broken from the good set of the missus. I'm going to Kobe to get one like it.

***

ATHOS III, handy size, 30,000 tons, black underbelly, red hull, residents twenty, an all-male village that never stayed put. So then, Mitsos Avgoustis, the water-logged captain; Kleanthis Birbilis, the second mate, half English, the other half from Mykonos, singed on the subject matter of women; Nikos Yalouris, from Syros and Psara, a former wireless operator, now a second mate and an antichrist to boot, always ready to paint eggs red at Christmas and decorate a tree at Easter; Pandelis Sigalas, a Tinian boatswain, both leftist and rightist, Stamatis Vekrelis, steward of Tinian-Lesbian descent, the boatswain's nephew, who'd agreed with Zoe from Petralona that she'd write to him in English, *to my darling husband, your faithful wife Zoe*; Miltos Lavdas, the trainee midshipman from Chalkida, not fondled since the cradle; Valias Daniel, an Andros lad, melancholy on account of a Marita; Makis Dachtylas, first engineer and father of three, two dark-skinned ones and an Apache Indian, which he contrived to find some way to present to his mum, the church-tender in their small village on Paros; Apostolos Michaloutsos, from Symi, second engineer with his brain steeped in red; Bambis Dokos, a dreamy descendant of Albanian stock, the cook's assistant and benefactor to a Filipino mother of a large brood; Takis Koronios, a wily youth, on a regime of ten coffees a day and an ulcer on its way. In addition, a bouquet of six Rumanians, two Nikolais, two Georgis, two Sorins, four of them certified sailors, the other two not so, plus the handsome pair of Russian twins, Sasha the third mechanic and Andrei the electrician, blond miniatures with a record of service in the nuclear submarines of the defunct Soviet Union, who'd driven the crew berserk the night before, wearing high heels and strutting along the boardwalk with tiny mincing steps, raising the men who came hurtling out of their cabins, some barely managing to slip on their underpants and others to slip them off in the nick of time.

Twentieth and last but not least, the one with eyes large and cool as vine leaves in the spring, Gerassimos Siakandaris, the fifty-five-year-old cook, who was intimately acquainted with everyone's issues and quirks, was genuinely interested in the tax affairs of the foreign languages school of Yalouris' sister-in-law, in the female troubles of Michaloutsos' daughter, the psychological problems of the wife of one of the Sorinses, the asthma of the son of one of the Nikolaises, the lack of progress in the violin of Sigalas's thirteen year old daughter and in all of the unavoidable screw-ups in the seamen's family lives.

–I saw the eyes of all crew members turning black, including the blue-eyed among them, cooked them up a storm with sausages from my village and, by the second round of drinks, they'd all gone back to normal. They're happy as larks now, was his report to the captain after such incidents. As for individual black moods, whether one or two or three episodes daily, those, too, he had his own way of mellowing out. A sugar roll and an apple fritter accompanied by the vivid description of a cool ravine, with the emphasis on the nightingales' song, would loosen a pair of unsmiling lips even if it was only to snicker, there would always be someone to make fun of him, but he'd succeeded in his goal.

January 5, a Sunday night, Gerassimos Siakandaris took out of the oven the two large metal trays with the roast, Avgoustis didn't let his crew go hungry, he demanded from the ship owners the best food for the men and everyone who had sailed with him testified to relatives and colleagues, we ate well and then some, a few even teasing their wives that their mousaka was mush compared to the carrier's cuisine.

Twelve years on this ship, ever since Avgoustis took it over
out of dry dock in Holland and, before that, seven years on the
PENELOPE, four on the ALFIOS and two and a half on the
CALYPSO, always with the same captain who took his cook
with him to every new address.

A couple since 1972, twenty-five-and-a-half years without
any infidelities on either side, they should be celebrating their
silver anniversary, the journey's monotony could well do with a
joke here and there, just to keep things cheery.

So, then, off went the dishes to the canteen of the lower
crew, in came the steward for the tray with the captain's light
dinner, two slim slices of lamb, two spoonfuls of veggies, throw
in a well-roasted potato, why don't you, he suggested to the
cook, but Siakandaris brushed him off, he absolutely needed
to take the food to the captain himself— he liked, among other
things, to serve in the capacity of butler.

He found him in his small apartment, the door on its hinge,
Maritsa on his slippers, Vicky Moscholiou singing the refrain,
because hands are ropes and bodies are sailing ships, and the longhaired captain sitting on the double bed, walled-up inside his
creaseless suit, gazing out at the void, the abundant void of
those two and seventy square feet which their tenant found
insufficient with another couple of bodies present, though when
he was all by himself, they spanned out like an open courtyard.

This is how it was every night in the space with the gray and
olive-green furniture and all the rest, the daytime Avgoustis,
present simultaneously in any and all of the ship's nooks and
crannies, turned into the twilight version, barring unforeseen
events, of the unapproachable monk in his cell.

The cook bowed, not in honor of his god, but to place the
tray on his knees, sniff his face all over, kiss him on the lips,
stand at attention and concede.

–You haven't had any ouzo.

Avgoustis gingerly shifted the tray onto the bedclothes,

leaned over the bedside table, turned down the music and making his way slowly to the sink to wash his hands, without seeming hungry this evening either, without even feigning impatience to taste the cook's work, asked out of politeness, so what have we here tonight.

–You saw.

–Did it come out good?

–Is not the fragrance answer enough?

–Lamb.

–Well bathed. Have a taste and let me know.

–The meat goes to Maritsa.

The cook executed the order with a long face, the best portion would again go to that faggy tom who scoffed down the lean steaks and the tenderloin he prepared with all his loving care for Avgoustis.

The displeasure in his face needed to be, once again, as emphatic as his appreciation of the captain's relationship with cats, yet, their daily understanding was also based on griping, which they needed and had gotten used to, it didn't interfere, because they knew well that affection and caring are expressed in any number of ways and, sometimes, guileless griping builds a familiar tempo and becomes the strongest accreditation of a relationship's longevity.

At all events, Gerassimos Siakandaris was preparing with these true and tested ruses the atmosphere of equitable intimacy in which to divulge, over and over again, what had long ceased to be secrets.

He, nevertheless, always had a method for gaining a bit of extra time, he disliked to hasten his leave-taking. All the more so tonight, when preoccupation weighed on the captain's gaze. Several times, he looked alternately at the floor and at the ceiling, grasping for an idea that would freshen up the silent nocturnal pantomime enacted for the umpteenth time, for an inroad into the silence that soaked up the four walls of his soul mate. With the oppressive deadlock of the sheets of tin as his only inspiration, he volunteered as guide for a brief tour of open, boisterous spaces, something that'd do the captain good, with intermediate stopovers and a port of call that would do himself good as well.

–New York had fifteen inches of snow, my village eighteen, he started while placing the cutlery on the table. Detroit is 60% workers, my village 95%, Paris makes expensive perfumes but Kyriaki in Viotia smells nicer, it has the fir trees of Parnassus, he went on while waiting to clean up after Maritsa.

–Come straight out and say you want off the ship.

–Isn't it about time?

–For good?

–For three, four months.

–And who's there waiting for you?

–Nobody, not any more. I'm homesick for the stream that picks its way from lake Kopaida to lake Yliki.

In a bit, he bent and picked up the cat's plate, glanced at Avgoustis who was taking a long time to get to his dinner and said what he deeply felt, that for anyone to form positive impressions of life they had to gaze at vineyards often.

For a few moments neither spoke.

–Leave in May and stay till the harvest, till summer peters out.

–Let's see which May you'll get off this ship. Which May you put your arms around your children. Which May you get a thrashing from your son.

The cook didn't wait for an answer, every attempt in the past few years to sift through Avgoustis' intentions had been crowned by absolute failure and, in the end, he didn't mind that, and even pondered how he, himself, had been given the green light for Kyriaki three times and hadn't gone, nor was he really sure that he'd end up getting off the ship this coming May. So, he filled the captain's glass with ice water—it was time to withdraw, he had, at all events, done his village plenty proud this evening.

–The truth, Gerassimos. Are you afraid my years are weighing my steering down?

–I used to be a wuss, I came on board out of need and only at your side did I get what courage I have. I've seen you give Death the slip ten times over.

He said that thing about Death and turned to go. But Avgoustis wanted company.

–Stay. Stay and talk. About the things you talk about.

Those things were dozens of stories about the secrets of the profession, which it was the cook's passion to recall out loud, standing, leaning against the wall between the framed picture of Meteora and the one of Mount Athos.

–The ship was just not flying, he began. I took it to heart to get it off the ground. And I succeeded, one Sunday afternoon. I bathed the lamb with wine, cleaned it up from all the piss and while it was basting, I basted its little body with a tiny broom of oregano sticks. The crew finger-licked even me. They came over one by one and they were kissing me. I'd found my knack again. After four months on the CALYPSO, the spell of bad luck was broken.

Gerassimos Siakandaris did have a knack for thievery, he stole the tricks of the trade from barbers, tailors, engineers and parted his lasagna down the middle, embroidered his beef with pasta, entombed legs in salt and delighted afterwards in the men running their mouths off about him.

Unmoved by the crescendo of the cook's disclosures, Avgoustis didn't respond, his mind having slipped off elsewhere, as it wasn't tales of the adventures of a chef he expected from Gerassimos but rather the companionship of a human voice talking about no matter what.

Siakandaris felt this and was perplexed because the story of the lamb that had pissed itself never failed to make an impression, and so he went for another version of the same, with his voice raised in volume threefold and warmer by ten degrees.

–The ship was just not flying, he started again.

How to get it off the ground? he wondered, searching the captain's eyes.

–I concocted spectacular salads and wild garnishes, he went on. Nothing worked, he confessed. The crews weren't yet mixed up helter skelter like in the past ten fifteen years, he reminisced, all then were Greeks, all the same body type, all their stomachs made in Greece. To win the men over, he'd had to fire the heavy artillery of Greek cuisine, roast lamb with potatoes, my last hope, he emphasized and went on with the familiar tale, how one Sunday morning he sent an SOS to St. Ephrosynos, patron saint of cooks, and had at last the divine visitation, the kitchen saint revealed the trick, in order for the animal not to stink, my esteemed colleague Gerassimos, bathe it in wine.

The test of repetition worked, Siakandaris caught for the second time Avgoustis being absent minded and not having heard a single word, captain, you give me grief, he said worriedly, stood still for a bit, then walked past Maritsa and went out.

In a while, Avgoustis forked a boiled carrot, returned it to the plate, back went the beetroot as well, in the end he had a couple of slices of zucchini, another two of sour-apple, then he got the orange glass mug and a bottle of whisky out of his cupboard, poured in a thimbleful and lit up a cigarette straight away.

Fine then, since the sight of vineyards is good for you, he closed his eyes and pictured himself in Elefsina many years back, at dusk, passing by the dark grapevines of Chadzirodias, the amber ones of Violetis, the sweet, small sultanas of the village porter, the pink fruity ones of Boukouvalas and arriving at

the pearly beaded arbor of her with the drawn-out, husky voice
and the host of remarkable noises, the squeaky, opulent thighs,
the wing-fluttering in her breasts, the hiccup in her thing, and,
two hours later, while his good self was picking his way back
through unfrequented paths, having a tulle stick all over his
mug, the web of a spider that reached from the fig trees on one
side of the path, across to the sparrow eaten grapevines on the
other.

Did it do him any good, this old scene with the female vineyard that used to get him drunk as anything? He put out the
cigarette, got up, released the hook and closed his door, there
were the charts to draw for next day's course and the way he
struggled with work in recent years, half the night would be
spent over the desk with eyes like slits and heavy cursing.

**

Mitso, I love your arm.

*But hang on a sec while I go get a napkin. I don't need
it, but I just got it into my head, I want to have a napkin in my hand for the duration of the visit.*

*I don't know what you expect to hear from me. Not that
I care. I saw you. I could've sent you away. Because I got
the urge to talk with no holds barred and there's no telling
what might come out.*

Let's go again.

Mitso, I love your arm.

*That is how I started all the letters, feeling his arm
across my shoulders, heavy and warm, till I was done with
the rough, splotched copy and while I rewrote everything
properly from scratch.*

*I would have liked to have watched the hairs on his
arm go white. In time, his arm was like those weird cacti
he brought me for my Mexican porch, the gray, fluffy*

snakes, the furry melons and the peeling ship ropes, coiling around themselves twenty times over, that come up with those tiny, bright-red, drunken flowers.

This time of year the stars come out after nine-thirty.

I spent last night standing by the window, shrouded in this miserable old robe, with the ceiling light off and only the night-light on, thinking of his work-roughened hand. While he was playing with the matchbox. While he sprinkled some salt on his beer. While he started his stroking, all of it nice, topped by his small finger zigzagging down my spine.

Those massaging caresses weren't bad either on my swollen ankles after two straight days of standing up at the salon, that one time I had four weddings all at once! I had to see to the hair of brides, mothers-in-law, best women and sisters-in-law, with all those springy curls that were in fashion then.

One night, the whole night long, who knows what was keeping him awake, he had two of my fingers locked in his palm and he massaged those till dawn. It was windy outside and, from time to time, tiny sudden storms knocked on the shutters of our northern window.

Another time he was sitting across from me on the couch, I was sewing two buttons onto his shirt and confessing that I didn't have the know-how to cook the rabbit any way, but in onion stew and all the while, with his left arm in the air, he was caressing me from nine feet away and making fun of the rabbit I was talking about.

Menidiatis would sing and Mitsos played the tune with his fingers on my nipples until they turned to stone. With Menidiatis, they turn into stone very quickly, he'd say jealously, even before the refrain. They turned to stone with Kokotas, too, but slower. In recent years they turned to stone with

Eleni Vitali and Litsa Diamandi even without fingering and I'm thinking, maybe it's the songs themselves that turn me on.
I don't love people who don't love songs.

In April '71 we were listening to the clarinets on the radio, on account of the anniversary of the junta. He was getting ready to leave again on a trip. He opens the drawer with my underwear, empties it on the bed and starts running his hand through them, undoing the bras and doing them up again.

Wear those when I come back again, he said and put aside a pale blue slip with braided trimming and a black bra with lace cups. He didn't want me wearing matching ones. God help you if I catch you with a matching set, he threatened me and while the clarinets were raising the dead, he rubbed the fabric between his fingers, brought it to his mouth and undid the tiny white bow just at the navel. Leave it undone, I'll tie it for you when I get back, he consoled me.

It might have been his way of finally apologizing.

Ever since I was young I was on the chubby side but, still, I loved wild and showy clothes. Everything leaving the shoulders bare, short and tight, long before the miniskirt was in. Once I had a short gold skirt I wore day and night and he kept at me not to wear it any more. I got grumpy, we split up, he disappeared for two years and he turned up again married. I sent him on his way. The first time. After another two years he came again. And I kept him.

He didn't marry me because I didn't take off the mini skirt.

Two decades later, by which time I had forty years under my belt, lo and behold! he turns up one night, from Jakarta. He digs into my wardrobe, unburies the gold miniskirt, won't you put it on for a spell? he says.

With pleasure, I say in turn. The zipper wouldn't do up and my legs weren't exactly show-off material. The left has a bunch of green veins on the inside of the thigh and the right has a forking of purple ones behind the knee.

I didn't mind making a fool of myself for his sake. Whenever he fancied me a circus act, I obliged at once, because I am style-challenged but have a gift for joy. And this has proven very useful. The laughter we shared when I dressed to the nines was something else. Our lovemaking was drowned in laughter.

Tritsis, you must have heard of him, the one who founded the race around Athens and gave diplomas to everyone who ran, had given me an idea. I get up to Kotsonis's on Kifisias Ave., who sells flags, trophies and sports bric-a-brac. I buy three printed diplomas, I fill in his name and a few words of my own and I award the lot to Mitsos in a ceremony with pasta with garlic. I hadn't had all that many men touch me.

First Prize in Caressing, on the back. Second Prize in Caressing, on the cheek. Third Prize in Caressing, on the bottom. More laughter, more madness.

His caresses live on in my body. So does that which didn't happen in the end though I had it planned for the afternoons, after have retired. The licking time, was my name for it. Five thirty, he's still all sleepy eyed from the siesta, coming out onto the porch in his sleeveless T-shirt and briefs, I'm in my negligee serving the coffees and he puts me on his knees, brings his hands to the front, clasps my belly and then he bites me on the arm and gives me one or two licks on the back of the neck. Our life is full of all the things we anticipate but don't ever end up happening, we are not given the grace. In my case, a lot of things happened, but only in the three-day allotments he would steal for my sake. Wild passion between the sheets, wild feasting at the table with all the treats. And afterwards, the daily grind all over, perms and dyes and much ado about curls.

Now, I am the one licking my memories, both real and imagined, I can't afford for any of them to dry up and go belly up on me. I need all of them at one time or another.

If you think I brought up his caresses in order to punish you, you couldn't be more wrong. Because, listen to this. As far as caresses go, I just may have liked it even more when he caressed the things in the house. The empty oven tray on the table. The olive-oil container. The curtain tassel in the bedroom, usually in the morning when he was looking out at the weather.

He was away and I was very close to my things. I counted on them. The bracelets were sitting in the box. The mauve liqueur glasses were sitting on the shelf. The two modern mirrors sat on opposite sides gazing at one another.

Whatever happens, I've decided not to be mute all the time.

The silent house is like a plane in turbulence. It suddenly dips and you lose your footing. I go in and out of the rooms, I circle the yard, I talk to all the things, to the walls, the household objects, the tree branches and I tell them everything. The news, lies, silly stuff, crazy stuff, hurts, whatever. I come up with some scenes from my life, too, when I should have let things rip but I bottled it all up instead and now, ten, twenty, thirty, coming to forty years later, I'm finding the right arguments and the courage not to hurt myself any more. It takes a lot of courage not to hurt yourself.

His eyes are constantly before my eyes and I get to thinking that the sea was born after Mitsos and it was made all blue and cool so that it matches his gaze. A gaze that leads me to excesses by the ton, to faith without measure, to patience without excuse, so much so that sometimes I wake up and I feel contempt for myself.

Straight away, to be sure, I struggle to erase these views in ten minutes flat, the complaints and the worries turn to dust, because I know he did love me a great deal and that he, too, suffered from not having the guts to do the right thing.

Your visit seems strange to me. But, finally, I am glad to have seen you in the flesh. You, especially, played a big part in how things turned out.

In my life I only ever wanted to love.

I wasn't dreaming of anything grand. A lively bed, to be listening now to his hammer putting in the nails for the small picture frames and to be picking up his crumpled newspaper.

This isn't how it goes.

The years must somehow pass even for those who've missed out on the so-called watersheds of life, a marriage and children. They can't stay stationary at a date on the calendar, waiting, in case something animates the deadness and the engines start up events, whether large or tiny.

That's why, in order to be pleasant to myself and also, so that the melancholy which sometimes gets me right in the chest doesn't show on the outside, I've placed all my bets on the hoe. I've spent my life with my garden.

Right by the exotic flower bed, this year I've got this purple jungle with the fifty cockscombs for the cat to creep around in when he plays at being a tiger.

In amongst the blooming cockerels, myself a hen, crowing away my news, just like I am doing now.

Spring is a revolution.

And the summer that's frolicking around us fills me, as always, with gratitude.

***

Skyscrapers, pagodas, Muslim temples, coconut palms, the Singapore they knew but could not see, hidden behind the blue curtain, ten nautical miles to their left.

ATHOS III sailed past it and started climbing northwards, while Avgoustis sent off the boatswain with his political prattle and remained smoking in the lookout, unaccompanied.

Day after day, night after night on the sea, what may be said had been said and what may not wasn't going to be, followed by more of the same in the umpteenth, comfy repetition. Best for life to be described in a broad outline that contains few things and if anyone wants more, they find those in themselves and place them in what order they see fit.

With his beard expertly laid out and set with hair spray, his hair impeccably parted, his uniform pressed to perfection, always immaculate in his grooming, with Maritsa ahead of him or else weaving in and out of his legs, Avgoustis was making his way slowly, as if calculating the distances all over again, as if his paramount sense of orderliness required daily confirmation of the one hundred and eighty footsteps from the holds to the forecastle, the one hundred and twenty from the chartroom to the chain locker and the twelve leading down below to Siakandaris' kitchens.

Apart from his legs, his palms also did some walking, locating tiny scratches on the white and red surfaces and there was no need to order, rust hammer, he merely called out the sailor's name and the man got to work on the double.

However, on Friday afternoon, January 10, rust was far from Avgoustis' mind.

Second cigarette, third, fourth.

Seven years on the rounds according to the Indian-Pacific Consortium Express Protocol, ATHOS III was coming and going in known territory, mainly Freemantle, Geraldon, Port Piree, for grains, as per the Austwheat charter party, Belekeri, Koundalore, Mangalore, Mazoulipatan, Samar Island, Marinduke for iron ores as per Charter-Party C., Laoutoka, Souva, Pouloupandam, Bacolod for processed and unprocessed sugar, charter party Queensland.

The telex from Pireas two hours ago was succinct and imperative. The Shipping Maritime Company had placed ATHOS outside the Protocol, after all these years, rendering defunct the known parameters and the familiar work cycle. This was an end to the charter parties arranged by the Tzelepis company, to the cargo deals and the rest of the reliable bureaucratic arrangements, an end to the security of the cyclical journeys, a blackmailing move, pure and simple, aiming to leave Avgoustis and the ship without support so as to force the captain to resign and go back with his tail between his legs.

Fifth cigarette, smoking way too much, way too tough a call and it was all his.

The others, about their business as usual.

Four afternoons later, Tuesday, January 14, the second mate Birbilis noted on the unofficial diary that at 1620 a port pilot came on board to lead ATHOS III into Bangkok harbor, at 1740 he noted the roping of the tugboats, one hour later he noted their disengagement, another hour after that the beginning of the ship's docking on the right-hand side, after half an hour the maneuvre's completion and the placement of a ladder so that half an hour later, at 2040 to be precise, the local authorities could come on board.

At 2100, while the tray-bearing steward was making the rounds in the ship's lounge offering the usual refreshments, his cell phone rang, the faithful wife Zoitsa wanted to make sure that everything was alright and to tell her darling husband *I love you, Stamatis*, as well as something her English wasn't up to, their brother-in-law was in the hospital with pancreatitis, now out of danger, thank God.

Thank God, Stamatis concurred and, after a brief silence, soon as you hang up it's like seeing your wife turn around and walk away, he said, speaking to himself but overheard by three or four men nearby, married ones or else engaged. Unmarried seamen always have one fiancée or more, and they were all in agreement with the pensive steward, it showed in their eyes, a miniscule quiver of the eyelids, the instantaneous reaching over oceans and deserts to land at the kitchen table at home, across from a woman of their own, not with all these seas but just two cups of coffee and a plate of wine-must cookies between the two of them.

So then, 2110 was also the end of the report to Zoe's.

They'd cleared off by 2130, the unloading was for the following morning, but with the sound of the password *clear!* before those hanging out for a feminine touch had time to scatter into the port's side streets, a dozen women clambered like cats onto the ship and within five minutes each had found her master, known from last year's visit and the one a year before that.

The one most gifted at fishing, holding a basket of fresh groundfish, hooked the cook again, who paid a fair price for all her tasty treats at the table and in bed and saw her off with a few boxes of aspirin and a bag full of chocolates for her kids.

Within half an hour the ship's forecastle smelt of fried fish and ouzo and in another half, the singles went off to sleep and those who'd found a match left the mauve moon and the pink stars to the sky and dove into their cabins for the rest.

Also in his cabin for some time now was Avgoustis, who abstained from both fish and women that night, having quit pairing up a long time ago.

His mind was divided in two. Half was on his replacement. Would he show up? When would that be? Tomorrow, the day after or at the next port of call? In the last six years Chadzimanolis junior would ask him a couple of times each year, at first politely, then not at all so, to leave the steering to someone younger, meaning someone he could control, and because he didn't have the gumption to send to hell the ingenious captain who had all of Pireas under wraps, he cursed his own father for his persistence in still owing his savior, fifty-five years after the war's end, when all the hotshots were in agreement that gratitude is a serious detriment to the business and only entered in their memory banks whatever best served their interests.

If Chadzijerkoff junior did send another captain, Avgoustis was determined to throw him overboard and if the bully himself turned up, he'd be twice as glad to tip over the rail the useless scoundrel who had come into a fortune all set up and didn't mean to get it in his head that an Avgoustis does not die on dry land and that he, in particular, would never take part in that old age which slowly and wordlessly undulates from one train stop to the next, from the left side of the sidewalk to the right, from the morning bench of this square to the afternoon bench of that one.

The other half of his mind was daydreaming about imitation electric stoves and condiments that had been interfered with. Nobody snuffed at pepper that was past its expiry date, nobody spat out their food because it hadn't been cooked on an original German appliance.

Avgoustis knew just the right person to clinch the deal. He was in Pireas, right at the Company's living, breathing heart.

Hermes Flirtakis, sixty-five, a former captain of love boats, professional seducer of past-their-prime American females cavorting around the Caribbean.

A long long time ago, as a high-school kid, he used to be embarrassed by his ancient first name and his silly second one, in middle age he didn't miss any opportunity to introduce himself, to the ladies in particular. He intoned the first name turning his head with the dyed hair to the left and right like a model and continued with the surname, accentuating the Flirt and pronouncing the -akis separately, a humorless joker like no other. Still, some of them took the bait. Not on account of his looks or his humor, both of which were nonexistent, but for lack of anyone better or as a quick fix of revenge on the husband or just for the hell of it—the guy fit to a t their hollow and boring married lives. An experience, is what they said afterwards.

Among them, the bored forty-year-old Kassandra Chadzi-manolis. Thirteen years ago Mitsos Avgoustis had paid a visit to the apartment of the chief captain in Kastela, bringing his wife thirty thimbles, souvenirs from Latin American countries. Poor Tasoula who filled shelves upon shelves in her living room with porcelain, clay, wood, silver and tin thimbles in order not to think of the tin-plated fool she'd married, was away visiting their son, a student in London, but the boss's wife was at her house. Avgoustis came upon her fully clothed bar her stockings, hurriedly putting on her earring, but Flirtakis, who'd answered the door, had his shirt done up crooked and his trousers half unbuttoned.

–It's fine mauling the pink-assed Dutch women that he screws, but his wife, too? he asked him a little after the ship owner's wife had left.

From that point on, he had him at his beck and call, theoretically, anyway, because he never would actually spill the beans to Chadzicuckold, but Flirtakis was now officially his hostage and whenever there was need, he covered over both mishaps and full-blown crimes. Now, given that the bosses hadn't divorced, on account of divvying up their joint properties being a major hurdle, maybe it was time to gossip to the rightful husband about the steamy scenes at Kastela.

Would the threat work?

It did work, because Avgoustis was in an advantageous position and the company's chief captain knew it.

During the ten minute call, Hermes Flirtakis resisted marginally at first, keeping up pretexts, the ship had now been taken out of the charter circuit, the boss will come after me.

–You always came through up till now, managed to rig up some extra cargo for me to load. You're going to do it again, because you aren't in a position to refuse.

–Ah, Mitso you're killing me.

–You've got two days to take care of things.

–Don't I get four?

–From now on, I'm going to be in a hurry all the time. I'll be keeping the anchor in my shirt pocket.

He said other stuff, too, very uncouth, mincing no words. Hermes Flirtakis eventually promised to do his damnedest, Fine, I'll get you something, I'll make ends meet somehow, but this is the last time, at our age we can't afford too much stress, he whimpered to Avgoustis, you, dear fellow, don't know the meaning of God's mercy.

–I don't need to, I'm acquainted with his delegate, old Chadzimanolis senior. Who is going to be on my side yet again.

End of phone call.

Mitsos Avgoustis was going to cut down the off-loading from four days to two, he would take on any cargo that came his way and then be off. Next morning, as if everything was fine and dandy, he would give the second mate a roll of five twenty-dollar bills wrapped with a rubber band, like he did at every port, to go out after work, choose something expensive for the captain's wife and post it to her.

Birbilis with the selective taste, thirteen years in his employ, had shopped for Avgoustis' wife wall carpets of silk, a fur jacket and two dozen bracelets, without as much as having seen a photograph of her.

But all questions on that subject had been nipped in the bud.

Avgoustis had turned in early, saying to the others who were impatient to lie with the women, that his temples were throbbing and he was going to sleep. So, he made the critical phone call at his convenience and, after that, all of the rest of his routine followed, as it did every evening, without deviation. He put down a towel in front of the door so that no light escaped from the crack and covered the keyhole with a sock for the same reason, then sat at the desk, opened the drawer and set out before him two envelopes, the red one and the red and white one, and the rest of the implements.

He was taking precautions so that nothing went wrong and this constant vigilance was wearing him out, but more than this, he was scared of his own implacable stubbornness.

***

Not pepper and not soy either, that son of a gun in Bangkok had another four ships to fill up, they'd been first in slipping him the bribe and Avgoustis didn't have the time to wait in line.

Flirtakis, slow 'n easy does it, didn't work any miracles.

Instead of ferreting out some monkey-brand electricals, he asked Avgoustis to strike a deal directly with the real monkeys swinging off the coconut palms and sent over a suited Belgian who'd fallen on hard times, to see to the rest of the details. Finally, after Avgoustis had unloaded the animal feed and the wheat-grains and washed out the holds, he took on board twenty thousand tons of tapioca, deliverable to Kobe, a produce that was delicate and troublesome, needing to be aired and kept at the proper temperature to stop it from getting too warm, but still a good charter, Chadzimanolis heard the price it would fetch and agreed on the spot from where he was, at the bar of some casino, skinned.

While Birbilis prepared the crew list to deliver to the agent for the local authorities and oversaw the restocking in foodstuffs and water, the merchandise was divided between the holds, half filling two out of the three, everything taken care of on the double and ATHOS III was off, on its way again out to the open sea.

The piece of bad news came the next day, Saturday 18.

–When did he die?

–Yesterday morning. Didn't you know?

–In the hospital?

–At their Kifisia home. He was being looked after by two foreign women. The Bulgarian cooked, the Russian washed for him.

–It was about time. Eighty-eight.

Chadzimanolis senior had ascended on high wearing a classic cashmere suit, freshly shaven and smelling of soap, as soon as he'd completed his life's work and after thanking the two migrant women present at the closing of his curtain, as well as the absent members of the play, his wife, dead for many years, the son and the daughter-in-law who visited every New Year and others, elsewhere, some of them dead and some living.

During the phone call his wife with the flue, just back from the funeral, enumerated those present, the entire mean and twisted tribe of the Tzelepis Co., not a single wreath from you and your ship, Mimi, (she didn't favor "Mitsos"), and she started on him again, come back, why don't you, come back, certain on the basis of past experience that at about this point, her husband would finally hang up on her, which he did, causing them both to sigh with relief.

For years now they would talk once in a blue moon, when some event dictated it and sometimes when she, especially on certain particular nights that brook no lies, recapitulated the past and felt the urge to holler even if only in order to spoil his mood as well.

Tonight's call was made on account of the missing wreath, because a couple of lowlife bandits from the shipowners' gang, on the pretext of being in mourning and deeply concerned about having an impeccable funeral, up to the kudos of the deceased, fell in step with her and pointed out its absence.

The news found Avgoustis in his cabin, it weighed on him, the monks of Mount Athos will erase his sins and send him on even higher up to the heavenly convents, he said to Maritsa and to himself and he meant it.

But why did not the son himself inform the captain? Or Flirtyflirt? The rush of the funeral, the turmoil in the Company and in the family, the numbing that death stamps on the living—no matter that it may have been a long time coming—were no sufficient explanation, the other two ships had been notified and the forty-year-old captains, who'd had no direct transactions with the old man, had done their duty as per the bloody wreath.

Avgoustis pushed aside all thoughts about the consequences of his friend's death, his priority for now was the silent bequeathing of honors to the deceased.

They'd met in 1939, Chadzimanolis also from Asia Minor, from Aivali, in his thirties, first engineer, Avgoustis sixteen going on seventeen, an apprentice sailor, crew members of the MYRTOON transporting a cargo of tanks from Halifax to Dover which it never did deliver; German submarines attacked and sunk them, dispatching twelve British gunmen and two Greek stokers to the bottom of the sea. The youth saved the grown-up. He put his own life jacket around him when they tumbled into one another in the waves, the older man having swallowed half the Atlantic, knowing that he was headed straight down and half waving, half drowning.

–I wouldn't have saved you if I wasn't sixteen. I didn't know then what life meant, he told him after the war, a man now.

–I've known that since fifteen, when I let someone drown, the answer, with no more details forthcoming.

Together on ships and separately, the sea alongside them and between them, for years on end.

Life is a return. Memory shifts gears and backs up, unburying a host of small stories scattered through the years, while after sixty-five, seventy, the speed accelerates enormously and ten minutes is all it takes to turn around and scoop them up only to realize they are no more than loose ends, leftovers from a past that's farther away from you the older you get.

At fourteen, he'd turned his back to soccer, to his favorite team, *Heracles* and to the Orpheus Philharmonic with his drums, had bid a rushed farewell to the resin traders, the barrel builders, the horse-and-carriage porters, the bagel vendors, the orchard keepers, the fishermen and the dockerworkers, had danced an extroverted mating dance, a *karsilamas*, and taken the road leading far from all that and into the deep. These events were surveyed dryly and summarily by Avgoustis, the kind of guy who did not wax nostalgic about his youth and refused to end up a crummy old fart who spends his entire waking life reminiscing.

So, he made a point of treating the dead man to some top-notch cussing, you spawned a fuckwit for a son, he started his monologue just as Siakandaris made his entry bearing the boss's and the cat's dinner and was brought up-to-date through the foulmouthed, more than sorrowful, necrology. The captain had a history of abusing even the dear departed, terrorizing the living, too, about what was in store for them after their death. Avgoustis's main target was the spoiled only-son but the shrapnel also caught the father, a fine piece of work himself, lest we forget, leaving control of the Company in his dotage to a jackass heir.

His tears were overflowing and the cook, all scrunched up in a corner, was waiting for the blessed silence to arrive, which he would honor for a bit and then would break, gently, softly, in order to assure the captain that the sweet memorial dish of kolliva would be served in memory of old Chadzimanolis.

–You have pomegranates?

For years now, the unidentified noble soul who'd been

procuring ten large, juicy pomegranates yearly to the captain in case of memorials on board the ship, had desisted from the kind offer, once Siakandaris had asked if that person was still alive, along with his pomegranate tree, without getting an answer and, as the foreign pomegranates he bought at some port looked dried up and acrid, he had subtracted them from his recipe, what with his talent for making do with what was available, wheat and raisins at whatever cost and, in addition, sometimes almonds from the assistant cook's family property, sometimes walnuts from the boatswain's in-laws.

But the captain was already up and gone, without supper, to the wardroom to find the men all gathered and say a few words for the departed and then, in his own good time, send the scoundrel son the telegram with his condolences, heartfelt, as was the dead man's due.

That night, the next, the one after that and the six yet that followed till Japan, were spent by Avgoustis in his tiny living room, sleepless, right across from the closed door of the ship-owner's bedroom, the quarters, on and off, of the cats and of every Maritsa, since only once, at the very beginning, did any boss rest among its sheets, what with old Chadzimanolis having had his fill of the ocean and the son keeping his fond distance ever since 1979 when he made his first, and last, trip.

Thus, then, sat Avgoustis, silently mulling over his friend's death and, since as he was in a tight spot and needed to be battle-ready, he launched himself again full force into mnemonic exercises, not ones to do with his personal affairs, but the other kind.

He repeatedly circled his mental map of vermin. How many scoundrels did he know and where? A great many and at every port. But the business needed to pass through the hands of one only. That frigid-ass Flirtakis. No matter how utterly untrustworthy the guy was.

***

Seven thousand dead from the 1994 earthquake in Kobe and, three years later, the port with the sheltered outdoor markets, once again gathered seamen from all over the world, shopping for shoes and videos.

It was a Saturday night, January 25, one third of the officers and one fourth of the seamen of ATHOS III remained on the ship, as they were supposed to, and the rest of the crew went out, with advances in their pockets, first off for some famous Kobe-steak, the meat of a calf, as tasty as anything, raised in the dark, with beer and massages, pricey, one helping divided in three, just enough for a taste and then doing the rounds of the few bars that were open to foreigners. The expectation of female company wasn't fulfilled because of a flu going round, that'd sent the whores off to bed, on their backs with no remuneration.

Earlier, under the instructions of the captain who hadn't left the boat for years, the second mate Birbilis had located the three-story glassware shop from where, faced with four golden teapots, he had had to call Avgoustis before he bought the right one, with the braided handle and the pale blue leaves, the one which the missus never used, he said, though once, on his patron saint's day, with relatives and the boss's family in the house, when he'd asked her to bring down all the porcelain, the teapot was discovered crookedly glued back together, minus the blue leaves and the culprit wife was unable to string a sentence together for all her stammering.

Such desperation over a teapot, her husband had thought at the time feeling sorry for her as he did all over again while recalling the incident.

My beloved Mimis, don't get confused again, our daughter is the one asleep in Xenoula's lap, the chubby one at my feet eating the ice-cream stick is her niece, she wrote to him behind a photograph that she'd sent him at the Canary Islands and this eloquent specification all this time ago, nearly thirty years, contained the distancing and the forgetfulness which with time, and with all the captain's continued, yearly digs in the extramural vineyard of Elefsina, had turned to frostiness and enmity.

Sunday morning, with a double coffee and overcast skies.

Maritsa executed her number impeccably all round the rails to an audience of freshly wakened Japanese dockerworkers and leisure walkers who poured out a storm of curt, one- and two-syllable words, never ever having seen a cat such as this.

Avgoustis, at his post, breathed in the sea that had no smell, no cooling effect, cement that'd turned solid and trapped on the spot dozens of ships in a row. Siakandaris who brought the second coffee with some feta and a piece of twice-baked bread, counted thirty docked beasts, white alternating with black.

He'd spent the night with eyes wide open and lips tightly sealed, when he got up in the morning his mouth was covered inside and out with a dried yellowish crust, it took some time to work his tongue free, his palate, his cheeks and test his speech with the good morning to Maritsa, who, for some days now, was being stoic and respectful of the boss's introspective mood.

The crew's comings and goings increased, the men bid him good morning first and Avgoustis merely nodded, he wasn't in the right frame of mind to address them with their nicknames, hey Callas, for the off-key Lavdas, hello Schwarzenegger for the miniscule blond Russians and so forth, today, bathed, to be sure, in fragrance, and impeccably dressed up, certainly, he stood deep in thought over the calculations of the trade's illegal math, about to put his notions to the test, in a couple of hours' time.

Sunday in Kobe was flowing under a gentle drizzle with the crowds perambulating on the seafront, cranes swerving high with orange containers in their pincers, porters on bicycles transporting three and five enormous paper boxes at once, joyful dogs in groups and kids with bikes checking out the seafaring vessels one by one, BALTIC SEA, ARGENTINA, SPANISH STAR, questioning each time the sailors in English, where they are from, where had they just been and where they are headed.

Avgoustis was in his office, during his lifetime at sea he had docked at each port ten times over, Kobe included, he knew the lot of them by heart, both the well-frequented ports of wealth and the ones buried in third-world misery, one dock, two straps, you load up, you move on.

He'd unloaded the tapioca and was hanging around for a new cargo. Would Flirtakis come up with a solution? Were things tighter still, now, in the absence of a commending word from the deceased? And was the golden boy of Pireas really trying or was he purposefully stalling the negotiations?

–Have thirty thousand tons ready for me before noon. Whether fridges, slippers or dog turds, he had made perfectly clear over the phone.

–Or else?

–Empty.

–To where, pray tell, Mitsos?

–To old friends.

It must have been getting on to eleven when the ATHOS III started receiving Sunday visitors. First up came a Japanese, a philosopher of wrist and ankle massage, who performed a demonstration on the bodies of the Russian volunteers.

The second appearance was by the agent with the mail; he distributed the letters, the men read them and got their fill of loans expired and taxes due.

Third, around twelve, came a lady in a taxi, dressed in gray blue. She showed her ID to a Georgi who asked no questions, let him take her suitcase and went up haughtily though twisting her empty hands madly, as if she were grasping and then releasing imaginary objects.

They say a good crew doesn't ogle the legs of the captain's wife.

First off, the woman was now middle aged, second, she was wearing trousers and third, she was a stranger to the men, none of them knew Flora Avgoustis, not having seen her, the captain wouldn't put a photograph up in his office nor had he ever taken the time to describe her.

The tall, gray-eyed woman introduced herself, shook hands with the first three seamen on the bridge, allowed them time to give her the once-over, looked approvingly around the ship, passed her palm over the bolts and alighted her gaze on the deck showing the footprints of the fugitive whom she had every intention of ferreting out and gathering in.

With the boatswain in the lead, the chief behind and the captain's wife third, they crossed the deck exchanging a handful of painless questions and answers, the weather in Greece, the relatives' health, they perked up a bit with the news of the national Athens-to-Thessaloniki highway, cut in two by the farmers' mobilization and they got overexcited with the ten CDs, several by Christopoulos, old gold, by Paschalis Terzis, the new god across the country, and others, too, which the somewhat clumsy empress took out of her bag and gave as gifts to her subjects. For all you guys, the top-notch voices of Greece, lest we forget.

As soon as they got down into Mitsos's stronghold, they felt his fever, he was on the phone again with golden boy, he was slashing prices, cutting down on the normal days for going from one place to the next and to the one after that, he was going for broke. The second mate and secretary at his side was keeping track of the gesturing instructions, he double-checked all the sums just to be on the safe side, working on the keyboards like a man possessed just to keep up with the captain.

–I'm busy, go away, he sent the visitors away without as much as raising his head, completely engrossed in his negotiations.

On entering the office, her gaze, amazed and severe, was riveted to his very long, very white hair, no picture from him in years, and to one small, fresh bluish mark on the side of the left eye.

He hadn't seen her, was now saying goodbye to Flirtakis, satisfied.

–You stand to gain. We've stolen so much petrol from that ass-licking son, that there'll be no place reserved in Paradise either for you or for me.

The deal was clinched and a good thing it was, some options opened up out of others' cancellations, fifteen thousand tons of industrial parts plus twenty thousand pieces of sinks and toilets, destined for frosty Xingan.

He made the sign of the cross, sniffed at the air with eyes closed, feminine perfume? he asked, feminine perfume, he repeated without a question mark and turned to face the three.

–Mimi?

A few minutes ticked past in silence, no welcoming, no hugs, till the seventy-five-year-old captain, said curtly to the men, go, and close the door behind you.

He got up walked to the porthole and took a deep breath.

–Why didn't you say on the phone you were coming?

–You wouldn't have let me.

–Still, you might have told me.

–Five times in the past twelve years I've gotten ready to come and you refused.

–I had my reasons.

–For not coming to Greece in twelve years? Not setting foot in your own house? Your children's house? Have you written all that off?

–I said, I had my reasons.

–And I for coming.

–Don't start all over.

–Now that, at long last, my hands are free, I'm going to feed my husband to the fish, because he's fucked me over and I owe him. That was meant for you, Mimi.

Chadzomanolis junior had said this to her after they'd buried the old man, just as they were piling the funeral wreaths on the grave site. Avgoustis, nevertheless was incensed primarily by the unexpected arrival, I was just talking with Flirtakis and the fucker never let on that you'd be coming, that you had come, that you were here. I pleaded with him and I also threatened him, Flora admitted and was in turn punished with his silence. After a full ten minutes, she was the one who took the initiative of making some move, of disturbing the almost ominous silence. She looked at the cat rubbing against the carpet, bent down and pet him without touching him, another Maritsa, she stoically noted, and moved next to her husband's side. She wasn't going to stoop to asking him to touch or kiss her, although, surely, she needed to be closer to him, now that slowly and gently, she'd decided after thinking about it, gently, she'd deliver the dramatic line, Mimi, you've lost your guardian and protector.

***

Brandy and an evening update on their children. In order and summarily. First, something about the oldest daughter, who didn't know how to string green beans and spent a morning watching the family videos until she found one of their vacation at the village, with her mother-in-law stringing away a bucketful of climber beans so she could mechanically imitate her, while her thoughts were on her marriage that was on a downhill slide.

About the lively little Laura, whom she'd brought him in

the kindergarten's Christmas video, dressed up as an angel, dancing and singing a fabulous number by Anna Vissi with the words changed.

About the second daughter, who changed her men at six-month intervals, would brook no talk of marriage and had turned into a fat-ass, nothing but chocolate mousse and pocket novels and, she sends you biographies of Einstein and Charlie Chaplin.

Her words regarding the youngest son, very circumspect. He'd thankfully given up on hooliganism. After Boston, though, Belgrade didn't seem to be working either, stuck in second year for the third time running, anyone could see he wasn't meant to be a biologist, wasn't meant to be a student. Whenever in Athens, bent over his drum kit for hours on end, not asking her not answering her either, closed up, dark, hardened and, yet, the best of their children. Did you even call him, Mimi, even just to wish him happy nameday? No, he hadn't.

Flora Avgoustis took a pack of photographs of Laura out of her purse and three miniature Plexiglass picture frames out of her suitcase. In the double one, last year's portraits of the girls, in the single, small one your son, she said and placed them on the cabin desk. Her husband looked at them fleetingly, unlocked the drawer to his desk, put the three frames inside and locked it again.

After some silence and a vain wait for some comment, for a phrase of delayed paternal fervor, the non-familial news followed, even more summarily and without the slightest hope, anymore, of dissolving the frostiness of the couple's first tête-à-tête in twelve years.

Flora said she'd grown tired of the white walls and had painted their apartment yellow, that she'd thrown out the dreadful squat couch, that Vouloubakis of the funeral parlor had died, that the two-story at the corner had been torn down

and turned into a mall with a delicatessen,
and a slimming center, Pireas no longer r
block in apartment buildings, she fores
logue omitting several items along simil
with the various acquaintances still keepi
lasagna and card games, followed by ten different kinds or
syrupy desserts.

Mitsos was listening. When Flora had said everything she
had to say, he once again unlocked the desk drawer and
brought out the cigar box. A second drink, an Havana and, at
long last, some questions, even for the formality of it, every
how often does the mayor collect the rubbish and if the garage
of the Smyrnian is still where it was.

–They come by for the rubbish every Monday, Wednesday
and Friday morning and the garage is no more, Abatzides
died and his son enrolled in PASOK and got a post as gardener at a TV station, Flora answered, at that same moment
thinking that she was, indeed, prophetic since she did usually
imagine, whenever that was—not often—her husband on his
own, sitting against a deep blue background, smoking away
for all he was worth. You are smoking again, she observed,
though gently.

–I picked it up again at sixty-seven.

–And you are not wearing glasses.

–I gave them up at sixty-eight.

They went on to thoughts they didn't exchange, as was to
be expected, they had no tradition of listening to one another
for very long.

A long time ago, there had been an intensity to their silence,
in the phase after that there were sporadic, intimate insinua-
tions and in the third phase, which became the status quo, they
were free at last to be oblivious of each other's existence, to not
intervene, for better or for worse, to restrict their intermittently
joint life to diplomatic coffees in the kitchen, to the cold kiss

atriation and to the farewell embrace which the presence
hird parties mandated.

So it was that Avgoustis, on the first day of his reunion with
his wife after twelve years, was smoking and thinking of scenes
as removed as possible, in Canada, at a restaurant in the company of two French captains sampling green sea urchins, white
crab and seal pâté from the Saint Lawrence river, notwith-
standing the loud protestations of the animal-besotted Brigitte
Bardot, the all-time best French ass.

Twenty years ago the seals in that place only numbered four
and a half thousand, with the protection measures they'd gone
up to five and a half million and one of those had crossed the
North Atlantic and the North Pole, gone down into the Sea of
Japan and was now enthroned across from him, both their
gazes turned backwards, watching the past.

They hadn't separated after the first daughter, not separated
after the second, they didn't manage it before the son, and not
afterwards either, the period when Flora was obsessively
dreaming that she could certainly have a better time of it with
some other man.

And there did exist a certain Marinos Limoyannis, neighbor, widower, hanging his laundry and casting glances. He had
a hardware shop, two street corners away. June of '73, she went
in to buy a small filter for the sink drain and first noticed him
from up close.

Forty-two? Forty-three? Not over forty-five, no taller than
five' seven", not more than a hundred forty-five, a hundred fifty
pounds max, brown hair, glasses for nearsightedness, the com-
monest appearance, one among many, with the exception of the
voice, deep, sweet and peaceful, nice day, Mrs. Avgoustis, how
are your little girls? and the eyes, enormous, twice as much eye,
so big you would go right in and walk round.

Flora, impulsively, hurled herself into their expanse of light
brown to stroll up and down and the hardware shop owner

removed his glasses to facilitate the meandering of his neighbor, who was going back and forth in the hospitable territory leaving the shopkeeper's question up in the air.

–For which drain?

She did explain which, a long while later.

–The sink.

–So that it gathers seeds and peels, I take it.

–Yes.

–Plastic or metal?

–No matter.

–They come in threes. Put one in the bathtub as well. It catches the hairs.

Her hand flew up to the bun on the back of her head but she didn't have to undo it, Marinos had seen her thick, brown hair coming down to the waist, they both remembered when, it was May, dawn, she'd gone out on the veranda to have her coffee and give the railing a wiping down.

On his name day, July 17, evening, Marinos Limoyannis in a new summer suit and freshly combed hair, was alone, just leaning on the frame of the balcony door, slowly drinking his beer.

The filters were followed by other purchases. At least once a week, Flora Avgoustis crossed the threshold of the paint shop for a plastic bathroom mat, four knobs for the kitchen drawers, new keys and an assortment of tidbits which she stuffed all mixed together, in their wrapping, in the closet under the sink. When they spilled over, she passed them on to her surprised and lazy in-law, presenting him on his name day with the traditional bottle of drink plus twenty sheets of sandpaper and on his wedding anniversary, with the traditional bouquet plus two boxes of extra long nails. Before her husband's ship docked in Pireas, Flora had called Limoyannis over twice. The first time was to put up a clothes-rack in the hallway with his Black and Decker and the second to set up a plastic pergola in the small kitchen balcony for the ivy to latch on to, which she intended to put in come spring, seven months hence.

There's no cash flow in the market, construction isn't moving, how many sugars in the coffee, one and a half, ah, is that all, they didn't say any more, they went into the rest with their eyes, desperately, but no further than that.

During that period, Flora was secreting away all her smart thoughts about the economy, politics and a life well lived, so as not to waste them on her husband who played deaf, she would no longer labor for the sake of Mr. Longgone, but in order to deliver her smart, well matured sallies to this one, who seemed like he would attend to her, all eyes and ears, when, at long last, the obstacles were out of their way.

Flora Avgoustis interrupted her daydreaming, enough for now, she thought as she watched her husband get up from his armchair to go to the bathroom.

She took the pack of Laura's photographs and put them back in her purse. She perused all the things that mattered to her very little, the bronze plaques of the inauguration by ATHOS of two new docks in Australasian ports and the metal ring in Maritsa's leg to stop him being driven mad from the magnetic waves.

She rose and stole a glance at the unlocked desk drawer, no family photographs there either, only exotic matchboxes, exotic decks of cards and magnifying glasses with phosphorescent handles. She reached to the jacket hanging on the chair and thought with secret pleasure that he, who let no one touch his clothes, had sewn on a button with brown thread instead of black, proof that old Mimis was neither self-sufficient nor unerring.

They'd gotten married thirty-five years ago, Easter of 1962. She traveled with him twice, fall of that same year and fall of next year, ten days each time, luckily she had good weather but she went without a wink, she could only sleep on land. She was bored by the shipping agents' tours around shipyards and fuelling tanks and despised the small rotting ports permanently stormed by mosquitoes.

A little later on, past midnight, with lights out, the Avgoustis couple in the double bed, the third trip for her on the wide-open seas of insomnia. She was thinking that she was smart, but without no courage. She lived gruesomely for years on end and she never moved a muscle. Same with him, often people with a lot of gumption, who manage well in everything else, can't make a clean break in their personal lives and turn into martyrs far forever and a day.

After twelve whole years and not a single kiss, Mimi? Not a single touch? She may not have been expecting it, still, it should have happened, because straight after old Chadzimanolis' burial, at the coffee after the funeral, Flora waged a battle to convince the scumbag son, before he rousted her husband from the ship with no questions asked, to let her go find him and bring him to his senses, not to spare him the humiliation but because, suddenly, she was looking for a pretext to resume her life with him any way possible, now that divorce would be meaningless, with him at seventy-five and her pushing sixty-four.

The half-forgotten Limoyannis wasn't going to be revived tonight, Flora was not about to stay awake rekindling some episode from her passion for the hardware shop owner, which had been blinking on and off for several years until the poor man realized it was going nowhere and had pulled away.

She did, at the beginning of the evening, find recourse in her memory of him, terribly piqued by the frosty welcome but also feeling that she was engaging in a farewell. She bid farewell post haste to one Giorgos and one Sotiris, at forty she had obliged the fifty-year-old and at fifty the forty-year-old, exceedingly short flings of one week, Flora Avgoustis wasn't suitable for her lovers for longer, she worked hard at making a point of her unsuitability.

So, then, here was her husband, well into full-fledged old age. This unsettled her. She had him next to her in bed they were turned away from one and another, ass to ass as it were, but his irregular breathing signaled that he wasn't able to sleep either.

Their great disappointments were known, solid and mutual and, so, all Flora wanted at that moment was to air a small complaint about his relentless indifference.

–Mimi, she said in the dark, with a gruff Pireas tilt, ever since forty-something when I started going gray, I meant to dye my hair and I kept asking you. Day before yesterday, before getting on the plane, I went at long last and switched back to my natural color, the old, light brown. Why, for God's love, didn't you say something?

***

–Oregano?
–In the yellow container.
–Mint?
–In the other yellow container. It's written on the outside.

Monday morning, at nine, while her husband was overseeing the loading, Flora Avgoustis stormed the freighter's kitchens, took off her wedding ring and put it in an empty saucer, rolled up her sleeves, put on an apron and started kneading five pounds of ground meat, to treat the crew to meatballs from a woman's hands.

–Why, whatever's wrong with men's hands? I rather suspect my pots and pans have been confiscated, murmured the cook to his assistant.

The shy thirty-year-old listened to him supportively, withdrew into a corner where he wasn't in plain sight and decided it was a good time to clean a ten-pound bag of sesame seeds, so it'd be handy for breads and bagels, when needed. The blood flowed downstream peacefully in *his* veins and he turned away from conversations that were begun in order to decide a winner and a loser, whatever for.

Gerassimos Siacandaris was apprised of the operation woman's meatballs from the previous evening, when he'd received instructions to take the ground meat out of the freezer and, in order to draw strength to face the invader, while putting the net on his curls, as he wasn't bold, unfortunately, not like other lucky chefs, he purposefully started his morning with a three minute dip in a sweetly pleasant scene from Kyriaki when, years ago, he was looking through paper boxes with junk in them, trying to locate a lantern and the lost packing needle, and came across a plate with a border of tiny yellow lilies, the sole survivor of his mother's tea set from her dowry, washed it, stacked it with biscuits and spent a contented day holding it to his chest, munching away and gazing out the window at the yellow leaves in the courtyard outside his kitchen with the yellowing vineyards on the horizon.

—Vineyards, was his single-word retort, too, to the assistant cook's glances from afar.

The entrance of the captain's wife had foiled him. He didn't like her airs and how utterly cozy she seemed to find his kitchen. She ought to be more circumspect, not to twirl with such élan among the benches with his pots and pans, not to dip so freely into his cupboards, not mix up his condiments on the shelves, or else he couldn't be at all sure that he wouldn't throw her, along with her gift, a sissy tie with pink crab pincers on it, in the oven, all ready and waiting for the two trays of his macaroni cheese.

—So was there a Marianthi to be found in the end ?

Flora Avgoustis was drawing on everything she could remember about the cook from old comments of her husband's and the Marianthi affair seemed appropriate for getting on Siakandaris' good side, as, at thirty, he'd gotten it into his head to fall in love with a Marianthi, he was so fond of the name, which combined the blessed Virgin with flower beds, that any merely passable Marianthi who might have come along would have him wrapped around her little finger within a month.

But every Marianthi there might have been, proved mysteriously scarce, Siakandaris turned thirty-five, forty and forty-five, remaining steadily luckless and, so, he declared to the captain's wife that after getting skinned at home by female man-eaters of different names, at fifty he himself turned hunter, slashing away at the snakes with the lustful eyes creepy crawling around his dick.

This intro plus some additional questions by Flora Avgoustis, about Japanese volcanoes, when did they last erupt, the eggs, when do they expire, and the rain, when will it stop for a stroll into town, were just the warm-up for getting in league with the cook who, watching her grate the onions awkwardly and listening to her transition from the formal address in the plural to the singular of familiarity, a prerequisite for a mood of guilty mutual trust, surrendered gradually to her covert method of interrogation and in the end, while admiring her punching of the ground meat, sided with her now unabashed aim of shedding light on everything, she would be doing the digging, but he would, surely, also get some tidbits himself.

–What do you mean, he eats boiled zucchini? Hospital food, he used to call it.

–He's looking after his health.

–Was his checkup bad?

–He hasn't been to the doctor five, six, seven years.

–Does he let you know every time he goes?

–He lets me know every time he skips his tests.

–And what's the Company doing, then? Don't they ask for a health certificate?

–Tests for alcoholism and drugs from the new guys.

The cook, an old hand at the game and enjoying prodding her now, stuck to his own version of things, captain Mitsos had cured two bleeding gastric ulcers, had treated three breakdowns, had successfully operated on an infected elbow and had put stitches on half the crew when, fifteen years ago, they'd gotten drunk and pulled out knives to fight over the merits of Kazadzides, the voice of the Greek Diaspora. He couldn't brook the time wasting and the going back and forth to doctors, nor throwing his money away, so he did tactical maneuvers and eluded them.

–This morning he tricked me as well. I had a checkup with a Greek, he said, and all's well.

–In 1989.

–That far back?

–After that we entered the Protocol and moved to the Pacific. That was the end of Buenos Aires for us.

–Is that where his doctor is?

–Was. He died in 1990.

Flora listened to all this mad and improbable bits of news in rapid succession. Anyone else would be overwrought by all this, she was thinking.

–At his age, she said soberly, Mimis needs a good pathologist at all costs and a live one at that.

–The dead bloke was a gynecologist.

The woman stayed with her arms sunk into the meat, unmoving, watching Siakandaris slowly stir the cream sauce in the pot and listening to him tell how in the past, whenever they passed through Argentina, the captain would go to his gynecologist's office, but the last time, in 1990, it was the doctor who came on board, at dawn, to see Maritsa's acrobatics around the rails as well, which he'd loved, he'd followed the reddish, plump cat, enchanted, walking on tiptoe himself and muttering softly about the marvels of animals.

In their occasional meetings over the years the two men

drank and talked, no one knew the nature of their bond, and why should anyone, they might as well just have smoked their Havanas together, Sifakakis being extremely generous with cigars.

–You mean to say his doctor started him smoking again?

–Most certainly.

–Good on him for it.

–Don't you fret over your husband, he's got a lot of mileage left in him yet.

Flora Avgoustis put the meat in the fridge to sit for a bit, threw out the onion skins and eggshells, had her second coffee of the day next to the bread-kneading trough, the first had been with Mimis, at six in the morning, she'd taken out of her purse the two return tickets and showed them to him, she asked for no report and no record of the past twelve years, she merely requested that he allow her to start getting his things together.

He unwrapped before her the package with the golden-blue teapot, locked the closet and the desk drawer, dropped the keys in his pocket and left for the steering house with a casual, do with your day as you will.

Toward eleven the cook's assistant was grating lettuce for the salad, the cook was spreading the cream sauce evenly over the macaroni and Flora's first installment of meatballs were already sizzling in the frying pan.

This is nothing like Japan in here, this is a wine tavern back home, Siakandaris smiled.

After the exhausting tug of war with the captain's wife, some emotion was due, related to Kyriaki, so, while adeptly feeding the trays back into the oven, he made the statement that his eyes were surrounded by tears that had come from a long way off.

Flora glanced at Siakandaris' moist lashes as he came to stand beside her to count the floured meatballs, at least here's someone who's nostalgic for home, she thought, even though he has no children and grandchildren standing by.

–Do I still have a grandfather? That's what the little girl asks.

–Why, he could as easily mollycoddle her a bit on the cell-phone, no? This new gadget has changed our life. An invention for seamen.

–He did talk to her. Twice. And how do I know that's really grandpa? Disbelieving and tough. She took after him.

Siakandaris asked if she was playful, the photo came out of Flora's bag.

–All wile and guile, a little woman through and through, age five, sighed the cook and what lovely name, Laura, it shimmers and it gurgles even without the initial F, since she must have been named after you, Florence, Flora.

No, the captain had never shown him the child's picture, there hadn't been an occasion, nor did he decorate his cabin with the family, he probably doesn't like photos of this kind one bit because they pull him into the constant wistfulness for home and hearth. He's not like us. Different in everything. And for the past few years, all stubbornness and silence. No candles at the churches, no visits to the sights. He, who always went to the end of the promontory so he could gaze at his ship from fifty yards away, hadn't been off it for more than ten years.

He did, nevertheless, extol his thousand other virtues and passionately praised his skills, he'd sailed, before Avgoustis, on two schooners, no more than tragic rust buckets breaking the embargo on Cuba.

With captain Mitsos he felt safe and he felt dignified, free to seriously apply himself to a cook's vocation of providing succor with a meal properly cooked. And just as he had no qualms about bombarding males with recipes, he now picked on culinary figures of speech, hellish onion stew and heavenly risotto, bent on annihilating in the gastronomic arena a woman who, however, wasn't following him anymore, didn't see him turn off the oven a moment later, nor did she register him rearranging his already orderly condiments and nudging the assistant, busy at the sink, gesturing for the two of them to go out for some fresh air.

As in turned out, Flora Avgoustis was smarting a lot more than she thought back in Greece over her husband's having written off not just herself but their children, too, and, unavoidably, while she was mechanically dropping more meatballs into the hot oil, her thoughts, unable to rest on the present and the future, turned back to the critical fall of '73. Not to her involvement with the hardware shop owner but to the other events that had happened in tandem.

At the end of November Mimis had come off the ship for three months, determined that the two of them should end things, but, because of the night curfew imposed by the ruling junta, he'd get back home early, would walk in and out of rooms restlessly, spend time with the girls until they dropped off and then, during the bitter post-midnight explanations, accompanied each time by half a bottle of whisky, two farewell fucks took place and, come spring, Flora was pregnant with their third child and Avgoustis was floundering about the Baltic, still a married man. The news cost him a minor stroke, thankfully while in port. He made it through and gave up cigarettes in the bargain.

Their only son was born on August 31, 1974, the captain got the news in Bremen, he wired money but didn't take the plane for a flash visit to see his third child and his wife in confinement.

This didn't go unnoticed by the men of the crew, in seventh heaven at that time over the fall of the junta, and Flora read it in the minced words and the manner of the two seamen who visited for the well-wishing, the first one, by the name of

Balodimos, who didn't live past the next year, had come back to Greece posthaste to hug his niece released from prison and, shortly after, the second, by the name of Papalexakis, well over six feet tall and thin as a rod, had come to be present in Chania at the ninety day memorial for his pilot godson, killed during the events in Cyprus.

Deaths and lives make up the connecting tissue of families, this here was no less than the birth of a son, eight pounds two ounces with a good sized little pecker and ballsies, as the infant nurse had admiringly put it, and the father was away and was going to be away for another year and a half.

He first saw the kid spring of '76, a white lily in the apartment's blue bathroom, being shampooed by his mother, his little dick proudly bouncing and dripping soap suds all over.

His name Antonios and not Triandafilos, that of the deceased father-in-law, Flora had already had the child baptized at one year and had, naturally, honored her own father, a small revenge to comfort her in her graceless and, by now, irrevocable captivity.

Daughter of the owner of a well-off grocery-shop, The Nile, foodstuffs local and imported, she always gave her father a hand at the store during the festive season, renewing the cans on the shelves, sticking on the labels with the pinched prices, weighing halva and pickled foods for the days of fasting, adding her aristocratic tastefulness with the fish roe and the white tarama.

That is exactly where Avgoustis chanced on her, in the days leading up to Easter of '61, he'd gone into the grocer's for a selection of choice tidbits, a pound of luxury items for a bachelors' feast.

The pretty Flora Avgoustis, with a weak spot for the two shades of white, that of snow and that of pearls, besides being haughty and taller than him, was also a single child and the heiress to the corner-store business, packed high with all the good Earth's riches. It was that, after her gray gaze, like a trident, pierced the customer, whose eyes, still red from the world's two largest oceans, contrasted with his blindingly white, starched shirt, she left him writhing there a fortnight or so, long enough for her grocer dad to check on his political convictions, for the single stone ring to be proffered and the silk suits to be tailored, for the elaborate luncheons at the different family branches of the Zagoraioi in the Ano and Kato Patisia districts, for a down payment to be made on the four-bedroom apartment in Pireas, and for two smart evening outings, at the Mocambo and the Coronet, jazz, black evening dresses and all the musts of a showy engagement.

Mitsos Avgoustis got married capitulating to the overkill largesse of his father-in-law and hypnotized by the manhandling of the horny Flora. The twenty-nine-year-old counted three relationships on her record, the first with a student, the second with a graduate student, the third with a postgraduate stuck on his dissertation, she hadn't been with a man for a year and a half and, there was no doubt, the captain was decidedly more accomplished in bed than the student body.

Two months after the honeymoon trip, Easter in Castoria, at the Hotel du lac, Zagoraios went bankrupt and within half a year, the first signs of bankruptcy started showing in the newlyweds' passion as well.

The first time Flora thought of divorcing, a novice mom nursing her baby girl, she looked through all the ads in the paper for a job, but mainly for pianists in Cyprus and dancers in Beirut.

The two hundredth and last meatball came out of the frying pan, the apron was returned by the captain's wife to its hanger, her sleeves were rolled back down and her wedding ring left the saucer and was returned to its familiar finger, a wedding for the eyes of the beholders.

***

Hate requires vigor. You need to be well rested to be able to afford the fierceness and intensity that will lift you to something so rough and unyielding.

On the eve of her departure for Japan, Flora Avgoustis had spent five hours, from eleven at night until four in the morning, inside the Punto parked high up on the Kastela hill, in the driver's seat, scarcely saying anything, her son silent in the passenger seat, until at one point he got out of the car, walked for some thirty yards upside down on his hands, with his feet in the air, came back and at long last opened his trap to say to her, you're married to a guy who's not coming back from the Pacific, not ever.

When younger, she'd had the strength and the will to hate Mimis, she would wait for his return in order to highlight their resignation, to parade before him their sorry state and hold him accountable, to ask pressingly that he quit the sea on the off-chance they could make things work again. In recent years she'd grown accustomed to not asking for anything, to desiring neither war nor peace, rage had been succeeded by weariness and weariness had set the stage for submission. He was doing his own thing far away and she, after completing the three year cycle of a movies, plays and wining and dining, was now nibbling away at the slow-moving time in her car, crisscrossing Attica and its surroundings, Evia, too, with any divorcee or widow she found available and willing for ouzo, marking time and badmouthing the male sex.

Sometimes, when she'd had more that a small carafe to drink or when the weather was the sickly kind that gets people down, she'd look for something to latch onto to dig up things from the past, some pretext to open doorways to half-forgotten events that had some juice or to yet another fight with the absentee husband or to nostalgia for the initial and short-lived good times, a summer night spent on the sand with the waves fizzling out next to them just as they themselves were fizzling, groaning, smiling, breathing heavily and screwing like dogs, and a Sunday when she was grating the carrots in the kitchen and Mimis had brought out from his suitcase in the living room tiny aromatic soaps, putting one under her nose to sniff, then going back to the suitcase to bring the next, a total of eight soaps of different colors and smells, eight round trips between the living room and the kitchen.

A good suit needs a proper coat hanger. Good clothes need a proper wardrobe. The captain's rich wardrobe, underwear, shaving kit, everything in order around her in Mimi's cabin, where Flora had returned alone after dinner.

The midday meatballs had been devoured at a quick meal with an infectious awkwardness spreading to one table after the other. Mimis came to his seat last and was the first to leave. Siakandaris cottoned onto the mood and, in order to keep her occupied, didn't let up on the delectable red mullets in goat butter and the five-yard-long meatloaf he'd made the year before last for the captain's name day. Two or three silly seamen mistook her for the kind that swoons over unheard of natural phenomena and treated her to a description of a steep white sea-rock, off the African coast somewhere, with a thousand red tiny birds in its ridges and to information about some kind of Filipino bat that lives on flowers and fruit. Birbilis, in particular, the scrounger secretary dripping with diligence and servility, had a go at bringing a tear to her eye with the sob stories of a female elephant, a goat and a crow.

Flora swallowed a meatball, nice, and a couple of forkfuls of spaghetti much nicer, and remained ladylike to the end with these men who, in their own company, would crack jokes about cuckolding and about dicks like quicksilver, standing to attention in the tropics and laying low at the poles.

She saw the afternoon out alone in the cabin, in the absence of the master, Maritsa didn't fancy sleeping in the presence of the mistress, and with dusk impending, she let lie persistent questions and troublesome thoughts, washed up, put on the tight black skirt and the good beige blouse, went walking round the ship, a little shamefacedly, and found herself again at the officers' wardroom and at the table of the captain who, standing up like a proper gentleman, gave out the order to the steward, throttle champagne for the missus.

As an hors d'oeuvre, an anecdote about red crabs with black pincers of beautiful Tasmania was served, as a first dish, Patagonia which is packed with king crabs and as a main, the requiem for a monster crab weighing fifteen pounds, from ten years ago in Alaska, which they had to split open with a hammer and chisel.

Might these short tales, and all the others she'd listened to during the midday meatballs, the morning coffees and yesterday's stuffed lamb, have actually been tasty, might the little poem recited for her benefit by the Russian twins, who emphasized how the love of Pushkin is a family tradition have in fact been a genuinely pleasant rustling in her ears and could the request of the Romanian what's-his-name to make them some meatballs again during the trip, been also a genuine expression of fondness on the part of the crew she would have felt welcome in their midst. Wouldn't she be well advised to take a deep breath, give out some big smiles left and right and throw in a couple of jokes herself, the first one modest, the second a bit more risqué?

She promptly put thought into action. She turned friendly, she teased Siakandaris with his own weapons talking about ministers not worth their salt and mealy mouthed politicians, she complimented Birbilis on his taste in coral bijoux and, in order not to overdo it with racy jokes and piss Mimis off, she humbly adopted the part of Holy Mary, patroness of Mount Athos and complained that the captain hasn't made his pilgrimage to the Monastery of Megistis Lavras.

All this was part of her scheme to gently dissuade her husband from heading in a few days' time for Xingan, in the north of China, for unprocessed phosphate as Flirtakis had been arranging, and for the two of them to leave for Greece. Mimis, though, terribly correct but remote, almost a stranger in the champagne-induced din, was slowly picking at some Gruyère cheese without the slightest trace in his eyes of nostalgia for Pireas or his home, places that had been crossed out.

I don't want the men talking, he turned and said almost in her ear, for a fortnight or so I won't be sending you away.

Following this statement, he said out loud, as if talking to himself, that he had the lists of the payroll and the seamen's pension fund to see to, got up and left and when, a while later, Flora went to the cabin, she found him bent over the papers, unwilling to talk.

She took from her bag a women's magazine, already read from cover to cover during the long flight, and while thumbing through it indifferently, she resumed the troublesome queries that the afternoon had interrupted.

Why would her husband be locking the drawers in his very own cabin? What was the meaning of the five hidden magnifying glasses with the fluorescent handles? How come he sewed his buttons with brown thread instead of black? Why hadn't he seen the videotape with his granddaughter dancing and singing for him? Why didn't he comment on her dyed hair? Why, at lunch, didn't he serve her some more wine himself when she had asked but had the steward do it instead? Why was he, Flora had noticed, never the first to address any of the men? And why did he avoid doctors and never leave the ship and why, in the last few years, every time he sent a gift with a half-page letter, were those dictated to his secretary and why had he turned into a sphinx that was now leafing through nautical documents without jotting anything on them but on some separate scraps of paper instead, until he gathered them all up and locked everything in his drawer?

He seemed absorbed by his own private thoughts, unreachable. What could he be thinking about? Was it just work?

At dinner, he'd said a couple of words about his first trip to Japan, forty-five years ago, carrying English bombs from World War II for scrap metal, and about the second, forty-two years ago, carrying old railway lines from the USA, another thirty plus times had followed to all the different ports of Japan and this one, Flora said to herself, he had at all costs to be the last one.

Maritsa was snoring inside his beloved master's slippers, by the desk. Flora bent down to pet him, failed, straightened up, smoothed out the black skirt and the beige blouse, picked up a cardigan and suggested to Mimis, let's go for a walk in the port so I get to see it as well, and for you to say goodbye to it, she added mentally. Go by yourself, his answer.

It's midnight, I can't possibly go alone and besides, I'd like a short walk together, she persisted, I'm not coming, he cut the conversation short with a doggedness barely able to disguise his nervousness and impatience for a speedy return to the assurance of silence. Mimi, Flora pleaded, let's try not to quarrel while I'm here, let's go out even for a cigarette on the deck, for your men to see us at ease together.

Avgoustis stood for a bit undecided, then unlocked the drawer again and took out a cigar, let's go Maritsa, he called to the cat and then Flora, putting her heels back on, added to her list of why this and why that, yet another item, why had Mimis looked for the cat in his slippers, in vain, when previously the animal, to avoid her petting, had leapt onto the bed and its white fur stood out a mile against the background of the gray-blue blanket.

With a lightening motion she took off the beige blouse and her beige bra and went out first, Maritsa behind her let out a meow and, further back, Mimis closed the door.

They must have gone seven or eight yards along the corridor when she stopped in front of him, took his hand and brought it to her naked breasts. Criminal, she said to him harshly and frightened at the same time and he, paling, pushed her away, dragged her back into the cabin, closed the door and while Maritsa was scratching on the wood from outside, asking to be let in, Avgoustis got hold of his wife's arms with both hands, shook her, slapped her, nearly missing, and called her a snitch.

The hours till dawn passed with Flora Avgoustis asking him when he went blind, it's been ten years now, in both eyes, in both, worse in the right one, can he see only a bit, shadows, silhouettes and strong lights, does anyone from the crew know, how could they not have figured it out, I know the ship like the palm of my hand, how does he manage, using my head plus Birbilis, a man's best right hand, charging him with taking the men down with him, others drown them in the wild seas not I, castigating him for being irresponsible and a fool, my mind's in perfectly good order, and threatening him, as soon as day breaks I'm sending Chadzimanolis a telegram with the truth, and, I'll inform the crew, and, I'll call the children, and, I'll let the Japanese in on this, and, this ship is not going to sail again with a blind man steering it.

Next morning Siakandaris was holding the box with the porcelain teapot and behind him Birbilis was dragging the suitcase of the captain's wife who came third, lagging behind to explain herself to any of the men who chanced on the procession, their grandchild is at the Children's Hospital with acute laryngitis and is bringing the place down, where is my grandma, I want my grandma.

She would be escorted to the airport by the cook, the captain had urgent business to attend to, he'd said, not caring whether anyone was convinced.

They said goodbye on the staircase. He gave her a lukewarm hug. She kissed him with her eyes brimming. Two hours ago there had been tears in his eyes as well. Dawn was about to break, sleepless and exhausted, he'd made the ship's round with his wife to show her Maritsa's extravagant performance, so she could relay them like a fairytale to Laura who was in perfect health, naturally, with no laryngitis whatsoever.

Flora Avgoustis was stealing glances at everything he couldn't see, as if she suddenly appreciated the moon trembling on the water, the silver shavings on the waves, all the while taking deep breaths and keeping an eye out for the cat, to catch it in case it slipped, for her husband, too, to support him in case he happened to stumble, though by now she knew he'd been managing the thick cloudiness of his vision for years on end, tricking humans and vile seas alike.

–Mimi, she'd said to him mildly, wishing to touch his arm but not daring, we'll go to the best ophthalmologists. You can have an operation. Lasers can work miracles.

–So can I.

She let him simmer down a little so she, too, could think of what might make a real difference to this state of things.

–I think you need to see your children, she said at long last.

–But I can't see.

–For them to see you.

–That so? Listen, I've seen what was mine to see. It's been plenty.

Leaning against the rail with Maritsa between them, rubbing her muzzle against Avgoustis's sleeve, they had one last cigarette, shared a three minute silence and straight afterwards, they exchanged the last three questions and answers. And this was precisely where he, both protected and trapped under the cover of his dark world, couldn't help the tears from brimming.

–Mimi, whatever it is, tell me what's happening to you.

–The swell has planted trouble in my mind.

–What's the real reason you won't come back?

–The sea won't give me back.
–What are you still looking for, now?
–I have no will for the land.

***

The sound of the exhale one snowy dawn, teeth clattering in the cold like rapid typing, the scratching of the match, the sailor on duty zipping up his raincoat, the morning cigarette cough of the men in their bunks, the Rumanian talking to himself, the boatswain's creaking shoulder, arthritis with a vengeance, the clicking of the worry beads of the elder Sorin, Birbilis's nail clipper that gets to work every Saturday afternoon before the secretary's royal ablutions, the tap-tapping of the no-filter cigarette against the flat square pack, this is the avid smoker and Communist Party member, the sigh coming out of the chef assistant's chest in installments after sundown, the mosquitoes' rapid fire in the swampy ports at nighttime, the seething sibilants that escape the tightened lips of men in place of the fully fledged cussword, the tearing open of envelopes and the pieces of paper being extracted, their unfolding, the counting, one sheet, two, three or more by studious twelve-year-old daughters, a cataloguing of sounds of special significance, especially in recent years when his ear functioned as a radar to cover up for his sightlessness, so he wouldn't be found out.

And, of course, after eight at night, in his cabin, the sound of the dry palate that welcomes the first mouthful of whisky and right after that, the rhythmical knocking of the wedding ring against the armchair, the only practical use of his marriage, and of its relic shoved onto his finger.

Tomorrow the clouds'll have things to say, I hear them preparing their speech, the captain stood listening to the weather as well.

He'd learned to pick up and unravel those vital signs of everyday living that signaled to him who the unspeaking sailor next to him was and what was up and with whom on the ship's every square inch.

In his own cabin, apart from Maritsa with the monotone snoring and the luxuriant meowing, he cohabited with the sounds of his own routine, as if he needed to alert himself, too, about what was going on and what each thing meant.

The lamp of the body is the eye, according to Matthew and the body's doorbell is the ear, according to Mitsos, he'd poke fun at himself in the aftermath of some sudden thud, some strange creak, even at the seagulls' squawking, when entering or leaving a port.

Having lived for fifty-eight years with the swell setting the rhythm of the very blood flowing in his veins, he had trained his ears exceptionally well, his brain and his entire body to fall in step with and prepare for every change in the weather, to sniff out the storms, only half of those came through in the weather bulletin, the other half were from his permanently choppy wife and the Company cocksuckers, Avgoustis' red ship, to them a red rag to the bull.

The eye is a fine instrument, like that old Optical store add said.

Eleven years ago in Antwerp, he was watching at a distance of ten yards the very first Maritsa, grandfather to the present one, weaving on the rail, come here you scoundrel, he called out as an endearment and the cat got scared and flew away, it was a seagull.

And the next day when he went into town for business, with that conjunctivitis and the chronic blur darkening his world and making his step hesitant, which he'd been blaming on the tropical climate, he had wondered what the seven black shapes might be that were gliding along the street, until a dozen awkward notes sounded by a transporter made him realize this was a piano removal taking place from one store to another.

He went to a doctor, the optical nerve a mess from that god-forsaken lightening bolt at Mount Athos, the left eye half gone, the right, an eye for the sake of appearances, merely. The sugar levels in his blood slightly pinched as well. He left in a panic. He didn't even tell Siakandaris. He reduced by himself his intake of his beloved bread, he cut out all sugary sweets, he cut right down to two swigs of whisky.

And after about two months, by which time his vision registered the surrounding life like the static on a broken black-and-white TV, nighttime, the ship docked at Biscay, he was in that self-same cabin again, pounding and scratching at his eyes in a rage, tempted to pluck them out with a fork and feed them to the cod shove inside the twin orbits his balls, which did still work.

Next morning, to the men asking about the bruises and the swollen eyelids, he'd dryly replied that, instead of using hair shampoo, he'd used hemorrhoid soap and had made a mess of things.

For the first time, out of fear of hurtling down the stairs, he started to grip the rail with force and to take his time going down or coming up the stairs, pretending to be distractedly gazing out to the horizon.

For the first time, he started silently measuring the small, endlessly repeated distances, ten steps from the bulkhead of the prow to his office, another ten from there to the steering house, another ten to the chartroom.

For the first time, once in there, he stood in front of the maps and looked at them from memory.

The eyes give the mind a rest because they do half the work on their own. Without them, Mitsos Avgoustis, on alert night and day, sorted through what he needed to remember in order to carry out his deceit, collected the data in his head, ordered it, checked it regularly, giving himself tests and as a result, during the first year, there was space in his head for absolutely nothing else, apart from this mnemonic thesaurus of his trade, a fact which made him move along the walkways like a sleepwalker.

There goes the blessed respite, a lifetime's habit of reading twenty pages each night from the biographies of the great. There goes the morning's meticulous shave, he cut himself three times then grew a beard, he let the hair grow long, too, only nipped it back with the scissors when it got overlong. An end to the outings at the ports, as well, it wouldn't do to be promenading with elbows hooked with the cook.

In August of '87, in Fortaleza, he'd seriously thought about the thirty tons of coffee being his last cargo, he would deliver them in Hamburg and from there go back to Greece and stay put. Pireas and the family out of obligation, Elefsina and Litsa out of love? And how to present himself to either party blind? He put off the decision for the next trip, then for the one after and, in the meantime, he learned to make his way and, port by port, to make do with and hide behind the pleasure and the competence of his deceit. By 988, he'd given up for good the search for his own wave that would wash him up on the shores of retirement and deliver him hostage to the turbulence on the shore.

He had quit answering Litsa's letters and let communications with the family grow scarcer still, the son, especially, was growing up like an orphan, with his father's lack of interest resoundingly obvious.

Greece unavoidably meant Litsa and Andonis, let the day never come when he'd have to settle with them at close quarters, the day when they would mete out their just retribution.

The sea it is, then, and we'll take things as they come, with God's help.

On the captain's last visit to Buenos Aires, doctor Sifakakis supplied him with a piece of paper, just in case, an ophthalmologist friend of his had signed without undue questions, a diagnosis for a susceptibility of the eyes to the drastic shifts in climate, from minus 10 to 40 degrees Celsius within six, seven days.

–So, then, that explains it, Birbilis commented on the doctor's report, on his previous ship the abrupt shifts in temperature had caused acute rheumatism to a seventeen-year-old sailor whose body and mouth became inflamed, his life was in danger, a helicopter came to pick him up and carry him to a hospital.

It was about then that Avgoustis got on the phone several times with the Pireas crowd and suggested that old Chadzimanolis schedule the ship for the cyclic trips, it's in your interest, he proved it by showing him figures, persuaded him and then asked for the Pacific.

–Isn't that far off for you?

–If only there was further.

–Instead of starting to circle closer to your home by now, you keep getting farther away, the old man said thoughtfully, without asking anything more, he did know the score, roughly. Their joint visits to Mount Athos lasted four, five days for himself and one, two at most for Avgoustis, who gladly used the alibi to secretly run off to Elefsina for his alternative pilgrimage.

The darkness in the eyes holds the tongue back, so no more running commentary either, on this, that and the other.

There was a time when he even enjoyed the topics of conversation with his men which are repeated in more or less the same words, like a wall that every year you freshen up with a couple of layers of whitewash. All of them were a lot happier with the oft-told things, because unscheduled conversations found them unprepared and obliged them to experiment and search into themselves with an uncertainty which, it was obvious, was the last thing they wanted right in the middle of the ocean and so far away from their homes.

It was enough for them to mix together for a couple of hours, for the time it took to empty a bottle, talk about skirts, politics and soccer so they could all take turns practicing, with guaranteed success, the art of sighing.

He himself spoke rarely, slowly and low, the others played out the main repertory and he, from the aisles, would touch on their talk with something infinitesimal. Sometimes, though, when the fun didn't spark, when spirits plummeted and they were collectively assailed by the blues and by that thick loneliness that overcomes seamen at night, individually and in groups, they did turn to him for the couple of expedient words that would light a candle in the midst of the dark talk.

Shut in his cabin, ironing his jacket himself as always, Mitsos Avgoustis remembered his mother who used to talk with her hand moving back and forth in front of her mouth, as if to send the words away, till she quit all exchanges with those around her and, at long last, attained the unblemished isolation she desired so she could put her own signature on her gentle and privileged passing away.

How come he had remembered the dead woman?

Sometimes death resolves the deceased person's issues with the living but Avgoustis was not the kind to invest in his own death.

He was on his way to China with a half load of industrial equipment and bathroom accessories. There'd still been no telegram from the Company delivering the expected thunderbolt, it seems Flora was weighing things up, should she turn him in or shouldn't she, she'd probably have a lawyer looking into whether there was any chance of them slapping a lawsuit on him and cutting a chunk out of his pension.

Would she have told the children the truth? he wondered. The son, especially, was bound to hate him even more. And hatred from a distance is an invincible regime.

So then, Xingan for the time being, unprocessed phosphate and see what happens, in a manner of speaking.

He hung the pressed jacket on the hanger and put it in the closet, gathered up the ironing board and the steam iron, he knew his space like the back of his hand.

And since blindness didn't hold sway over the life inside of him, which was eating him up, he could see there with perfect clarity the whole crowded world of his past and, alongside them, his mistakes, his lies, his wrong-doing and his deceit; he poured his thimbleful of whisky and replaced worrying about his spouse with the sly sorrow that he almost hankered after, every time he thought of that other woman with the potted plants.

***

Mitso, I love your arm.

Every time you come I'll start like I did in half my last letters, over a hundred, and I will talk to you as if I'm writing to you.

At least I won't have to be sealing the words in envelopes and writing a male name with my initials as the sender, Leon Tavrides and Lakis Taramas, pretend friendships from when you were in the army or mariners, just so no one from your crew suspects my existence. In fact, in order for the correspondence not to be too frequent, I collected my writings over two months and mailed them all together, a goodly chunk. He'd write three, four times a year, half a page each time and a full one a short while before he came.

I've lived through so much muteness in here that, for

me, the letters take on the role of a conversation. Since then, I've managed to have conversations all by myself.

In every next letter I copied a few lines from the previous one, having meanwhile found in magazines the right spelling of the difficult words, both so he could see my progress and because I like repeating myself. Repetition is necessary, so that things don't happen just once but two times or more, because then their significance increases and they stay with us forever.

I often get to saying the same things over and over and in the exact same way I was taught them as a kid, which is to say that time in life when they use the same words to put some bits of wisdom into all our heads.

That the first autumn rain is God's blessing.

That kindness is a balm.

That men are children.

That you don't go for a visit empty-handed.

That every garden is looking for its jasmine.

I planted mine in 1973 and it was used to decorate all the epitaphs in our parish after the junta.

When I was ten years old, at Aghioi Apostoloi, I used to stand behind my dad. I would hug him tightly around the waist. I lay my cheek against his cool shirt. And if it was the blue one and the dandruff was showing, I would spend the entire service flicking away the tiny white dots one by one.

As an adult, I tried to believe in God, but faith wouldn't slide into me because I saw on the dark church walls the saints, all stretched out, posing right up against each other, all of them tall, thin, with their goatees, standing up and frowning like those wordless coffee-bar patrons that spend the entire night at the bar on two drinks. I went myself a couple of times, and I got painfully drunk.

Mitsos, may his days be long, was partly to blame. The first years, I remember whenever he came to me and whatever followed. Then, it was the separations that stuck in my mind. So, out of habit, I went with two of my customers to the last of the Virgin Mary's Salutations and, on the inside, I was singing farewell songs. Still, the disbelieving Litsa goes on singing praises to the lord who plundered her youth.

The only time in my life that I believed in miracles was by the cement blocks of someone else's toilet.

The devout concentration of the deflowering.

Before that, I was sort of dating a soccer player, a solid fondness. But I didn't adore him, nor he me, so we only did it around the edge. With Mitsos at the cement blocks it was straight through.

Lots of things happened after that.

I'd see his hands get sweaty and tingly until they went into action on my body and immediately afterwards, those eyes of his that always had me pondering, would shut, not letting me gain unlawful entry into them.

I didn't let off those eyes, not for one moment. I hunted them down and I interpreted them. Maybe wrongly, too. That's also useful in its own way. When two people live separately, they are not only deprived of the language of talk, they also miss out on a lot of the things that are said through the hands, caresses and slaps and, even more, through the eyes: the oaths and the forevers.

You, too, lived apart from him. You missed out on a lot. And he, on just as much.

I was looking at the four photographs of his that you left me the day before yesterday. A ramrod posture and at seventy-five no less. And his eyes, the absolute best feature on this man, that gaze of his that lets loose lightening bolts and conquers. His by now snow-white hair and beard, certainly in need of shearing. And as for the cat, another Maritsa, I bet.

Let me just grab a pen, for something to hold in my hand while I'm talking to you.

I'm seeing now the clouds moving away, the birds being left up there on their own, having nowhere to hang onto.

As I said last time, I've hung onto the garden, a tropical mind in Elefsina that gets ideas about how to combine colors or showcase them, a cactus plant myself, since I flower with no water.

As I sit down to watch Antenna, that's the channel I've gotten used to, as for the others, it's as if I can't understand the language properly, I run out on the show host, go out to the veranda for half a minute to smell the carnations and then go back inside, to my chair.

When I was young I couldn't go to sleep for not knowing which way Hawaii lay.

Now, in bed, at two in the morning, I'm wondering, three purple carnations and four red ones or four purple and three red? I get up. I turn on the courtyard light. I look out from behind the window pane. In the end, there are four purple and three reds. I turn off the light again and slip under the sheets. And before morning coffee, as I'm removing the snails from the leaves, I'm thinking. But how can he live without a tree?

That's why, when I got notice of his arrival, I would prepare a special welcome for him. I would hang up potted plants on ropes, oil lamps in bloom. I'd set out dozens of tin cans of all sizes with plants inside along the front path, the sidewalks outside, the fields all around, green soldiers of the land forces this time and not the navy again, guarding our tryst.

All these years two thousand carnations have bloomed and he's only seen thirty-five, maybe forty.

Fortunately, he never happened to come over in February, when the flower beds are on extended holiday and the garden isn't showcasing a single thing.

I didn't only keep track of the flowers and the funny business. I have counted and saved the tops of the beer bottles he opened here. The razors he used. The empty plastic bottles of alcohol I used to rub his neck with.

I've kept track of all my questions he answered about the sea and all the places I wanted him to take me, even if he didn't take me to any. A licensed driver since '78, I sometimes used to drag him in the Fiat to ouzo taverns, past midnight, the two last remaining customers, like outlaws. I have jotted down the number of kilometers I drove and the four taverns I took him to.

I kept an accountant's records of our relationship. Losses and gains. The latter, plentiful.

I wrote to him.

Mitso, listen to me. Empty house. Switched off television. Switched off radio. A plate on the table. I am eating your favorite dish and I am happy. There are parties with one person, you know. I am forced to feast by myself.

But breathing feels so lovely tonight.

I've got this notion to take the chair out afterwards and spend the night sleepless under the pomegranate tree.

***

One of the first-born daughter's rare phone calls.

–She caught you in your cabin with a whore. That's why she came back willy-nilly. That's why you've made yourself scarce around here, so you can hump your whores. Get lost, to us you've always been lost anyway, you're nothing but a sex-crazed dotard, set on bringing us all undone.

There was more to her three-minute-long harangue, you are traveling but mother's the one slaving away to keep this home afloat, you are riding the waves but she's sunk, you send her away like a dog, here's your teapot and on your way, while she's covering for you with the Company, saying you are due back any day. I got my degree and not a single phone call to congratulate me. I gave the ministers a guided tour of the Acropolis, you never made anything of it. I left my work afterwards, like a perfect fool, you never talked any sense into me. You care nothing for us, you don't want to know what ails us, you don't want to know your only son, you didn't come to my wedding, you didn't come to see your first grandchild and you haven't kissed me since I was in high school.

Mitsos Avgoustis had no retort, he was listening to her and recalling the evenings of the cursed fall of '73, playing checkers with his young daughters, letting them cheat, telling them about the pink dolphins in the Amazon and then putting them to bed, impatient to talk things through with their mother about the divorce.

When Lily abruptly hung up, without even waiting for a word of excuse from him, scrounging around for an apology would hardly be in character after the event, it'd be unacceptable and rightly so, Mitsos Avgoustis thought of two things. First, that he did deserve his children's palpable hatred and second that Flora had talked about his blindness neither to them, nor to the faggot trolls at the Company.

Why was she giving him time? What would Chadzimanolis do? And what about Flirtakis?

He was smoking by himself at the lookout, the others on duty at their posts, exclaiming over Vekrelis's good fortune.

His Zoe had dreamt that, as she sat on the bishop's throne in a church of the Virgin Mary in the countryside of Lesvos, admiring the cross, flanked by the mourning figures of the Virgin and Saint John, and the dragons carved in the partitions, she loved those carved church templons ever since she was tiny, she heard one dragon call out to her in English, *good luck*, Zoe, dear, and at that very moment, she saw two swallows barge in from the small window above the altar that was without chicken wire, fly straight to where she sat and poop on her. And insofar as shit means money, she bought a Lotto ticket, the dream came true and, now, the couple, with twenty million drachmas in their hands, could start the first two grilled chicken diners of the chain which had been their life's ambition.

Stamatis Vekrelis celebrated his last remaining days as a seaman by belting out the entire repertory of Dalaras, wishing liberally to his colleagues, Greek and non-Greek alike, may you be next, and hearing, from the old-timers especially, that he must surely be the first guy in world naval history who, after quitting the sea, would keep on eating chicken, the one dish that every sailing man and his dog are sick to death of.

After Xingan, Osaka, scene of the farewell party for the steward leaving the ship, Wednesday, February 12.

On Thursday, February 13, late in the evening, they'd already unloaded the phosphate and cleaned out the holds, but were sitting empty.

–There's nothing going.

This was Flirtakis, from Pireas.

–I'll leave dead and weighing nothing.

–Where to, God's willing?

–For a carefree saunter. The open sea moves me. It is the place of non-attachment.

–When are you thinking of?

–Tomorrow morning.

–And what am I to say to Chadzimanolis?

–Tell him, I'll make him go bankrupt.

Next dawn the telex came that instructed ATHOS III to sail to Iloilo for eighteen thousand tons of manure and palm dates, then to Hanoi for fifteen thousand tons of bricks, rice and bicycles all to be delivered to Incheon, Korea.

They took off and while sailing, the same routine as ever. Days and nights with not one word uttered and suddenly of a night, all of them becoming parliamentarians and getting into a fight over party politics, another night, every man giving his all to slow-moving *zembekiko* solos with arms outstretched, the Rumanians and the Russians alongside the rest, the lot of them already past the age of thirty and well versed in the monotony of male company. On Wednesday, February 19, in the jungle of Iloilo, on Filipino ground, home of Soledad, the enamored chef's assistant's mood brightened to where he even sang a little *Glykeria* under his breath. His sweetheart, fifteen years his elder, mother of three and the recipient of half his wages for the last two and a half years—the other half found its way to his old mum—barged into ATHOS, kidnapped him for one hour and returned him a happy man along with ten cans of crabmeat, she'd gotten a job at the local processing plant.

The loading and the packing were carried out briskly, Birbilis sent to the Pireas boys all the documents with the requisite data, the men didn't get off because the place, marked end to end by poverty, didn't appeal and, now, full steam ahead for Vietnam.

It'd been nine, ten years since Mitsos Avgoustis last docked there. He wasn't going to get off, wasn't going to see it again and he didn't care. He'd sat his ass down on five thousand towing bitts all over the world, enough already, all seas are one, a body of water to sail through, all countries are one, land to walk on, all ports are one, winches for emptying out the holds and for filling them up.

–Won't you trim the beard some? Flora had said during her visit and her tone of voice meant, you're turning into a spectacle.

–I'm not trimming it.

–Cut back your hair, at least.

–When I dock again at Lisbon.

–You're not docking at Lisbon again.

–That's none of your business.

–Let me cut it back for you.

–For thirty years I've had it cut by the same untalented Portuguese.

–What do you see in him?

–I like his life story.

–He might be dead.

–As long as I don't go there, to me he's alive.

And for as long as he didn't go back to Greece, all the people still lived there who he wished were still alive.

He was very hungry, wanted to get his fill of food, so he needed to go to his cabin, apart from feast days and special occasions, he was obliged to eat by himself ever since when, in front of the telegram operator and the first mechanic, he'd confused the salt with the pepper and asked for that other chicken leg while on the platter before him all that was left was a breast and a wing. I was seeing double from hunger, was the best he was able to come up with.

The butler brought the tray along with another spiel about Kyriaki, the heroics of 1821, the frights of the Civil War, he served Turkish pilaf to the cat and the silent captain, realized this was no night for talk, complained that nowadays only lettuce has a tender heart and exited pointing out that the czar's first chef was getting a yearly wage of one hundred and sixty thousand rubles.

It would have been eight thirty, or thereabouts, when Mitsos Avgoustis, well fed and full of verve, opened the wardrobe to remember, by force and by touch, that the pale blue linen shirt was hanging first, the pale blue cotton with the too-small buttons second, third the sugar-colored one with the ivory cufflinks, fourth the such and such, fifth, sixth, seventh the so-and-so, tenth the one with the small checkers and the satin label in the collar and, lastly, the brand new one, a present from Flora, silk, maybe very pale blue, maybe a soft gray, over a month on the hanger, unworn, because the captain believed that with new clothes, just like with borrowed ones, you are not yourself entirely, you need time.

He fingered the Bible on the narrow ledge and his work's two gospels, the SOLAS on safety at sea and the MARPOL manual on the prevention of pollution by ships, kept up his training practice by handling his dossiers here and his little boxes there, prioritized in his head the business that was pending, extemporized solutions for every conceivable mishap and decided, in order not to delay too long in Hanoi, to bribe his very own crew, one hundred dollars bonus each, to do the job in less than seventy-two hours, pick up the new steward they were expecting, and get out to the open sea again. He wouldn't risk wasting time in ports with marine authorities and unknown back-stabbers, possibly in cahoots with Shipping Maritime.

He went for one last check inside and out, the kitchens smelt of chlorine and cleanliness, the showers weren't dripping, the crates were sturdily packed on the aft, the boat chains well oiled, Birbilis had the shift report ready and the sailors on deck, drenched by the mist, were patrolling with fake Kalashnikovs hitched on their shoulder.

He touched the plywood cutouts one by one, keep your eyes peeled, he told them, he lifted his collar all the way up to the ears against the humidity that went right through and headed for the sternpost aiming to complete his regular memory exercise, not with scenes of the son and the two daughters, they only had leading parts in the exercises of forgetfulness, but with scenes of the now invisible sea.

He was fired by a sudden longing for the spectacle, he would bribe with any amount to be able to see, even fleetingly, the seaweed blinking off and on, a myriad of green fireflies in the dark waters, and the small waves lined up, flower beds with white blooms in the black garden of darkness.

Exactly like the winter daisies in the flower beds of Elefsina, that he used to look at from the window, during his late-night cigarette.

***

–How old is the captain? the new guy asked worriedly.

–He has three dark-skinned beauties for lunch all by himself, you figure it out, Siakandaris shot back grandiosely.

–Is he legal? the first man persisted.

–He's made the laws in Merchant Marine. How is it with Johnny Walker, since 1820? It's like that with Mitsos Avgoustis since 1939, at sea ever since, unmatchable, came the second man's answer.

At Hanoi, Vietnam, Monday afternoon, March 3, after refueling with water and gas, they'd get food in Korea, the launch brought to ATHOS III the young Stelios Kazas and went back to the port without him, though it was a certainty that, out in the open sea, the new guy, both a first timer and more than likely a wuss, would feel safer with a captain at least twenty, twenty-five years younger. Two or three crew members made a bet that the tall, swarthy newbie would be spending all of his wages on cell-phone bills, calling up his mamma day and night.

The captain had welcomed him sparsely and then passed him on to the boatswain for the induction speech, the good seaman's set of rules decrees that you are respectful to seniors, take a bath daily, serve with your nails clipped, not be stingy with condoms, not gamble your earnings away, not get into fights with the others, and also, and furthermore, while giving him a tour of the entire ship till they arrived at the crew's quarters and he was installed in his cabin.

How old did we say the captain is? Kazas asked again, Sigalas laughed and patted him on the back, canaries live fifteen years, nightingales eighteen, seabirds and waterbirds live forty to sixty years apiece, so we, seamen, God's willing and the weather allowing, live twice as long.

The next day, though, out in the open sea, the delicate cloud formations of the calm scooted of, chased by a different kind, weighty and jet black, that broke out into a mighty storm with unremitting lightening, thunder and twenty-five-foot waves.

If swell winds bodies up, a gale force of ten on the Beaufort scale makes the crew go haywire. Everyone was walking around like dizzy chicken, five days at the mercy of Siakandaris, who quit cooking wet dishes and sauces, fighting to settle the upset stomachs with plain pasta, boiled rice, and reassuring tales from the inexhaustible Kyriaki, a tsamiko dance competition where he finished last because of clumsily stepping on the feet of the dancers next to him, and a funeral where, during the endless talk over the coffees, the sorrowful congregation counted the horns planted by the deceased on the foreheads of the villagers, got into fisticuffs and broke up the coffee shop to smithereens.

The seventeen-year-old ATHOS III was automated, the engine room could stay locked up at nights, but Avgoustis favored the opinion that humans are the surest alarm and the mechanics stayed on shift even when it was calm, all the more so in harsh weather with the sea's relentless pounding and the metal plates creaking.

Four days without sleep, from the engines to the deck and from there to the bridge, cut the wheel to the left, to the sailor, slow the speed down, now this, now the other, cool, calm and collected until he heard on the phone the voice of Chadzijerkoff.

–Avgoustis, you are giving me grief. I thought, for your wife's sake I thought I would hold back from extreme measures, which you ought to appreciate. But I can't hang around waiting for Flirtakis to corner you. On the 16th a legal rep from the Company is coming to Korea to take over, just so we end things nice and smooth. He'll explain to you where your interests lie. Make sure you see eye to eye.

–Whom are you sending?

–Athanasopoulos junior. Better than his father. Modern thinker with connections among the politicians.

–Fine, the captain answered, I will welcome your playboy in my best skirt and blouse.

He hung up and prayed not to implicate the Virgin Mary in the war with the hornet's nest at Pireas, but for the sea to calm down so he might gain some extra time. In such cases, always in front of his men, Mitsos Avgoustis crossed himself twenty times, said his prayers thirty to forty times and ended by saying out loud, woe to anyone who's being snobbish towards the Virgin and the Almighty, I don't fancy men who aren't afraid of death.

The freaked-out novice steward, very thin when he fist showed up and even thinner within a week, came onto the bridge carrying a tray with hot drinks, at the beginning of the prayer, *I the sinner, attached to the desires and pleasures of the flesh*, heard it to the end, times fifteen, *in favor of cleansing us from all sorrow, wrath, peril and neediness*, heard the postscript, too, the fearless sailor is a nincompoop.

Avgoustis didn't take note of the tea, his mind was set on the weather and on Korea. The ship's holds were filled with the goodies from Iloilo and the Hanoi cargo.

He spoke with the kitchens.

–Gerassimos, first off, pass everyone a box of palm dates.

–And second?

–Take rice from the cargo, put every manner of pilaf on the menu and figure out a proper way to economize on quantity.

–Why's that?

–Because the Virgin Mary has graced me with knowing we are not to delay in Korea for restocking.

–Let's do the shopping during the unloading.

—You look after what's economic. I'll look after the rest.

He opened in his mind the map of the Indian and the Pacific and jotted down Visakapatnam, Souvadivadol, Parandip, Haldia, Shembo, Pouloupandam, Amourang, Pindianak, the most faraway ports and the ones farther still, for after fleeing the unavoidable Korea.

He then asked again for the weather forecast and the course of the storm, triple check with the stations of Colombo and Singapore and Darwin, too, he emphasized. He was contemplating a small detour in order to leave the weather behind and save on petrol. He twirled things around in his brain, figured them out, gave the order.

The men didn't so much as look at each other, so he wouldn't catch them wondering, besides, they were all accustomed to the captain's whims, except for the newcomer who departed tottering.

Before, however, Kazas had gained much distance, a new heart-stopper.

—Alert, alert, alert, the captain's voice echoed from loud speakers all across the carrier, the monthly readiness exercise, this time for fire in the kitchens.

Avgoustis and the second mate went down into the kitchen, others turned off the ventilators, some ran to the nearest firebox, took out the hose, connected it to the extension and a Romanian tied with a rope and wearing a gray fireproof uniform made of asbestos, with oxygen bottle attached, hurtled into the fumes of the expired smoke bomb.

—Captain, afterwards, I need two minutes of your time.

—You can have two and a half, the answer.

—It's to put some eye-drops in your eyes to clean them out from the smoke.

—No need, I'm fine. Like Cicero says, *All worldly things are smoke and fire.* We're done.

Everything happened by the book, a routine exercise for

the expert crew, sheer terror for the newcomer whose fledging career hadn't gotten off to a good start.

At five thirty in the afternoon, he served everyone else in the sailors' mess, all talking about Albanian finance pyramids, riots, loan sharks and lost fortunes while he neither spoke nor put anything in his mouth himself. He didn't even honor the dessert.

It was the last Saturday night of carnival and Siakandaris had presented an impressive cake with mashed date palms and while serving it, he consoled the weary men with stories of pastry romances, how, once, he enticed a Chilean into bed with two sugar-coated dates and how he drove another crazy with his puffed-up pastry doughnut. For the foreign speakers, he translated himself into some basic English and did a good amount of miming, to which the subject matter lent itself. But he had a lot of work to do. He needed to think about tomorrow's festive veal, the Ash Monday platter, which would be served the day after tomorrow and, above all, to organize the menu for Lent. To calculate the quantities, using pen and paper, and search in his notebooks for all the rice pies, rice balls and pilafs from Constantinople, China and Thailand.

So, he took the new guy to the kitchen. You're not used to this, I see, he reprimanded him, see if you're any good to me, he sighed, then made him change his jacket and comb his front lock, gave him the tray for the captain and told him five times how to make his entry, what to say, how to act and all the don'ts, even though, in the end, nothing more was needed than a good evening and an enjoy your meal.

Mitsos Avgoustis in his cabin, after freshening up with a quick shower and a clean change of clothes, white work trousers, white long-sleeved top, with his long silver hair and beard drying, was pacing back and forth between the desk lamp and the bedside lamp and looked like a human-size votive offering to her grace, the Holy Mother.

He had fifteen minutes at his disposal to snack before going back out on deck, enough time to think about operation Korea, arrival at 1300 in the afternoon, unloading at 1400 and 1500 and that same night dropping anchor before the lawyer showed up. Where to? Somewhere.

The steward set the tray on the table, put some food in front of the hissing cat, locked up in the cabin through all the days of rough weather, waited for a bit in case the captain wanted something, but thankfully, he was motioned to go.

Only before closing the door behind him, he heard a question.

–Which soccer team are you a fan of?

–AEK.

–Good, we've got a flag.

**

–He's going to fall off!

After testing them to their limit for a week, the Holy Mother of God put the stopper back on the wicked sea and at dawn on Monday, first day of Lent, 10th of the month, Maritsa got an exit permit, shot out like a bullet and hurled himself onto the rails to reestablish the routine of morning dance gymnastics.

Stelios Kazas, relieved and grateful for the change in the weather, taking tequila and coffee to the captain who was stretching out at the stern, saw the cat balancing while it tread on its precarious wooden path and he freaked out. He let out a volley of shouts. He hadn't had time to take a liking to Maritsa but he sure wasn't going to get in trouble for letting the animal go overboard.

His yells brought to the spot Birbilis, Dactylas and one Rumanian all of whom assured him that Maritsa had plenty of lives to spare and set out for his benefit several advantages to having a cat on board a gentle companionship on the ship, something to caress. Eleven years previously, ATHOS had shed tears when one of their cats had leapt into the North Atlantic and nine years ago, their acrobat-cat made the news on Dutch television and received a gift of two magnetic rings. There's more. Four years ago, ten of the crew each had his own cat and when half of them gave birth to three or four kittens each, nineteen in total, a veritable zoo, the ship resounded with mewls, everyone kept stumbling on them, the cook was outraged because they sneaked into the food cellars, leaving hairs everywhere, until at Port Talbot they let them all loose on the wooden dock, keeping only the last descendant of the Maritsa House, who wasn't going to be contributing any more offspring to the family tree. His half-chewed-off ears were a souvenir from the last cat-fight. These things having been said, everyone went off to their business.

The captain's coffee was now cold, but Avgoustis was in a good mood. Tomorrow Korea. Unload, quick as lightening, and beat it. He wasn't going to hang around for his date with the lawyer.

For today, a different agenda.

After the canned pickles, the squid and the ever-present pilaf, with the sun out, the deck was filled with cyclists, with the captain's permission anyone who was through with their six hours took a bicycle from the cargo, and they were playing like kids, standing up while pedaling along the side corridors and on the deck and ringing the bells. Daniel, Georgi senior and Sorin junior were abstaining, cold fish through and through, sworn to moroseness, unswervable from their loneliness.

Despite the three, the red ATHOS, a sailing theme park full of wheels, shouts and whistles, with three cameras, one the newcomer's, two video cameras immortalizing the revelry after wear and tear of many days running, and Mitsos Avgoustis,

princely, leaning on the rails with the cat in his arms and saying to his men, the bikes are yours, one per man.

He didn't know anyone's face. Three Greeks had come on
board with him in the first two years of his blindness, he could
only make out their outlines, a half-size shadow was the
diminutive Daniel, who got christened with the nickname
underground, as Yalouris was *bride* with his white overalls and
his two hundred twenty pounds. The signal of Michaloutsos
was the steady cigarette cough, the signal of the assistant cook,
who'd joined four years ago, was singing Mitropanos under his
breath when he was especially moody and the new guy, the
youngster with the few words and the plentiful farts, made his
presence known by the scraping of his shoes.

The present-day Russians and Rumanians had traded places
with other Russians and Rumanians five and three years ago.

He didn't want foreigners in his crew, in times of peril, too
many different tongues can sink a ship. The son Chadzimanolis was pressuring him to take on the carrier a cheap Pakistani
or Filippino mob, he was refusing. He had in the past been
soft-hearted and let in four starving souls, two Indians, two
Pakistanis, sea-sick seamen, kept them with great difficulty for
six months, just long enough for their stomachs to stop rum-
bling and for them to send back home some canned goods and
a little dough. His Russians and his Rumanians, both the first
lot and the second, didn't stash bottles of vodka or Slivovitz
plum brandy in their cabins, were expert seamen with ade-
quate English and, besides, he'd taken them on out of necessity, when he had twice needed men in Australasia and couldn't
wait for Greeks, he had sacks of sugar on board and was worried they might liquefy.

Mitsos Avgoustis, a wondering Jew with his eyes peeled for
five decades and for the sixth, latest one, with his ears pricked
busy figuring out the foreign languages, the sizzle of Chinese,

tweeter of the Japanese, gurgle of Swedish, the boiling over of the brown-skins and the burbling of the Africans, seeing now with his ears, his nose and his hands, had quickly learned the voice, the smell, the palm and a little or a lot of each man's family history, without ever seeing their faces. But the older ones, too, Siakandaris and the rest, he knew as they were twelve years ago, he didn't see the balding heads, the white hairs and the lines that had meanwhile carved their faces, nor could he search their gaze, every man's most reliable identifying trait.

Nomads, the lot of us, he thought, escape artists.

With the sun warming up his old bones and Maritsa licking his fingers and rubbing whiskers against his coat sleeves, his mind flew to a sun-drenched Greece, childlike and time-weathered, he savored it and brought it up to 1985, he didn't know the Greece that came after that. For him, the streets, the squares and the buildings, the shirt maker's, the shoe maker's, the taverns and the monasteries, the trees and the cats were all frozen in 1985 and all the faces were stuck in that same year, neighbors, acquaintances, relatives, Flora with the look of a fifty-year old, his oldest daughter at twenty, the second one at eighteen, his son at ten, a child.

As for the sweet old soul at Elefsina, the reason his heart hadn't preserved her with the damage that time had more or less wrought was because the swell of his conscience was making a din, pitching and tossing him sideways and charging him with her youth going to waste as he devoured her twenties, wrung dry her thirties, demolished her forties and, then, disappeared for good, like a thief.

As he was getting older, she, forever young, innocent and sexy started returning persistently, a regular and now tyrannical presence in his mind.

He put Maritsa down and walked alongside the rails with eyes closed. The men had seen him walk like this on other occasions, too, even take a few dancing steps of kalamatiano, on the deck at Easter. For them, especially for the older ones, Birbilis, Sigalas, Dactylas and Siakandaris, after all those years at sea, Avgoustis had grown gills and scales and, every so often, dived in and swam alone to distant waters and dark depths.

***

I asked him about you. He wouldn't answer.

So then, just so I'd get it right, I imagined you at one time to be an itty-bitty thing, dark and blue eyed, or else, blond and brown-eyed. Sometimes tall and thin and sometimes stocky.

I didn't leave out any possible shape and size.

You are a good-looking lad. The thick, curly hair brings ideas into my head.

Two years before you were born and did me in once and for all, I'd come to Pireas, to your neighborhood and I'd spied on the other one. Not to get into a screaming match, I loathe that stuff, but just to lay eyes on her. I chanced on her coming out with your sisters, fillies then just starting school, with braids and spotted skirts.

She was wearing a showy red coral necklace. Mitsos had bought a set, sent the necklace to the wife and the earrings to the mistress. That afternoon, they were dangling from my ears. I barely had time to unclip them.

I held them tightly in my fist like stolen money, and I walked behind the trio of women, until they went into a school of English as a foreign language.

I recall her pretty walk, her balance on the high heels. And her high-class perm.

It made her look old.

Now his turn.

He never wrote again, never came back, I never went after him any more.

I thought, a pensioner now, killing time, he'll probably be hanging out at one Pireas dock or another, getting in the way, gazing at each ship from twenty yards away, like he used to do with his own.

I've seen him with my own eyes, from a distance. In 1965, in 1967, in 1971, in 1973 and in 1979. He was standing on the land by himself and was looking at his ship. KALYPSO, the old one, ALFIOS, the one after, PENELOPI, the one after that.

I avoid Pireas nowadays. And I never did sneak back to your neighborhood, to keep watch on your street, if you're still living there.

I didn't freeze when you introduced yourself because there was nothing in your face signaling bad news. You looked at me and at my living room in surprise and you cracked me a smile. That means he's alive, I breathed easy again. And I wondered to myself. Sent by him or by her? I was puzzled by your presence here, you see, since all of you are alive and well, thank God, and nothing untoward has burst out as sometimes happens with deaths that suddenly reveal a well-guarded secret.

How did I resurface? For thirty-five years of their marriage I lived like a submarine, following him from the depths, in case the enemy located my position.

I don't know why, but I like it that you came of your own accord.

Do you know what just came to me? While talking to you, to be walking around your chair, as if today I was dictating my letter to you. Don't bend your neck all out of shape watching me. Look anywhere you want. Here, hold the picture with the four white bears on the iceberg.

A mother with three children.

Every time I wash my hair, I sit in the kitchen with it all wet and while it's drying out, I remember him.

Mitso, I crave remembering you. I craved remembering him. Ever so thoroughly. Though, sometimes, not all of him. I could spend up to a week having in front of me, like an enlargement that took up the whole room, just his left unshaven cheek on the pillow in the morning.

I still often live with his slippers walking from the verandah to the kitchen and standing in front of the stove where his spaghetti is boiling. And it's enough to hang before my eyes, like a framed photograph, that most useful left-hand pocket of a man's shirt, with the tip of a cigarette sticking out. He did smoke some. By the time he quit, I had picked it up.

That's too bad, my dear fellow and mate, heavy cigarettes have made your voice like a man's, that's how he told me off, being used to living and talking with guys.

At night, before I lay down, I prepare the scene of my sleeplessness. I make two coffees and leave the cups covered with the saucer, one on the kitchen windowsill and one on the living-room windowsill.

And when sleep proves feckless and won't let me sink unconscious into the sheets, that are hankering for the old hanky-panky, I get up, I go walk about the rooms, I sit at the kitchen post for two or three sips and two or three drags from a cigarette, I stab the butt out on the dregs and I go back to bed. A little later, when I'm still in vampire mode, I go to the living-room post for a repeat performance. Those windowsills are sacrosanct, they hold great power.

Time molds a forgetfulness around everything. My forgetfulness is taking too long. I resist. Because he has written every line of my life. If I erase him, what's left?

A peaceful ocean with Litsa in the background. The ship

*is plowing the waters and the perky but ill-fated hairdress-
er is following it on foot, in her golden miniskirt, chasing
after the foreign seas.*

*I'd set in my head a time when the ship would sail into
a certain port and I would fly to the foreign dock, in my
imagination, to call out my presence.*

*He did the traveling, I spent my life a deadweight on
the dock. Thousands of daily wages of waiting.*

*The Mitsos I have experienced a great deal of is the
absent one. The Mitsos I contemplated and studied, from
a distance of thousands of miles, is the man I brought up
in my mind.*

*I thought of him constantly so I could get my fill of
him. Other women live day and night with their man by
their side and don't have the feeling of him. I lived with
the man who wasn't at home but I didn't allow him to be
missed. I didn't let us not clink our midday and evening
wine glasses. There was one plate, two glasses.*

*I was curious about the male. What kind of creature is
he? What exactly does his gaze mean and how does it
change? How does he come to a decision? How does he
stay silent? How is he at a loss? How does he despair?*

*They have no curiosity about the man, those who look
for him, who'll tell them the things they themselves have
planned.*

*It was really nice, for example, when he told me about
the hole that exists on the wall of Norway. I listened about
the world's strangeness, open-mouthed like a child, without
thinking, cut out the tales of Norway and Ireland and tell
me when will we, at last, stand before a priest and a best
man?*

*Not that I didn't go through my phases of feminism and
rebellion. One spring, every Friday afternoon I did the hair of
a new mum with her blouse stained at the nipples from the*

milk, her breasts like running faucets. I had the worst w e e k-
ends, my mind darkened, arms crossed, palms on my dry
breasts. So then, that Easter, our seventeenth, after spending the holidays with you, he came on Pentecost Sunday.

I welcomed him with a resounding slap wearing Christ's
crown of thorns on my hair, platinum blond at the time.

Eternally crucified and never resurrected, I let him have
an earful.

He threw me on the bed, no surprises there, peace
among all men.

Did I mention my crown of thorns in the garden? I have
two tin cans full, its little flowers droplets of blood.

When I was young I was crazy for bougainvillea and rho-
dodendrons, for any showy climbers that you can spot from
far away. As the years go by, I love more and more the flowers that don't scream out from a mile away, the shamefaced
ones. Those that show their tiny blooms from behind grass-
es and weeds and bunches of leaves. The ones beaten by
the glory of the roses.

And my life's Mr. Parsley, at one time in his black
sleeveless T-shirt buzzing like a bumblebee, at another in
his colorful Hawaiian boxers flitting like a butterfly between
the rosemary and the sweet williams.

The fragrant plants were his weakness. He plucked the
tops and rubbed one or two tiny leaves between his fingers.

Mitso, I would explain, I want the flower-shrubs as tall
as children and the trees as tall as men, no more.

The garden in bloom sheds its fragrance on my unqui-
et sleep like a blessing. And my alarm clock is the smell
of the jasmine that grows strong with the first sunrays and
barges into the house.

That is when the sparrows, too, riot.

At six in the morning, the garden belongs to the birds.

***

Korea done. On the fifteenth they weighed anchor, on the sixteenth the lawyer got stood up, on the seventeenth sharp words exchanged with the Company.

–Chadzimanolis is frothing at the mouth.

–It's an experience, like your Kassandra would say.

–Avgoustis, I mean you well and you provoke me. Why did we come to this?

–Because every so often, I get fed up with that abundant common sense of educated servants and with all of you in general.

In the phone call with Flirtakis he said he wanted to go to Visakhapatnam. After all these years in the employ of Shipping Maritime and the flood of dollars he sent Pireas's way, he should be entitled to dock somewhere of his own choosing, and, find me on the spot thirty tons of metal ore that's eager to perch in the holds of ATHOS III and go on a trip.

Flirtakis went berserk, this doesn't happen anywhere in the whole wide world and you know it, he told him, Avgoustis answered deadpan that it should, he, in any events, was already setting his course for India.

–I just can't vouch that Chadzimanolis himself won't be waiting for you.

–So let him come. Whenever he sees me up close he pulls up short. And I take advantage of it.

Two hours later the happy call was made with the big news. Old Portokalakis, the notary, while dusting the spider webs off his drawers and cabinets finally found the stashed envelope he had been looking for and presented to the Pireas crew a sheet of paper, addendum to the will of Chadzimanolis senior. According to his last wish, Dimitrios Avgoustis would serve as captain for as long as himself saw fit and with his retirement, whenever that was to take place, he would get one hundred thousand pounds cash in hand.

The complementary will was written by hand, with concise phraseology, a sturdy signature and dated 1989, one year after the initial. The son's only hope of contesting it would be to prove that the old guy was not of sound mind, which he was going to investigate through lawyers and doctors.

–Even dead he keeps watch over me. He sees what I'm going through and is taking action from beyond the grave. He is sending me what I need. Time.

Another three days seafaring, meetings with SANTIAGO, TASMANIA, IONIAN SKY, chatting and mutual support among the captains, Avgoustis, a household name amongst Greeks and foreigners in the trade, received thrice the question, still on the tin bucket? I'm a piece of work with a one-hundred-year guarantee, the standard answer, they wished him well, he wished them back and on we go, on the fourth day a telex ok-ing the mineral ore impatiently waiting at Visakhapatnam and further down the track, on the fifth day, a very early call on the mobile.

–Well, well! How about that? I almost forgot what you sound like. It's been two years since you last showed up.

–You haven't called either. And it's been five years since you wrote.

–Is it money you want?

–Don't talk to me like that. I've called to tell you I'm cutting short my draft deferment. I'm presenting next month.

–Will your studies add up to nothing for a second time?

–I'm entitled to do much worse with you for a father.

–Go wherever it pleases you.

–When will you be back?

–What, so I can stand proud, watching you swearing allegiance?

–To be with us.

At this, Avgoustis pulled himself up, thought it through but dealt with it as usual, his tongue knew of one way, the cut and dry.

–I love my family but from a distance of ten thousand miles.

–You told mother that the sea won't give you back. It's as if you are doing everything in your power for us not to miss you.

–If I was there I'd be a worse pain.

–I'll send you some photos in uniform.

–The army is no concert and rifles aren't drums.

–Don't criticize me before you have to.

He repeated that last statement with an imperceptible break in his voice.

The clipped dialogue confirmed the abyss between them. Even if he met up with his son, he wouldn't be able to see him. But Avgoustis had made up his mind to stay away from them all for good, even though he had no arguments and explanations they could comprehend, even though the enmity gained ground inside of them, even though he was getting a unanimous vote as the worst parent ever, even though he cursed himself sometimes, in his cabin, on his own, over having made a mess of things, having trampled people's lives, you can't have back the lost years and amends delayed for so long look like sorry signatures on the contract of a now-expired reconciliation.

It wasn't him, he'd spelled it out to the Virgin Mary as well, and had had an argument with her, you want me to turn pathetic and you're as stubborn as a mule in this requirement of yours that everyone must repent, some situations, though, can't be handled that way, time doesn't stand still forever, the time for an apology has come and gone, since it can't heal any wounds it is now meaningless, a word defunct and suspect.

But Visakhapatnam was five days away and Avgoustis was obliged to put out of mind anything not related to his job, he'd no idea what might came up at the next turn, it was enough for him to plan and execute one step further at a time.

At the Malacca Straits the fake Kalashnikovs again came out for duty, they made the crossing unharmed. And because the health inspectors would certainly be waiting for them in India and the pesticide certificate had expired a month ago and they had run out of time, he went down to the kitchens and instructed Siakandaris, if they dig up a rat, give them ten chickens and a case of the cheap imitation whisky.

The cook was anxious and fretful, fanning himself with a bunch of papers, the stock deficits detailed in tons, pounds and dozens. According to the regulation, the cook is not a member of the committee for food supplies, but this particular one, exempt from rules and regulations, made decisions left right and center, with everyone's approval.

–We need water and several foodstuffs.

–What, precisely?

–A bit of everything.

–With me, they've been royally fed on fillet and rump steak. Buy cuttlefish and put them all on a compulsory fast.

–I need fruit and vegetables.

–Get the cheap ones. And the apples can be small. Cheat a little on the scales.

–We need pastry, too, flour and coffee.

–Get ones past the expiry date and don't breathe a word. I need the cash for emergencies.

This was the first time in twenty-five years that the cook heard his captain ask him something of the sort, he was puzzled and angry and he refused, Avgoustis clumsily brought his fist down on the table, get out if you want, go back to Kyriaki, the sooner the better, he said, certain Siakandaris, his true sea-wife, wouldn't abandon him in hardship and even more certain that, if his eyes worked, he would gladly go himself to the damn village as an in-law for a week, in case there was solace to be found in the vineyards with the light spring clouds overhead.

He hadn't seen a green leaf in donkey's years and as for grass, the last time was in the South Atlantic, when a sudden squall threw the waters up high and winnowed the seaweed even higher, to where it covered the sky, then fell and stuck in thick layers on the ship that ended up looking like a huge yellow-brown haystack.

On Monday, March 24, eve of the Annunciation of the Virgin Mary, at five in the afternoon they set down anchor without docking, and the launch brought on board the Authorities, three sorry sods counting on the baksheesh. According to the certification at hand, the ATHOS III was seaworthy for another two months, and they were just fine with an old pesticide certificate. Avgoustis offered them his hand with three of the fingers blue and swollen from the inopportune fist-banging on the table, the shy steward offered them cokes and Turkish delight well past its prime and the cook passed them on the sly the chickens and the booze.

They concluded all their business by a quarter to six, the crew dined hurriedly, at Xingan, Osaka, Iloilo, Hanoi and Incheon they hadn't had time to get off and, so, they were asking to step on dry land even if it was among tin sheds, filth and flies.

—Wash your tools and off you go.

Avgoustis, standing by his desk, was sending them off one by one, while the second mate was handing out advances and keeping the records.

—A small advance for the new guy, as well, Birbilis suggested discreetly.

—He pays with the gold in his trunks, the captain loudly retorted.

Everyone but the steward laughed, it was true that only youth screws for free. Nevertheless, the envelope with the one hundred and fifty dollars, an advance from the first salary, had already found its way into Kazas's pocket.

Within twenty minutes the boat was gone, everyone was gone, even Siakandaris beat it, he wanted to have a big stroll in the night, alone, away from the magnetism and the hypnotic effect of Avgoustis, so as to ponder more freely whither the boat was heading and was, possibly, the time coming up for a change of tack.

He was more or less apprised of the Company's pressure and his exchanges with Flora Avgoustis forced him to no longer turn a blind eye to the captain's irrational stubbornness. He had been his idol for years and today's order for expired foodstuffs was a major insult to the cook, a stain of dishonesty and fraudulence at the crew's expense, first one ever, but also a sign of deep despair.

True enough, for Avgoustis, weary, near starved and forsaken in his cabin, with Maritsa out of doors dreamily gazing at the port lights, was fallen across his desk with the drawer open and his hands feeling the picture frames. He caressed by carving the Plexiglass with his nail. His thought was a scratch on the son's unknown face, sight unseen, a vague dark head under the magnifying glass. A soldier, then.

When the knock came on the door, he hurriedly shoved the glasses and photos deep in the drawer and let in the steward who hadn't wished to join the rest on account of not feeling up to it and had consented to the cook's request to serve a plate of food each to the cat and the antisocial captain who, once again, would dine late, by himself, knee deep in his papers and his scheming.

–You've asked the others how old I am, let me now ask you the same.

–Twenty-four.

–My son's twenty-two.

Avgoustis asked the young man to sit, I'll eat later, tell me a couple of things about yourself.

The first question, do you have a cat at home? No, The second, since you're afraid of the sea, what are you doing on board a ship? For some quick money. The next questions brought out the rest. With his sister Kazas he ran the photocopying business their parents had opened in 1980, their father died, the two siblings took out a loan to buy the small shop they had been renting, a good spot on Exarchia square, and, out of necessity, he'd gone to sea to get some money together.

At the last question of the interrogation, how was it that the sea came up as a solution, he said that some time ago, he went to the same English classes as the daughter of the Company's first captain and had had his seaman's papers issued thanks to her mediation, Aleka Flirtakis was a very reliable, very trustworthy kid.

Then, he asked a question, too.

–Is your son a seaman as well?

–He's an idler and a lay-about. He cost me fifty thousand dollars for a year in Boston, the University wasn't to his taste, he went back to his mother, left again to become a biologist in Rumania, prime holiday destination for prodigal sons, a two-bedroom in Bucharest with his own car and traipsing down to Greece every chance he got.

The youth was listening flabbergasted to the captain's vehemence toward his son, but was allowed no comment, he was shaking his head in embarrassment and looking down at his shoes.

Just in time, Maritsa came back, the steward opened, the cat leapt on to the captain, rose on his hind feet and started playing with his master's beard, as he asked another two questions, have you been to the army? For one year, on account of supporting a family. And where did you serve? For the most part on Kos island.

There followed a goodly silence, time for me to go, said the youngster but the old goat pointed to the desk and bid him take his seat again, grab pen and paper, he told him. He took from his shirt's breast pocket three bills, he had them ready, folded up, pushed them across the desk and dictated two lines, since the damaged fingers of his right hand couldn't press the pen on the sheet, so he complained.

Recipient, Andonios Avgoustis, address, 17 Neorion St., Pireas. Dear son, I'm sending you three hundred dollars spending money, for coffee and cigarettes while you're on sentry duty.

***

It's a must for men to talk about women.

When they are amongst themselves for long, at first they'll the Socialist and the Communist will squabble, politics always make for the best fights, then, they'll move on to soccer and in the end, especially if it's late, they'll start on the skirts, where everyone must find something to say, silence makes room for suspicion or somehow throws a wrench in the works.

There are plenty of ingenious extraterrestrial man-eaters on the scary and unfathomable planet Dryland, who reel sailors in like dumb fish and swallow them whole, everyone has something to confess or hide.

On the easy nights they start off with the lasses who haven't moved an inch from their port or island of birth, but have had men from five thousand different cities and villages the world over, their body a United Nations assembly, and with unabashed exaggeration, but also a measure of gratitude, continue to tell all about the one night stands, the one-off embraces with no kissing.

A date with no kissing's like a New Year's pie with no lucky coin, the cook's habitual retort to the conversations about the goings on under the rented bedcovers.

On difficult nights, whores are crossed off the agenda, firstly because whoever brings such a creature into his conversation, has singled her out from the army of the great unwashed and elevated her to the select company of mothers, wives, sisters, daughters and fiancées and secondly, because nobody considers their woman a whore, even while they mock themselves saying that if they end up drowned, wearing the ship for a hat, on the pittance of a pension that sailors get, their widows will have to put out more than generously, in order to bring up their orphans.

The difficult nights ensue because of the desperate lack of women's voices, the usual women's talk at home, Niko, you need a haircut, Apostoli, do you want the blue or the black trousers ironed, Pandeli change the station, let's listen to some laika for a change. On the ship, what can't happen appears important, their wife talking in the kitchen with her girlfriend or her sister-in-law about those lovely dwarf-rose bushes that pot-bellied guy has at the open-air market, about the love affairs in the TV series, about the damned chestnuts that won't peel no matter what and, finally, about how utterly bored they are with cooking.

Miltos, Makis, Lakis, Takis, chain-smoking, talking back and forth, one will honor his missus cause she was cut up three times, three caesarian births, another will bestow a halo upon his mother because she is his mother, someone will without fail resurrect his grandmother who loved a good joke and yet another will badmouth his former fiancée and mope because love holds him in disfavor.

One of the Rumanians will again tell about his wife who drives a school bus for half a day and a taxi for the other half, so the four fillies can study. His middle-aged compatriot will, in turn, softly sing an old song about female beauty. The Russian guys will take up the poetry routine, one by Pushkin yet again, they don't know all that many, or by someone else, they will recite it standing and will take turns translating the summary in bits and pieces, at the banks of the Neva river, beauties as pure as the snowy whiteness, as cold as the touch of a snake.

Inspired by the poetry, Siakandaris will pipe up to compare a woman's kiss to a refreshing ice cream, her soft knees to succulent brioche, a prominent belly button to a pastry bubble in sweet bread, synthesizing the parts into praise of the whole, women are the choicest morsels, life's most beautiful fragrance, and to promise that he'll decorate tomorrow's tarama with two black olives, a pair of a woman's black eyes or tasty nipples.

Seamen are the only men who don't go home after work, they stay on at the workplace, the sea is their stomping ground day and night and the younger ones, when they deign to join the gatherings of the gray-haired, show up full of pique that they aren't able to stroll about in their hometowns and feast their eyes on the girls of March, so befuddled by the weather that half of them come out of an evening dressed as if it was January and the other half as if it was May.

If it's a Saturday, first loves come back from the dead right in the middle of the ocean, each man's first sweetheart, the feel of the girlish breast and the fumbled moonlit caresses in the blackberry dusk or the night of the cherry trees. With the exception of Daniel, Georgi senior, Sorin junior and Birbilis who, in the event he talks, is as likely to contribute the tale of some tender doe, wolf or donkey, the two hours are plenty for the rest to run through the archives of their youth and the females who've become an entry on their life's balance sheet.

When, however, the ambience of woman is fully evoked, what's important isn't what each man says, truths or lies that have also been told on other occasions, but the atmosphere all these create, plus the glances exchanged by the men, plus the gaze of each one that imperceptibly changes on its own, minus their body movements which grow more sparse, until they all become a living painting, with no more words, with thick smoke tulips wrestling up on the ceiling.

If Avgoustis happens to be nearby for ten minutes or so, he joins them for a cigarette, there you go down the panty trail again, he ascertains, at the right moment he throws in an old-fashioned joke, love equals heart failure by two, or the admonishment, look out for your women with your lives, and then takes his leave threatening them in jest, now I'm going to write it all down in the ship's log.

On the day of the Annunciation, a working day outside of Greece, the men had worked themselves to the bone, loading, stocking and cleaning up the droppings of hundreds of seagulls.

Their evening was one of those centered around the subject of women. The trigger was the well-wishing for the name day of two Evangelias, the mother and the Congolese daughter of Dactylas.

Mitsos Avgoustis wished well and departed. While treading the familiar path up and down the deck, he avoided crashing into the females of his own life. The night's thoughts were devoted to his telegraph operator from the CALYPSO, the ALFIOS and the PINELOPI who, on learning that his wife was cheating on him non-stop, feeding her lovers in the *crystales regalos* he'd bought for her from the Santa Fe boulevard in Buenos Aires, laying them up in the fine sheets from Miguel Manolitsis and treating them to cigarettes out of the gold-and-red pagoda-shaped cigarette case that he, the perfect fool, had brought back from Singapore, he'd wily-nilly changed ships to go back to Greece and do away with her and was met with the calamity of piracy.

He had come out of it a cripple, got involved in a variety of shady deals and finally, had settled down as volunteer guard on a rotting old ship under a repossession order, anchored and haunted, the both of them, out in the open sea, far away and beyond the comings and goings of the gas-trailers and the freight ships.

He had to drink to his health. He went into his cabin, woke Maritsa up, poured a sliver of whisky and, since work puts off a bad old age and death, he pulled out the glasses and his papers and applied himself like an earnest high-school student. The loading and other ending business had to be completed by early afternoon the day after tomorrow, because after that, he needed a couple of hours for himself.

***

The whole sea the color of pomegranate juice and in the middle, the black and yellow AEGEAN BLUE II. Six thirty in the afternoon. The ATHOS III launch, after weaving in and out of the gas trailers to get out to sea, then came up close, maneuvered, the Rumanian sailor tied the rope and the rest of the three passengers took hold of the ship's rusty ladder and went up in a row, first Siakandaris followed by Avgoustis who, on account of his swollen hand, accepted a hand going up from the third, Kazas—the kind who made himself a fixture, a scout of curiosity, with his camera on a strap around his neck.

–But how come he didn't hear our engine? How can he not have seen us yet? Siakandaris had to conclude, he's either out or asleep.

They tied a rope around two paper cartons, gifts from the captain and lifted them up onto the ship, under repossession since 1992, on account of the heirs' bickering and the non-payment of the security deposit.

Trash all around. In the absolute calm and quiet, a noise of cans landing on the metal floor, led them around the other side of the stern.

They found Papalexakis in his pajama trousers, peacefully sitting on a dirty plastic chair with half the back missing, next to a pile of cardboard boxes and tin cans which he picked up one by one and threw into a basket hoop, nailed at a low height, rusted and with no net.

Handsome even at seventy, a bony daddy longlegs with gangly arms and legs and eyes of light brown, like raisins, as Siakandaris whispered to Kazas, hair of coconut-white, skin the color of grape-must pudding, so as to match the color of the rust eating away at the ship's hull.

–And pink pajamas, the steward added.

Damian Papalexakis, at one time a fuel mechanic and a sailor and a telegraph operator and anything you like on fifteen ships, in three out of those with Avgoustis, in two out of the three with Siakandaris as well, turned around, checked them out, threw the last two tin cans in the hoop and in an unnaturally loud voice, called out, welcome, compatriots.

He bent down, grabbed a red plastic broom handle from the deck and using it as a walking stick, got up, went straight to Avgoustis with quick, small geisha steps and threw himself into his open arms.

Siakandaris stole a bit of a hug for himself and started prattling, you old goon, I never thought I'd see you again, you old hermit, a seabird's what you've become, and Kazas, too, offered greetings and introduced himself, fetched another weathered, plastic chair and, after asking for permission, which, as no one paid him any mind he considered as good as given, started taking photographs, the red sun, a panoramic view of the port, Siakandaris posing here, there and everywhere on that dumpster of a ship and the two friends who, after a session of mutual sighing, first the one, then the other, at last found what it was they needed to say.

They didn't speak of the following: steep waves, hellishly dark seas, cut, off fingers, a ship-owing pack of hyenas, the poisonous blue octopus of Perth, toxic weddings and poisoned bonbons.

They spoke exclusively about their mamas, two seventy-five-year-old orphans, mama's boys for a whole hour smoking away like there was no tomorrow.

–My mother died at sixty-four, Avgoustis led forcefully.

–Mine loved snakes, Papalexakis declared in a stentorian voice, out of habit, virtually obliged to fill the deadness of the empty ship with voluble shouts, in order to multiply his lonely presence.

They went over caresses and chastisements, advice and short trousers.

Avgoustis remembered pulling at the coin-bag around her neck so she'd give him spending money. Papalexakis, her washing and kneading in others' houses and after the day's toil was over, gathering the leftover pastry bits in a white hanky and taking them home to fry for her five children.

Avgoustis was next again, and brought into their midst, at dusk, his old woman just as she used to sit outside in the afternoons, on a stool, looking out to the street and talking ceaselessly to herself without caring to share her thoughts with her family.

Papalexakis sketched a portrait of his mother's favorite saint, saint Mamas, a symbol of spring blooms, gutted at fifteen by a harpoon, a beardless, smooth-faced and truly praise-worthy youth, because it's probably easier to become a saint in old age, and even more so if you're a man, since society restricts women and spies on them to stop them from sinning, I seem to think this came from her, before she was proven wrong by the developments of the next two decades, including her daughter-in-law's making a cuckold of her son.

Avgoustis proceeded with a dream. He was at the freighter's cabin with the door closed and he saw her gray hair sliding under the door, inch by inch, slowly taking up the entire floor, small waves of a silent swell.

Siakandaris and Kazas silent, sitting a small distance off, out of respect, were listening to the two elderly devils until the cook glanced at his watch, got the steward up and they went off to do a bit of work. They picked up the two paper cartons and went into what used to be the saloon of the AEGEAN BLUE II.

Around them holy curtains, holy carpets, holy slipcovers on the couches and on one of those, the bored, malting red cat. The only ornament was a dried up sports newspaper with soccer star Nikos Galis, glued crookedly on the mirror above the bar.

They took the supplies out of the boxes, six bottles of good whisky, three bottles of ouzo, a radio, two Japanese porn magazines, a Tupperware container with haddock from the seafood fast of the Annunciation the day before, another container with feta cheese, bits and pieces such as toothpicks, batteries, band-aids and a couple of dowry items, it went without saying, a pair of sheets, two towels and some clothing, six pairs of boxer shorts and an unused silk shirt, the gift to Avgoustis from his wife.

Siakandaris served the cat two forkfuls and then, opening a bottle to make two strong drinks for those outside and two weak ones for those inside, he told the steward how in 1983, during a pirate attack on the last ship that Papalexakis worked on, the yellow-skins, waving jungle machetes fit to kill wild beasts, picked clean the till and all the watches, crosses and golden chains, took the booze and all the clothing and even completely stripped the captain, a proud Kefalonian, leaving him standing in just his sandals.

As a Cretan, poor Papalexakis who'd come on board with the Kefalonian so he could go back to Greece, couldn't not put up a fight and he kicked at them so that they wouldn't tie him up, he bit one guy's hand and their leader cut off his toes with a sickle.

–Take the drinks and the bottle out to them and, then, let's tidy this haunted mansion a bit, he told Kazas, adding, with Avgoustis we're as safe as it gets.

And he explained why. When they came near danger spots,

he left the spotlights on all night, even though it's prohibited, kept the hoses and all the fire extinguishers ready at hand and manned the watch with the fake Kalashnikovs on display.

He fell silent for a bit, figuring whether to say more, couldn't hold back. Only once was the ship assaulted in the open sea off the Ivory Coast. We were the ones who tied them up, we even took their inflatable boat, he said.

Again he stopped, thought things through and came out with the rest. Since they couldn't afford to wait for arrival of the port authorities in their own good time to pick them up, the captain had them thrown in the sea, all seven of them, and he showed Kazas his five splayed fingers plus another two in the victory sign, enjoying the terror he had inspired.

Speechless and pale, Kazas took at long last the treats to the old men and scuttled a bit further off to listen to the rest.

Avgoustis' mother used to plant maiden ferns, Papalexakis' used to tame horses, the first used to sing a song from Asia Minor on her husband's name day, the latter sang hymns at Easter, the former loved all the children in the migrants' settlement, the latter all the elderly olive trees in the village, the former used to say you catch a cold through the naked soles of the feet, the latter through the kidneys, the former used cinnamon cloves to cure the evil eye, the latter used a belt. Their common ground was tidiness, the joy of setting the rug straight, of distributing the curtain folds justly along the entire length of the curtain rod, the pride they took in their tidily arranged poverty. In short, lovely tales from the dear departed, matching the peacefulness of dusk that had dyed the sea, the sky, the boat and the people with a mellow beetroot color.

–Wake up.

Siakandaris' voice brought Kazas back to order and he went back inside, the cook had finished one round of sweeping and the numb steward folded the old sheets and laid out the fresh ones on the couch that served as the old man's bed.

–You mean to tell me he let seven people drown, he said at some point.

–He threw seven buoys in the water for them and notified a Greek fishing boat nearby. After about a quarter of an hour at most, they were picked up.

–All of them?

–Six. Listen here, sweetie pie, the sea isn't the countryside of Kyriaki, spit roasts and strolls, laying about on a bed of anemones and breathing in the firs.

The cook collected the rubbish in two bags, took a break for a couple of minutes—no need to go telling this stuff elsewhere, he said pointedly, slightly regretting having opened his mouth, and closed the subject with the words, underlined one by one, Our life has also terror in it, plenty of it and for everyone, not exempting Avgoustis.

Just then, from outside was heard the refrain *world made of glass, what if I cracked you with a single blow*, the two grandpas were done with their warm-up, which consisted of kindling the flame of debt and devotion to their mammas.

–Now they'll put the torch to their loneliness, Siakandaris said sadly and joyfully and, seeing the cat come out, he joined the chorus, too, from where he sat on an uncomfortable stool which he dragged closer to the bar so he could sing softly while gazing up at Nikos Galis.

For half an hour Papalexakis' awesome voice chose the songs and the rest played along, not quite the repertory of young Kazas, though of course he'd heard in the mechanics' garages and the hamburger stands the well-known hits, I Exist as Long as You Do, Bats and Spiders, My Whole Life a Cigarette and again, I Exist as Long as You, and then, Everything's a Lie, dedicated to the Rumanian who came at the appointed time in the launch to get the three and walked into the party, no mean singer himself and, unavoidably, a devotee of Kazandzides.

There was no sun left, every color darkened, the lights of Visakhapatnam all in a pile half a mile back.

With arms around each other, Papalexakis and Avgoustis walked stiltedly to the ladder, kissed on both cheeks and, wordlessly, said goodbye for good, content and grateful for the gift of this satisfying meeting, from the tepid caress of sunset right into the inebriating fragrance of the night.

***

In a Hamburg park, fifteen years ago, Mitsos Avgoustis had seen a small Greek flag stuck in a tree trunk, approached it, and saw at its base the shriveled-up turd of a nostalgic compatriot. Still though, there is a difference between Greece in small doses and in one fell swoop, all the way up to one's last breath.

Thursday evening, March 27, alone in his cabin, eating his bread and cheese and, with every mouthful he swallowed, a different version of his retirement.

Some sailors, his own and others', Vios, Koutas, Arvanitakis, after going around the world thirty times, sank deep into their villages and struggled over three hundred square feet of soil, planted with field beans and cauliflower.

Others, Kaklamanos, Gerakas, Mortoglou, Dimitriades, sank in the morning into a chair in front of the television and in the afternoon, in the neighborhood's underlit coffee-shop for the veterans' melancholy backgammon, playing for their melancholy coffees.

Thanasoulas and Markonikos had taken their parrots back to Greece and were growing old in the narrow balconies of Abelokipi and Kallithea, not with Meropi and Eleni but in the company, respectively, of the yellow-and-red Dora and green-and-blue Aristidis.

Tsaousis, Zafirakis, Megrelis, Lionakis, Voutsadakis, colleagues from other companies with whom he'd had drinks at

Port Elizabeth, Vera Cruz and Gdansk, at the last moment before their retirement, remained at sea, a different ship and a different ocean for each, bless the waters that closed over them.

Karayiannides, Doukakis, Balodimos, Dapontes were resting in a wooden suit, he'd paid them visits at the Third Cemetery, with a candle and a bunch of violets, bless their resting ground.

Some didn't come back. Tzavelas became a coffee shop owner in the Amazon jungle, Pavlakis had been wheeling and dealing in Hawaii since his thirties, Siafakas a shepherd in New Zealand since thirty-five and Xenos a worker since forty at the fish markets of Melbourne, prying clams open, packing blue crab and cutting up baby sharks. Papalexakis he'd visited yesterday, out of action at Visakhapatnam.

Himself, even if he could see, was good for nothing like all that, whether alive or dead. Three or four times a year, on the occasion of a stiffness, a night of cramps, a good or a bad piece of news, he thought it over, just in case, at long last, the desire stirred to leave his iron castle, but it never did. His back didn't require leaning against solid walls. No house could contain him. His hands didn't reach out for tree branches. His feet had no wish to step on dirt, asphalt or sidewalks. His ears didn't hanker for car horns and bulldozers, nor for the crowd's Sunday roar at the sports field, nor for the slogans at the party rallies, the pages in his voter's registration booklet were mostly blank.

For him the swell was everything. And more than.

He took up his knitting for a bit, did twenty rows, calmed down, put it aside. He received the latest weather report via the intercommunications tube, the distant storm was changing direction. He studied the map with the magnifying glasses. With his mind all tense, he calculated that with a bit of good luck he'd have time enough to get out of the weather's way.

Twenty times he'd managed to trick the typhoons and get away from them and another twenty he'd fallen into their clutches, two and three and four nights and days with the ship collapsing to the left and to the right, being hurled to the top of the waves and tumbling down to their bottom and coming out safe in the end.

Avgoustis' bodyguard was the sea itself, she still wanted him, he hadn't had his fill of her nor she of him.

It was past ten when he came out for the requisite stroll up and down, forward and back, on the bridge. He went past all the posts, a night guard combing through the premises, was satisfied with the level of vigilance and went to stand on the stern, collect some fervid slaps from the wind and have a cigarette.

That's how his father used to sit, in the boat at night, drawing parsimoniously on the leftover cigarette, next to his cat, wordless. He'd spent time with him fishing, his helper and positive at that time, at twelve and at thirteen, that the sea was boring, the sea was poor and he didn't want any part of it. He was dreaming of commerce, buying and selling, filling and emptying out his storerooms.

Up to the age of fifteen he practiced selling off dozens of pounds of buck mackerel and bogue daily and running a lottery with the day's red snapper or dusky grouper.

After he was orphaned, he craved leaving behind the graves and the dirt, he went into the employ of the navy and never left. Not even after the Occupation, when for a short time he could find English woolen shirts at a good price, and make a killing reselling them at twenty-five and thirty drachmas apiece, he was practically in love with them, so fluffy that they stood upright as soon as he opened his sailor's suitcase, as if there was a body inside them. When Chadzimanolis called him, saying he'd just gotten a share in some small ship, he sailed off with him again, the wages were ample and secure and, besides, his youthful body had by now gotten used to the dried up salt and his eyes were yearning for the far distance.

He'd almost finished the cigarette when he heard fairly close Kazas's scraping shoes.

–What are you doing here?

–I was getting ready to go down.

–I want to know where you are from.

–I was born in Athens, the youth answered a bit timidly.

–Your parents Athenians, too?

–Yes sir.

–And your grandparents? The captain persisted.

–From villages in Macedonia, said the steward and, still inexperienced in the rules of proper conduct towards superiors and, in particular, towards the number one in the hierarchy, grew overly familiar and let out, though with some hesitancy, it seems as though you've started missing your village.

Avgoustis couldn't very well convey to the strange youngster the profession's peculiarities, the waters are my country from the foam to the bottom, the ship is my capital, my official language is the swell, my formal religion is holy cussing and my currency is the splayed out palm, the youth would think he was a nutcase. He looked for somewhat simpler words and he came up with these.

–The country is inside the seaman's satchel, it's the lining for the underwear, the letters and the money.

What was there for Kazas to say?

–To make things plain, as far as I'm concerned, my country of origin is a juicy tomato cut in four with thick grains of salt, the captain added and pricked his ear to enjoy the surprise of the inexperienced youngster, whose own useless longings life would soon cross out, setting implacable burdens in their place.

–But was there nothing you loved back there? asked the stupefied Kazas.

Avgoustis weighed the situation inwardly and as he turned

around to take another stroll down into the engine room, and as the wind beat against him, and the old chapters of his life sprung unexpectedly into his mind, he wondered himself if he truly loved something back there and came up with a definitive answer.

–The Asia Minor catastrophe and Litsa Tsichli.

***

ARE YOU LISTENING TO ME? As soon as I walk into the living room with the tray, you're going to see a funny tea set. Instead of handles, the teacups all have little gray frogs. The porcelain spoons have a green lizard for a handle. Around the cake platter a brown and yellow snake is curled, asleep. I am describing it before you see it so you don't get a fright. Unless the son of a gun has sent your family one like it. Here it is. I brought it empty. Without the tea. I don't want it to break. I served you in the usual cup that you know.

And, Mitso, I love your arm and another little something about the untamable nights, my oven trays, the flower beds and dung for the vegetables. I'm not buying that you, a lad brimming with vim and vigor, a player of the noisy music of the young, should come all the way out here for my sake. You are not interested in the wretched Litsa, it's him you are interested in.

I'm schooling you in your parent. I'm giving you a headache, too, with too much gabbing, but that's what you get when you meet people. Besides, the course is for free. And one-sided. In this house there is no dialogue. In here, visitors are rare nowadays, and in a hurry. You turn up without calling and you find me at my post. I was the father's Penelope and I've become the son's as well.

My little squid, you go set your life up, he told me when

your eldest sister was born. He was present at a call from a customer who was matching me up with a loaded Greek-American with two eateries in Chicago. He'd set eyes on me and was drooling all over.

Mitso, my brown eyes let fly showers of sparks and my white calves flash lightening, the plate-man says, I informed your old man of the lovesick guy's words.

The sequel was written with moans and bites until the wee hours and the half-eaten squid never made it into the frying pan of the groom-to-be.

The same again when your second sister was born. Another suitor had turned up, the owner of a glass shop with a great big operation of his own and the captain was saying take him, and, why don't you, while he was taking me in bed with a whole new bunch of tricks which he brought out for the first time ever.

The leading role that night belonged to my belly button, hiding place of a new blue mole that got him all excited and dawn found him with his face buried in my belly, kissing away and sighing, my Litsa mole, in its Litsa mole-hole. He could conjure unforgettable nights.

His talent in this respect left two Penelopes in his wake. The one wasn't enough for him.

Don't be shocked that I'm dishing it out like it is. You're no infant. You are a man. And I'm not telling you these things so that you hate him. I want you to love him. But do it knowing, instead of being in the dark. If we should only love saints and gentlemen, no one would love anyone.

I don't fit in with the dry folks.

That's what he said one winter night that he spent in the chair in front of the window, watching the clouds outside come to life and the branches warring.

It's the chair next to the one next to you, on which, in

spring, I sit the bowl with the blue lilies on. When the wind stirs them and I can look at a bunch of waves in the vase. The chair's come undone at the seams now and won't hold a person's weight. When its hind leg broke, I heard the crack and I felt as if my own knee gave way, it hurt, I stumbled and for a couple of days I walked with a limp.

What do you care about chairs set? And I talk too much non-stop and stuff you with my rubbish.

A young girl student in the neighborhood would, from time to time, bring me some nice summer novels. You read a book and in the end, more than the telling of the terrible and unlikely events, women strangled from jealousy, knifed by mistake, major revolutions, you're left with certain little things, squashed in two or three lines and tucked away here and there in the hiding places of the pages.

That's how it works, in the end. Every person's History with a capital H, is made up of their stories, the loose change that every now and then jingles in the pockets of their life or of their mind.

I have my own opinion because I think everything through. From the meaning of the house to the meaning of Cyprus. From the meaning of tea to the meaning of the army. Thinking doesn't go only with the thick black books of the lawyers and the professors, it also goes with the hair-curlers and dryers of a day working at the salon. I, too, have a right to philosophize, however much and in whatever fashion I'm able, à la Litsa.

I'm telling it to you straight through, as if I've had years of rehearsing my part, as if I've been reheating the words in this last while you've been coming to visit.

I'm prattling, I'm aware of that, but I don't much like to recount a happening in telegraphic fashion. I need to put in where it happened, when and whether it was at night and if it was in winter, the full monty.

First I'll say it was noonday on a Saturday. The bakers were taking out the individual little cross-buns, the bakers' wives were putting them in bags for the Sunday memorial services and all of Elefsina was smelling of mahaleb cherry. Then I'll say that my windows were open. Then that there was again the robin on the balcony rail. Then, that you could hear the loudspeakers of the election campaigners outside promising feasts galore to the poor. I will go on with the tablecloth which still has the hole from his cigarette. I'd better not forget my cat on the windowsill, who's watching a cat on television. I'll add the Christmas kourambiethes on the platter and only after I've said all this, will I say the last thing. That the phone rings and it's him, after a long time, telling me that he is having cocktails with a Greek doctor in Argentina. But I don't complain to him, Mitso, I'm turning thirty-five tonight and you've forgotten, why do I like so much listening to his voice, no matter what he says, and besides, his phone call is like a gift, the only one I get for my birthday.

I'll go on, though with my eyes shut.

I'd already started decorating the Christmas tree of 1974 at the beginning of November. In between the balls and the silver branches I hung the school pencil cases of the two children I would have, their tiny shoes, their caps, their abacus, their talcum powder. The year before he'd left banging his fist on the table, I'm getting a divorce. Beginning of December I received the greeting card of your birth. You would have been three or four months already. That's how long it took him to muster the courage to write to me what had happened. That tear dynamited my cheek. Only I can see the scar trailing from the eye to the throat.

I undecorated the house. I was finished with my hopes. And I did so love births, little brothers and sisters, little cousins, godchildren, kindergartens and primary schools. Small children should be the only serious excuse for half the things going on in the world. I did like births a lot. Ever since I was a wee thing. An orphan, all on my own, describing to myself in detail, the midwife in my parents' bedroom, at one time helping bring out into the world two younger siblings, at another even bringing out two that were older than me.

The old school mates at the Yellow Comb all have children and grandchildren. From '74 onwards, whenever he'd come back, I bought him condoms. I didn't want to get pregnant again. I've had three abortions, I never wrote it to him. Nor did he ask about it, maybe he suspected something, probably that's why.

I heard the familiar comments plenty of times since. Litsa, you raise me from the dead. Litsa, you're a garden, Litsa you are the joy of living. But those of us who are such fun are only good for illicit affairs. The brooders become the legal spouses, those who won't put up with nonsense.

I get back full speed to the plants. I seed, they grow. I water, they shoot leaves. They give birth to strawberries and then the shadow ministry of the sparrows gathers to feast and burst my eardrums. If I plant things on the tiles they'll grow, if I throw the seeds on the cement, they'll thrive, if I spit apricot pips in the middle of the asphalt, apricot trees will spring up.

May, I bring you to flower, me, Litsa. June, you can count on me to single-handedly make your jasmines fragrant. In Australia, the year switches the seasons around and makes the wisteria bloom in September.

Yesterday evening, in a foreign movie on television, the Atlantic was all dark and puffed up. Mitsos's nation, I thought. The sea is his justice.

And now I'm opening my eyes. Suddenly I want to see yours from up close. Lift your eyes, my boy. Ah, come now, you don't want to get all teary eyed with my piffle.

So then. Today's letter is over. Love, Litsa Tsichli. Beat it.

***

–You fulfilled what you had vowed at Visakhapatnam.

–My men went strolling through the mud puddles and they dug in their pocket again, to be told their fortune by the Indian palm readers. The news is good. Long life guaranteed. With me they're in no danger, which is why I won't give them over to some stranger's care.

This was the interlude of the phone conversation with Flirtakis. The full report took five minutes and the upshot was that the lawyers, looking to contest the will, went through all the Company's books and concluded that it wasn't in Chadzimanolis' interest to claim that his father had lost it, because there'd be repercussions on other decisions of that period, meaning the whole thing would go haywire.

–We again escaped together, the dearly departed and me. He from the stain of being a loony and I from the land.

–Don't rush into feeling happy. The boss is contriving a new scheme, to change flags and fire the whole crew. This is all on your head, Avgoustis, were his last words.

He went into the ship's saloon, heard the good evenings, counted the figures, five men not on shift were sprawled out watching *Hot Shots! Part Deux* for the tenth time and their hot and bothered captain sat down next to them. He adored all three hundred odd that had been in his employ. In the past he read in their eyes and in recent years in their breath, how fond they were of the short, longhaired fox that governed them, eliminating with cunning and stealth any and every obstacle. By his side they'd come to know the sea, as much as she allows herself to be known. Ten years ago, all of them without exception would have been prime candidates for employment on any ship, having served under Avgoustis was tantamount to two or three Harvard degrees. Now, all the bosses only took on Greek captains and engineers. Boulmetis, the old captain of ATHOS I had retired prematurely in January of '93. With a crew of twenty-two Russians who adhered to the old church calendar, he'd celebrated New Year's with watery lentil soup, it wasn't till the 16th that meat was served. And Kopasakis, the captain of ATHOS II, had been cornered with twenty-five Pakistanis and Filipinos and not a soul to talk to about his goats back at the village and his soccer team, OFIS, he had been twice in danger from the mix-up in the translating of orders, until he too was worn down and went back to his mountains.

If Shipping Maritime fired his crew, would they all find work again, and how soon?

There were other things, too, that Avgoustis thought of. He first thought of the DIANA and LIMASOL II, old hulls just like him, lucky freighters that made their last trip accompanied by a tug-boat and sank gloriously before arriving in Karatsi and being cut up to little pieces. Then he thought of the first trip of ATHOS III, March of '85, from Rotterdam to Canada bearing as passenger, for luck, the now-dead old Chadzimanolis, in his personal last sea voyage.

High up at the Seven Islands, near the source of St. Laurence river, the iceboats were out, the ATHOS was on a zigzag course through the icebergs and everyone was on the alert, watching out for a crash with the enormous white shapes gliding next to them, sparkling in the morning sun. A slow dangerous journey in the middle of an expensive, silver hell.

Old Chadzimanolis, with the eye of a hawk, was the first to see a slice of ice as large as an island fall away from the mainland and, stranded on it, a huge white bear with her three cubs. For ten days the carriers, cruisers and fishing boats saw and photographed the mother with her hungry pups, without even half a handful of seaweed to eat on the iceberg which, on its southward trip, grew smaller day by day. The telegraph operators were signaling to each other with information until on the eleventh day the whole North Atlantic resounded with the news that the iceberg had melted and the bears had drowned, someone had photographed the furry corpses floating in the water.

The ATHOS heard the news just as it had filled its three storerooms with ore, ready to sail for Middleborough.

In the following years, Chadzimanolis and Avgoustis, on the few and far between occasions they were in touch, India's still pulling in a lot of Canadian rice, those of us captains that married girls from Chios became shipowners, what does Chile have to say today, always ended with the refrain, remember the polar bears, remember the three cubs playing on their mother's belly, remember how we all cried over the animals forced against their will to migrate and meet with a seaman's death.

One old bear, Chadzimanolis, was dead and gone and the other bear, Avgoustis, had no reason left anymore not to destroy his hapless orphan. After the shipowners' fallout in 1979 at Souvadivadol, Avgoustis had been instrumental in saving his bosses from bankruptcy, other companies and top-notch shipowners were wanting to grab him and were waving fat promises, but he was not to be swayed, faithful to his old pal and benefiting from it, too, because he had been cashing in ever since on the cover-up of this affair and his continued presence at Shipping Maritime Company with freedom of movement and no strings attached.

Which should be his next moves? The margin was getting smaller, things were getting tough. He needed to think and to organize himself.

First on the duty roll, again, faithful old Siakandaris, he didn't, as it turned out, have the heart to not stand by his master to the end and so, forced now to make do very frugally and no longer surrounded by fresh zucchini, elegant steaks and cute cheeses, he took up preaching to the crew about the importance of fasting which *cleanses sins and transgressions, moderates the spirit, sanctifies belief, casts out demons*, and to forcefully expounding on the patriotism of bean stew, the wisdom of chickpea broth, the friendliness of potato soup and, every Tuesday, Thursday and Sunday the frugality of halva.

On every other Friday, late in the afternoon, the ship's loudspeakers played tapes with a collection of hymns hailing Mary the Mother of God, giving all the men extra points for holiness.

Friday, March 28, en route to Shanghai, the weather report wasn't all that could be wished for, there was a storm coming in from the South China sea, with a one hundred mile radius, heading South-South North at a speed of fifty miles an hour and a wind intensity of ten on the Beaufort scale and, on its present course, the ship would meet it head-on in about twelve hours.

Do we have enough flares? the new guy asked, pale with fear, while collecting the after-dinner plates and glasses from the crew's mess hall. We've got flares and we have storm lamps and buoys, too, only thing we don't have is a flag of the Bucharest Steaua soccer team, said one of the Rumanian lads. And only one flag of the Moscow Dynamo, the two Russians piped in, always ready to pull someone's leg and they explained to the steward that if anyone kicks the bucket on the spot, because, say, a mast falls on his head, the captain has vowed to send the dead guy's coffin back to his homeland covered with his team's flag.

The orders, secure all loose equipment, tie down the weights, all crew members on alert, dispersed the men to their tasks, and ATHOS III with engines at full throttle changed course and duly notified a possible delay in the cargo's delivery, on account of unforeseen circumstances.

On the bridge, Avgoustis felt nostalgic for about half a minute for the excursions, in the company of the deceased bear, to the heaven-scraping Mount Athos. *Hail Hallowed and God-trodden Mount, hail ensouled bush that will not immolate, God's only bridge into the world,* according to the hymn composed by the nun Claudia, she, too, a kindred soul, completely blind.

Well versed in men's monasteries, himself an abbot every one of his ships, he went out to meet his monks at their posts and, in his tread, he felt creation turned black and blue, he heard the sea's uproar and, alongside, the scraping of shoes of the apprentice monk, Kazas.

–You butting in again?

Momentarily taken aback, the young steward asked, eventually, in a shaken voice, A coffee maybe, or a tea set?

–What I'm thinking is that Flirtakis has planted you here, to spy on me. You tell him, I'm picking out which sandbank to crash this ship on.

Kazas excused himself saying he'd come out on deck because he couldn't get a connection on his cell phone in the crew's quarters, but there was no signal outside either, they were too far away from any shore and, then, there was the weather turning bad.

–And who do you have to report to?

He had to report to his relationship. His pissed-off girl was a graphic artist, posters, CD covers, things like that, she had balked at his decision to go to sea and she couldn't understand why the three letters and the parcel with the chocolate wafers, video tapes and CDs she'd sent, hadn't reached him, nor why she still hadn't received photos or anything else from him.

There is a special way that seamen communicate with their women, that evolves through long-term absence, after both parties have been well versed in lies and have acquired the wisdom to let lame explanations be. Overall, seamen get along better among themselves, too, when they say one thing and mean another, when they answer questions that weren't asked, ask about things that cannot be answered, comment on any odd thing that comes into their head, on the condition that it isn't of burning concern to whomever is hanging out with them. But not even Avgoustis had a steady record of good results with this technique, let alone this pup they loaded along with the bricks in Vietnam.

Stelios Kazas, a novice to the codes of the sea, stood at ramrod attention near his captain, holding on to the rail against the heavy roll of the sea, undecided about whether he should take his leave or stay, when, out of the blue, Avgoustis indicated he was in the mood for more.

–If she's worth it, do your best not to lose her. If she's a rotten apple, do your best to let her go, get the thing over and done with. There are women cannibals who roast the man on a spit for a lifetime and it's still not enough.

Kazas gulped and Avgoustis had no more steam to blow, there's no way we're not making a port, we're bound to, our agent's waiting in Shanghai, you'll all get their letters and send them yours.

He turned up his collar and lit a cigarette. You put me in mind of my folks, he said, took two drags and went on. The meek and the dead grow their hair long. What do you make of my head? I should be getting myself ready, in good time.

By the time he finished his cigarette, he'd said the rest as well. He never let the family come on the trip, never had women and children on board, he preferred bachelors, faggots and old farts with grown-up kids at high school or University.

The talk, three speedy minutes of unexpected disclosures, could have gone on at length, but it was cut short when the steward stated, simply and straightforwardly, that if he had a captain as a father, he would like to spend summers on board his ship. His father had died relatively young but, thankfully, he let me have my fill of him, that's how he put it.

Those words smarted. Avgoustis pressed his lips together to stop any unfair talk from escaping, he did often become infuriated with others when he should have controlled himself better, but, as stated, seamen are rough-hewn in conversation and masterful in silence.

He moved away hurriedly thinking that he had not only not let his son have his fill of his father, but not even a morsel from the dish that's cooked leisurely and slowly by a man and a little-man out of the reach of the females sweeping like tempests through the houses of Pireas.

The smoke that comes out of ships, is that from their fireplace? Has your ship's siren ever got stuck for one whole month, with the sound driving you crazy? The man drowning at sea, does he hurt? When you die, for how long are you to stay dead?

His son's questions as he was reaching up from seven to eight and from eight to nine and was writing to him every Sunday struggling to gain entry into his father's life, till he realized that he'd been left out and that all his desperate attempts were in vain.

And then there was this young scaredy-cat who, whenever he wasn't cowering silently next to the Russians and the Rumanians, kept bumping into him, still unrehearsed in the format of submission, awkward and impudent, without meaning to, saying things that called up the ghosts of Pireas.

On the next round he found him still there, walking back and forth in the chill.

It's past eleven, he told him, go wake up the Russians to sing you one of those lullabies they used to put sailors to sleep with in the submarines.

—Sasha lost a bet and he shaved off his awesome mustache this afternoon.

Avgoustis pulled up short. I saw that, he answered dryly, it's

his right to mow the thatch off his mug, he added and motioned
with his hand for him to be gone.

***

Right from the outset of his career, Captain Avgoustis yielded
some of the highest earnings among his colleagues. Before he
had settled on the port ahead, he would get information about
local strikes and quarantines due to epidemics, he slipped out
from bad weather to burn less oil, in some cases he asked for a
port pilot only at the very last moment so the pilot couldn't
possibly make it on time and Avgoustis saved on his fees, he
didn't lose a single day in overlay and, therefore, not a single
dollar either, his shipowners never had to pay part of the cost
of a crash nor those who chartered him damages due to piracy
or theft, he checked the quality and quantity of the cargo himself so that the Pireas team wouldn't have to pay any fines to
the shipping registry, none of the ships he ran ever got demoted
in class, nor did he ever have to voluntarily run any of them
aground.

In the absence of errors, naval accidents and losses, his
insurance fees were lower than those for many other similar
carriers and in exchange for the bosses' gains he got their
silence about illegalities which, in any event, he had his way of
covering up. After economizing on behalf of the Chadzimano-
lises he looked after himself, he collected the fees for attendance at official events and for port outings, though he never
did go on shore anymore, he withheld a percentage whenever
he had a chance, he stole petrol, he stole from the cargo, he
didn't say no to safe contraband, including his officers in the
scheme so they'd uphold their part in the obligations that
incurred, just as was the case on most ships. This was, is and
will be the code of the sea.

In the past two months out of the Protocol, he was at the

tender mercy of Flirtakis, a shepherd in the seaweed prairie, a diver in the depths of need.

Saturday, April 12, the ore had been delivered to Singapor with only half a day's delay, every wave a supplication to the Lord for mercy, for the weather to go blow off its steam elsewhere, for Mitsos to get safely into port, unload, wash off, get his correspondence, sail off and put his ideas into action.

In the office with Birbilis, he sent the telex to Pireas with their supply needs, the three-day report, coordinates, average speed, distance, engine turns, viciously formal, pointedly methodical. Then he put a call through to Flirtakis.

–Just so I won't be on your back all the time, do your damnedest and get me a good, pre-arranged charter for a couple of months down the line, so I can cut myself some slack.

–That's not what the lawyers are arranging. You've been warned.

–You'll have fifteen thousand dollars if you get me a worthwhile cargo, so we can shut people up for the time being. Look for something else around here, too, so I'm not stalling about empty till then.

–And what if I don't manage to oblige you?

Avgoustis then told him his other idea, too.

–You can't replace a captain while the ship is sailing. You won't get me at any port. I will sail around empty, I'll set down anchor in the open seas and I'll charge you two hundred and fifty thousand a month.

The find was silver from Martaban, an expensive product, available to load forty days hence, deliverable to Australia. The money-mongering Chadzimanolis couldn't bear losing out on the scoop and his other two ships were far away, ATHOS I was sailing with wood and produce from Vancouver to Conception and ATHOS II with animal feed from Paranagua to Amsterdam.

The pre-arranged charter deal was made before others got their paws in and the old man secured an extension of his time at the helm of his freighter. He felt satisfied with having won the round and, at the same time, deplored his inability to, at long last, pull out of the game.

In the wardroom he didn't touch his food and Siakandaris, on the lookout for the men's looks and exclamations of appreciation for the macaroni with octopus, sat next to him, got bored with his hermetic silence, threw out a comment about his own mum, I love cutting up the lamb into portions, missus Despina used to say, may God forgive her soul and The lamb's right hand-side has more meat on it, no response from the other, Where to get strawberries from, now, and all that girly fruit that you like, he apologized, Send me something later, Avgoustis conceded at last, With the new guy, this he emphasized and got up.

One hour later, the cook, still piqued by the usurpation, sent Kazas up from the kitchens with a well-turned-out dinner portion for Maritsa and cheese and bread for her master.

The cat, royally pissed off those days, all jerky twists and hellish mewling, had moved into the shipowners' apartment so as not to bother Avgoustis, and the steward served him there, next to the ship's small rotating library with the biographies of Al Capone, de Talleyrand and Prodromos Tsaousakis, in between *Myripnoa anthi tou Paradeisou*, *Apokalipseis tis Theotokou*, *Apostoliki Sagini* and five or six more leather–or cloth–bound tomes plundered from Mount Athos in the course of past incursions to the Sacred Garden by the now dead Chadzimanolis and Avgoustis. When in a good mood, Siakandaris would cook narrating to Kazas the life and miracles of his master.

Across the way, in dutiful attendance inside his own cabin, the monkish captain walked like a robot back and forth, touching the handkerchief in one trouser pocket, the key to the drawer in the other, the mini magnifying glass, in the breast pocket of the jacket as always, all of these tepid from the heat of his body, while he tried to formulate a question which he finally expressed in a direct hit to the hapless Kazas, as soon as he'd said good evening and set the tray on the table.

–What might the guts of an old man be like? Full of holes and shrunken? And his blood, red and vivid or purplish and flat? Do they still pulsate and get roused up and thunderous or do they crawl along inside their derelict fold?

Without waiting for an answer, he snorted like a wild beast at the smell of the cheese, took off his jacket and his shirt and stood only in his sleeveless T-shirt. Sit down, don't go, he asked Kazas, reached out his hand and, almost carelessly, felt for the tray.

He took hold of the bread separated the crust from the rest, left the white, doughy middle on the plate, brought the crunchy brown-gold circle to his mouth and ate just that, mouthful after mouthful, wetting his gullet with red wine a couple of times.

–Dead-meat arms but lively brains, he said shaking his bare arms and went on, I closed a deal for a pre-arranged charter a month and a half from now.

Kazas, who in the meantime had learned to tell apart the bollards from the load booms and the bow from the stern, though he still confused the lines with the shroud and the shroud with the bitt rope, was still a total virgin when it came to freighting schemes.

–We've got a long way to go together, smiled Avgoustis and bit into some cheese.

–Yes sir.

–So, what do you make of the sea? Are you a fan yet or what?

–All's well. I'm doing my best.

–You're the youngest on board. Do you smoke? Have a cigarette.

The youngster didn't smoke, the captain lit up alone.

–Kazas is not a Macedonian surname, said Avgoustis, took a couple of deep drags and asked for the steward's grandfathers' story. To start with, the Kazas are found in Arcadia, your kin must have sprouted from the Peloponnese.

The youngster, like all the young, hadn't looked into his roots, he said the struggle for survival kept his family squarely tied up with today, the talk at home was around photocopying machines, loan payments, and, at best, around the pranks on TV talk shows like Anita Pania's *Golden Bonbon*.

–You and your old man got on well, you said.

–Yes.

–How well?

–On Sundays he'd take me to the Planetarium, to soccer games. We did each other favors. I wish he was alive, he said, took out his wallet, shuffled through some photographs. That's him here, he picked one and passed it, hand to hand, to Avgoustis.

He pretended to be studying it, casually made a comment with which he couldn't go wrong, pity he's gone, and left it on the table from where the steward collected it and put it back in its place. There was silence for a while. Then, Avgoustis unlocked his drawer, frisked around the jumble of small objects, feeling for the three frames, picked the single one without looking, hatched it in his warm palms for a fair bit and handed it to the steward.

–My son, he said.

Kazas took it, looked at it, didn't say a word.

His lips looked locked on paper as well, the thick, curly bangs covered his left eye and on the far right-hand side you could see Laura's little hand pulling at his sleeve and handfuls of her hair braided by Flora like spaghetti with yellow and orange threads, a little mop-head.

***

The photograph had been taken by that crazy-ass Vassia during the last of the family's nightmare feasts, sisters, little niece, brother-in-law, parents-in-law and the umpteenth silly twit of a boyfriend of the name-day girl, targeted as a bridegroom, everyone at one, new year's wishes, on the table the overcooked turkey and the overboiled rice, Flora's doing; no end, either, to the syrupy tales with controlled innuendo about grandpa, whom we miss so much or to toasts, consumed way past the expiry date, to friendly seas and to the absentee's happy return, with all the family members inwardly wondering, yet again, where might the old bugger be and who might he be feeding dick.

Just on time, the dogfish's call from way over Australia to wish Vassia many happy returns and a happy new year to all, one last gloriously chorused crescendo of well-wishing and, then, onto the trail blazed by the patisserie, a cake of dark chocolate, the son-in-law's all time favorite.

As for Andonis, he hadn't opened his mouth either to eat, well-wish or chat, moody on account of a stiff neck from a cold, this was the standard excuse he used for all such get-togethers, with a pointedly provocative manner, so they would be well-apprised of his lie. So, he waited patiently for them to finish eating, to cannibalize each other over politics, for the women to score their points, invincible prattlers abetted by the trashy TV shows, and for the feast at long last to blow off, leaving everyone with the aftertaste, not of the meal served, but of deception.

He had this thing about walking upside down ever since his first year in high school. With hands down and legs up he'd go up or down the stairs of the 9th Gymnasium-Lyceum of Pireas, pretending there were no exclamations or guffaws from the kids, though there were a few of the former, plenty of the latter. Early on a Sunday morning, when the streets were empty, he walked up and down the pavement in front of their apartment building, with the blood going to his head and setting it on fire, the palms sturdily stepping and his eyes trained on the little dog of the old woman across the street which, every so often, turned puzzled, almost compassionate, towards the upside-down walker.

The whole family had gone to the wedding of such and such and to this and that one's baptism, once at twelve, another time at thirteen, and he'd gone into the church of St. Constantine on his hands, walked upside down around the candle holders and secluded himself in a dark corner.

Three years in a row, during Easter at Porto Heli with the women, he followed from a distance the Epitaph procession, last man in the crowd, on his hands. On the five-day high school excursion at Chania he left the others going wild in the cafeteria and walked upside down the entire length of the jetty, out to the lighthouse.

He'd exhaustively studied the asphalt, the eroded cement tiles, the sewer grilles, the pissed-on tree roots, the stepped on cigarette butts, the socks, the trouser legs, the knees, the skirt hems, the walking sticks, the purses and the leather briefcases.

The feet-up kid at first, then the upside-downer, finally Sky Walker, any alias would be one hundred times preferable to the surname Avgoustis.

And yet, he disliked drawing their attention, he wanted not to be like them, no way, not like anyone in their lot. And to give them the slip. That's why, at fourteen, he threw himself into the drums, violent sounds, violent rhythms sending everyone scurrying away, at long last and good riddance, so that half of them would stop asking of him to still be an infant while the other half got pissed off that he wasn't already a well-rounded adult.

Since fifteen he'd also quit summer vacations, he sent his sisters and his mother off and had a whole month to himself.

The adolescent Avgoustis of August ordered daily two sou-
vlakia for lunch and another two for dinner and spent eighteen hours a day in the empty apartment building, playing percussion to Nirvana, Joy Division and Rage Against the
Machine, anything at all, as long as it sounded like a bombing
raid. When he needed to give his arms a rest, he did improvs
on the drums with a patience he didn't have in other things
and he came up with the bitch's slaps to her son from the
Lotto shop across the street, the clicking of high heels on cob-
blestones, the horse's gallop, the swallows' furtive nestling in
the eucalyptus tree at the square; he invented outfits of sound
for a life that would be to his liking, and at night he, who dis-
dained orderliness and cleanliness, put his uniform of black
jeans and black shirt, in the washing machine and sat for
hours dusting and polishing the double bass drum, the snare,
the two toms, the high hat, the crash cymbal, the ride and the
china.

Yesterday evening, the picture that he contrived to show
the captain as a photograph of the departed Kazas senior, was
none other than one of the old man himself! How could the
sightless man make out his own proud posture in the officious
uniform, fifteen years earlier, statue-like next to the statue of
some horse-riding jack-ass at the famed port? The only reason
the boy hadn't thrown out the photograph in all these years
was his wild fondness for the Beatles, Ringo Star and Liver-
pool.

Formerly Stelios Kazas, a stolen first and last name, as trib-
ute to his one and only chum ever in the first year of high
school, whom he lost, along with their talks about tits, Bruce
Lee and Formula 1, when his family left for Stuttgart; presently
Andonis Kazas, in the buff at his bunk with the light on, sleepless and stuck.

He racked his brains trying to remember when the last time
was that he'd cried like a normal person, went over all the

hurts of recent years, about this, that and the other, he'd made it through it all dry-eyed. The only tears he could bring to mind were the common, childhood ones at the school's stone-throwing battles, the first ones around the age of nine, his poor head split open by a pebble big as a chestnut, the second ones at eleven, when he came around, eventually, from four shots of vodka, the third at thirteen when his mother wouldn't shell out the money for him to buy a scooter and he was calling her a Tight-fisted shrew and suchlike, with outbursts of sobbing in between the words.

Later on, two of his fellow students crashed in a Yamaha, he called them nitwits, his godmother died, who cares, Vassia's dog snuffed it, apathy. He always had a vitriolic swearword for the dead of his adolescence before he left them behind.

He didn't get into University, they can go fuck themselves the bastards, he went to Boston, all Americans with their dick in their hand, went to Bucharest, wusses and buttheads, some Rita snubbed him, who gives a hoot about that pervert, some Evi dumped him, what a nitwit, for each one of those a two-day farewell marathon on the drums and an upside-down night wander through Messinias street, then Thrasyvoulou, Clemanseau, Skevothikis and Neorion streets, and now, here he is, in the middle of the Indian ocean, with lead in his head, cement in his chest, his whole body turned to stone, needing to break down, to retrospectively allow himself the forbidden wailing and flailing and not being able to, in case he fell apart at the seams, in case they heard him.

–He can't see a thing. Walks around like a zombie. Beware of the cook. He's a slippery one. Don't talk too much with the crew, they may not be bright but they sure are more hardy than you and someone'll see through you. I don't put it past you to piss yourself at six Beaufort and spoil everything because, then, your own father, barbarian that he is, will kick your ass tum-

bling down the dock at the first port, like he did me. Don't let
the Company know first and me afterwards, me first and we
see how we go. The shipowner's interest is not the same as ours
and the lawyer, too, he needs time to think the case through.
Flirtakias was loathe to arrange your travel papers, he did forge
them for our sake, don't you forget it. He wants you back with
the booty in one month, tops. Be careful. This was your plan,
I wasn't for it.

Yes, indeed, the outlandish ruse was all his suggestion. The
night when he found out from his mother that the old man's
blind, he got scared stiff, the blood rushed to his head, first
thing in the morning I'm going down to the office and turning
him in, I won't be the son of a culprit.

Flora objected, it's against our interests. They fought. He
gave her a piece of his mind uncensored and merciless,
reduced her to tears, then stepped back down.

He asked her several questions gently, what is happening in
that guy's head, he heard what she said. He went into his room
to struggle with himself privately for the rest of the night. As if
his issues weren't enough, not knowing what to do with his life,
not having a desire for anything, not even the music worked,
here was this update. Should he go himself and arrest the mad-
man who had no will for the land? If he turned up as Andonis
Avgoustis, the old guy would turn him away on the spot.

The idea came to him in a flash in the morning.

–I'll go as another. I'll make up a fitting tale. I'll disguise my
voice somehow. I'll watch his face the moment I'll tell him,
yoo-hoo, this is your sonny. And I'll get that braid cut off that
gets on your nerves.

On the airplane, direct flight for Vietnam and for the old
man's *Apocalypse Now*, the self-ordained Rambo of the Tropics, thought the whole thing over, asked for a sedative, which
they gave him and, a while later, they brought him some oxygen, too.

What had gotten into him? Why not just airlift the old man from the ship by force and have things over with?

He used to ask his mother. Will he come? Did he say when he'll come? Since he didn't come last summer, will he be coming this one? After her no, he'd say, best he doesn't come. With time he stopped asking, he wanted to get to where his father didn't matter to him, wasn't in his memory, was thoroughly and truly non-existent for him and in recent years, the two had indeed become thoroughly and truly non-existent for each other.

Before setting foot on the ship, he'd imagined that, already in the first week, he would draw him aside, bend his resistance, set him up just fine with three direct sentences, if you start yelling, I'll start yelling, too, I won't back down like my mother and, this way, with no big scene in front of an audience, they'd get off at the next port, supposedly separately, each going his own way.

The first fifteen days locked up mid-ocean in this pathetic tin contraption, with the ship's roll messing up his stomach, its heavy odors messing up his nostrils and the incessant claptrap noise of the engines messing up his head, he'd trailed the old man on three or four occasions intent on mustering the courage to finally tell it to him like it was, but had ended up just rooted on the spot, gaping in admiration at the prehistoric monster sauntering about his kingdom, with himself a participant observer in a field trip on dinosaurs.

He was unprepared for surprises like this, hadn't figured how it would feel living for the very first time right next to his father, a man already well into old age, and finding out about all those far fetched tales, from Birbilis, for instance, about the unbelievable old guy with the twenty-seven cats, from the commie Michaloutsos about how in Seattle, in 1967, the captain refused a cargo of canons for Vietnam, from Siakandaris about the dowries he put together for the five daughters of two Pakistanis, members of an older crew, all the girls seamstresses and land-workers, at forced labor since age seven, from the Rumanians who had no idea, naturally, that the new guy spoke their language and was eavesdropping while they sang the praises of their boss, that they wouldn't take time off just so this catch of a captain wouldn't hire others in their place on the derelict floating Hilton.

Meanwhile, whenever there was signal on the cell phone, Flora's stormy calls kept up on a daily basis. We'll miss out on the hundred grand of the will, and, their lawyers aren't backing up, and, you're taking too long, and, move it, will you, and, I faked a stroke so that Chadzistupid would take pity on me, and on and on.

He'd been on the ship for nearly a month and a half and he had another month and a half left for the rest of what had to happen plus God knew what else, into the bargain. On the stretches of dry land time evaporates while on board the ship, it looks as if it can hold very little, even though a thousand things still come and pile up into one's head and time congeals like the concentrated milk which it was time to water down for the bowl of Maritsa, the live trademark of the House of Avgoustis.

Dawn.

***

Siakandaris' test number two. Here goes.

–On ship, the bread ought to flow plentiful, same with the water. Seventeen years back, my first time in the Persian Gulf, two hundred ships anchored in mid-sea for three, four, even six months. Us alongside the rest. And on deck, you remember, the huge high-pressure French cauldrons for Iraq's nuclear reactors. Sweet Lord, the cargoes we've ferried about. The heat's awesome, 113 degrees Fahrenheit and the dough is fermenting away, it just won't rise no matter how long I wait. I'm staring at it all sweaty and desperate. I've cooked green beans and green beans need bread, of which there's none in sight. Saint Euphrosynos is standing idly on the sidelines, my heartfelt supplications are wasted, there's no enlightenment forthcoming and my brain's all addled. It takes him one whole hour to take pity on me and to say, squeeze a couple of lemons into the dough, throw in three ice-cubes on top of that, and it all turns up roses.

In order not to mooch around like deadbeats with no cargo till that happy hour of the Martaban ores, Pireas sent them to Colombo to lift twenty-five thousand tons of rubber and five thousand tons of cinnamon to lay down at Singapore for reloading for the USA. Every good freighter owner wants his ship loaded and Mitsos Avgoustis had again managed it so the waves weren't lapping away at them with no recompense. Nonetheless, in his cabin, pensive and morose, nighttime with his chores still unfinished, he sat and gave himself a manicure, with, laid out before him on the table, a small pair of pliers, a nail file and hand cream to soften the paper-dry skin and the welts between his fingers.

The cook hung around for a bit in case the captain opened his mouth for a single, blessed utterance that would turn this early evening into a normal one like the thousands of their life together, nothing going for three minutes running, so, then, he started all over, the heat of the Persian Gulf, the nuclear arms, the shrunk dough, the lemon juice, still no response.

Avgoustis stayed silent, moving his lips from time to time as if sucking on and then swallowing morsels of silence, his only meal since he'd let the fried yellow cheese and the olive-bread baked to a crispy pink à la Kyriaki, especially and exclusively for him, to go cold on the plate, untouched, right next to the glass of white orchids, taken out of the fridge by Siakandaris who always made sure there were some fresh flowers around for special occasions.

–Is it alright that from time to time I dream of flower bouquets? he tried a different tack and was again met with resounding silence.

Sometimes it's inhuman to be with others, to not be alone, tonight's special circumstance was the cook's need for the reverse. The electrician was playing *White Fang*, the crew was desultorily watching the movie and he was playing truant from the children's party, like a kid that the others had excluded and had gone looking for his dad.

–I only need your attention for a bit but you are ignoring me. I'm bending over double to take care of you, to whet your appetite, hot morsels and flowers, I couldn't do better if I was gay. Your punishment will be to miss me when you'll be swallowing down the obligatory menu prescribed by the pharmacist, a pound of pills per sitting, he said out loud, got up, picked up the tray, said goodnight even louder and opened the door.

–What do you think of Kazas, Avgoustis asked him at the very last moment, as if he'd been pondering whether to start a conversation on this subject or not.

–My assistant cook, rabbit ears, sheep eyes and turkey voice, spoils the beauty of my kitchen and your steward, a misfit in our midst who takes pleasure in being bored on deck with his shakered coffee and is playacting at being a seaman, interferes with my menu management. He's found out the expired foodstuffs.

–When? said Avgoustis worriedly.

–Day before yesterday.

Two days ago and still not a word on the subject, the captain made a mental note and when the cook wondered jealously why all the interest in the *jeune premier*, Avgoustis gathered all the manicure accessories inside their plastic bag, took it to the bathroom and answered from there.

–He's young like my son and it makes me feel guilty.

Later, on his own, he ran through the daily events, Friday

had expunged the sun since nine, had gathered around its clouds by ten, and the remaining hours had been spent in its saturnine company, the ocean gray cement which the ship bore through, half of it to the right and half to the left, utter calm which facilitated the maintenance of the lifeboats, the splicing together of ropes and wires and a host of other jobs.

It was getting to midnight, the most potent hour of the twenty-four because it holds something of the day that's been and has something of the day to come.

Friday left him a ship well oiled and squeaky clean, Saturday was coming on, bringing yet another day's wages in his fifty-eight years of prodigality.

He took off his shoes and socks and touched the nails, thick and hard as pebbles, the chapped heels like hardened mud, a savage reminder of age. He smelt the fragrance of the moisturizing cream in his palms, slid his cheek along his hand, his aged skin like paper tissue, about to tear to little pieces.

Mitso, I love your arm, he recalled the other one as well, Litsa and the son, the two sides of the coin of his forfeit, his twin avengers, his twin convictions.

Where the hell did he leave his cigarettes? He searched through pockets, drawers, felt along the seats and on the bed covers, told off Maritsa for sleeping on his pillow, found them under there.

He lit up and in order to send his distress away, he sent his thought as far as he could, to Abraham's prairies and the hazelnut island, to the white-tailed deer and the whales he would never see again, but whose image he had always kept close, right behind his closed eyes, in case of need, the blue herd, the fifty bouquets of rain, the splashes which, even in imagination, cooled his weariness and pacified his stormy mind.

While lighting a second cigarette he blew it, because, relaxed and half-dozing, he didn't resist the thoughts of his son and his offspring once again invaded him.

Flora, during their call the day before yesterday, Mimi, you're throwing away one hundred thousand dollars, I will not be bought, you've obligations to see to, I have you more than well provided for, one more chess-like conversation, my turn, your turn, to see who will checkmate the opponent and bring him crashing down. Andonis reported for duty at Tripoli, she told him in the end, everybody's fathers were there except for you who cleared yourself by sending three hundred dollars, well and good, he replied, because to you, I've always been the check.

And how could he not be? The money orders were frequent and with a satisfying number of zeroes, for the daughters' newly erected penthouses and cars for all three children soon as they turned twenty, though letters and phone calls were few and far between.

The last photograph sent by his son himself was from antiquity, the boy at eleven, barrel-bodied, dressed in red and white, the colors of the Olympiakos when everyone in the family proclaimed themselves fans of Panathinaikos, and, on the back, the dedication, to my dad so he never forgets the express goal that Anastasopoulos posted from centerfield to Minou's nets.

Ever since, not a line of communication between them and the photograph, along with older ones and subsequent ones, the eldest daughter at her engagement, her marriage, at the birth clinic, the youngest one in Paros, Milos, Nios, Laura on the slide, on her tricycle, at Zappion gardens, he'd all but gouged his eyes out with the magnifying lenses trying to make out the smudges, had been locked in the safe of the shipowners' cabin, a pack of people he had ignored. There, too, the rich collection of the unexpected poses of the eternal other woman. Past midnight, she too came back and got ensconced in his mind along with her flower-print sheets and her flower beds in bloom, the night recklessly allows every sleeping remorse to rise and the deadened senses to come alive.

His life had cost the lives of many others, it was like some of the novels Vassia read, like some legendary biographies with a large participation by the dead, in every chapter a dozen people lay buried.

He lit up the seventh and last cigarette in the pack, squeezed his flabby arms, pressed down on his recessed sternum, listened for his heart's irregular beat, the tremulous flurry of a trapped bird, and for the first time he didn't puff with pride, like he always did after a successful naval feat, that his old age was worth ten misspent youths.

The senses live on for donkey's years and guilty feelings are immortal, there is always one on the ready for you to resurrect, if you badly want to, like Avgoustis did, all primed at three A.M. to go for a wander into the far reaches of his hell.

Sorrow is a place, a bitter garden. And still another place is fear, an abysmal gorge and another still is loneliness, a cold desert at night and further on down the stone prairies of sorrow and the side streets of lust. Pain straddles the mountains, the intoxication of pain becomes a whole country and guilt becomes a continent.

***

–Kazas, my boy, what are you stalking him for, all this time, what are you expecting to see?

At fifteen yards, Avgoustis with Maritsa mewling up at his trouser legs, was bending over time and again, checking the triple-layered canvas that covered the hatches to the holds, with the suspicious steward watching him, virtually half hidden around a corner, when he got an earful from the furious cook who'd caught him in the act.

–You've been on this ship nearly two months and you're still afraid, does relentless youth have no mercy for even such vigorous old age, after all, the captain was no moth-eaten relic but a hawk-eyed samurai.

–That's why I'm watching him.

–Ask him for an autograph.

Siakandaris reached out, touched the youthful springy arm, sighed and mumbled softly to himself that in times gone by, old age was popular because experience and wisdom had value, the highest premium in today's world is on youthfulness and all the gods are younger than twenty-five and couldn't tell you how many beans make five.

Friday dinner was calling out for him from his kitchen.

I took my breath of fresh air, he said, you make sure you scrape the rust off your head, give your brain a new coat of paint, he advised the rookie paternally and turned about, leaving him in the company of his thoughts.

The day had started.

Laundry was laid out on the rails, underwear, shirts, jumpers and jeans stiff from the salt, summer clothes and winter clothes mixed, since they crossed the Equator every ten, fifteen days. Alongside everyone else's, the laundry, too, of Avgoustis junior who had by now joined the ship's routine and was getting a taste of the wicked itch of loneliness, more or less like all the others.

What sort were these others?

To him, the crew's living quarters were a habitat of ghosts, madmen and commies. One guy didn't speak to anyone, another mumbled to himself, these guys over here buried themselves in endlessly thumbed magazines, some others were given over to a passionate melancholy with champion amongst them the assistant cook who expected nothing from life but the gratitude of the Filipino woman with the three kids. Moving further along, there is Birbilis, the second mate who had in his office a collection of the *Indian Times*, the *Buenos Aires Herald*, the *Capo Verde News* and so on and so forth, not any longer in order to read the first page with the coups and the prime ministers but, rather, for the middle page stories about guanacos and otters and condors. Still further down the line, the red-dyed Alien, fan of the communist-party leader Florakis, forever mouthing some ancient rhetoric from the party newspaper, then the pint-sized workers' rights guru who knew by heart the collective agreement patents; next came the apprentice Zulu who spent his youth all over Africa, freighting combustible materials to get the ten percent safety increment in wage and was now spending his time round the clock with his eye on the new recruit so he could serve him a new episode each day, at one time the cotton catching on fire and two men getting immolated, at another, the timber going up in flames and four turning to cinder, then, the methane exploding and everyone perishing bar one, himself.

–Nothing worse than being the sole survivor, was the closing refrain to all of his lectures on death.

Avgoustis junior who, to show his devotion to Papakonstandinou's passionate voice and guitar, had bought the *Southern Cross* album ten times between the ages of fifteen and seventeen and, out of hatred for his father, had broken it as many, was cursing the entire regimen of strong-armed men, what a load of drivel all the talk had been about a life of action and exotic adventures, this here was a hand-to-mouth existence on the tin madhouse, and nights spent in solo sessions with their dick in their hands; nevertheless, a few weeks later, he had discovered several reasons to dig the men on the ship that raced back and forth between the Indian and the Pacific, including even the old man's guardian and god-fearing better half, the cook of cooks, who went from "you are forbidden to touch the elements of my stove" in the first month, to "listen, boy-o, seeing I'm feeling dizzy, why don't you go ahead and make the captain's soft boiled egg, you boil the water, throw in the egg, say the Lord's prayer and you're as good as done."

Greeks, Rumanians and Russians, their cleaning and scrubbing as worthy as any housewife's, expert menders and housemaids to themselves and, at the same time, working like dogs under the old renegade, his father, who was refusing to give in to old age.

As he bent over the canvasses, his long white hair waved and shone in the afternoon sun. He went to him, captain, he queried, do you need any help?

–We're good, Maritsa and I, we managed just fine and the job had to be done cause tomorrow the weather's getting worse, he answered and stood up.

The sonny was looking at the green sea and the golden streaks in the sky which daddy next to him couldn't see, standing by his side and thinking of blind men he knew, Ray Charles, Stevie Wonder and some ancient prophets, Tiresias or Calchas, he got those two confused, and there was that other guy in a tragedy who humped his mother and his father, all of them as ancient as it gets, Greece is still producing relics out of acquired velocity, he thought, some of them unbeatable, he admitted.

–Kazas, if you have some film, why don't you take some photos here, to send to your girl and to remember these rascals and this part of the sea, Avgoustis said ponderingly.

–I'm going to get the camera and gather everyone, the son obliged and ten minutes later, those not on duty gave up snuggling in their bunks, one or two gladly and the rest grumblingly and turned into Maritsas on the rails, the whole deck thundering with backward flips and tae-kwon-do figures, finally the whole crowd lying down on their backs under the billowing assortment of underwear.

Sasha offered to act as photographer so the steward could squeeze in a group photo, join in an acrobatic quartet and pose in two duets, one with the star cat and one with the captain who also asked for one on his own, so I can send it to the

country's defender along with his pocket money, he said to
Kazas.

Nice afternoon, the dark-green sea turned purple, the golden
streaks turned pink and the oncoming sunset sent the men off
to lamb with rice and potato dumplings.

Two hours later, Siakandaris figured that the captain must
be finished with the bureaucratic chores of his station, so he
prepared the tray and though he'd have dearly loved to take it
in himself and concoct for the captain an atmosphere of Kyriaki in the spring, he generously stepped aside in favor of Kazas,
instructing and advising all in one, if you find him riddled with
his stuff, leave it and go, if you see he's in an easy mood, stick
around for company, you do him good, your sight lets him pull
out some of the weeds from his past, his family life all thorns
and weevils.

Thorns and weevils or a bombing site? A bombing site or
an inferno? An inferno or an out and out Auschwitz with his
father enslaved by his sins and justly condemned to blindness?

–Comb your hair and go.

On the tray, the cat's food and the old man's, accompanied
by two green leaves, from a sweet-smelling lemon tree, I keep
stuff in the fridge for him, I spoil him because, in the end, he
deserves it.

The son, who kept postponing the moment of reckoning,
pondered whether tonight he might find the courage to tell him
how things stood, to face his rage, his amazement, maybe an
unscheduled fainting spell, an all-out heart attack, just so they're
left stranded in this fucked-up weather with no captain, and
almost wished to find him snoring, but no, he found him awake,
listening to Frank Sinatra and knitting a yellow woolen scarf.

–His eyes and his suits match his songs perfectly, he said
pointing to the tape deck, that's what women say about Sinatra.

–Your wife?

–Another. A woman called Litsa.

–Asia Minor destruction and Litsa Tsichli, so you mentioned the other day, the son recollected in a low voice, while serving Maritsa.

–Litsa Tsichli. Guileless eyes and a body like a flame torch. And her soul, a handful of wheat strewn through the house. An old story, Avgoustis sighed, put away the knitting needles and the scarf, leaned back into his armchair, closed his eyes.

And the son wondered who this woman was, where might she live, in Asia Minor or in Sinatra's America, was she still alive, when did she pass through his father's life, before his marriage or after, for how long, what part might she have played in the family mess, did his mother know the score, and all of this, while listening to another three songs in succession, with the volume turned low, My Way, you can say that again, New York, New York, didn't care if he never set foot there again, and Strangers in the Night, their own story spot on. That's the two of us, dad, he should have said, and at long last launch into all the rest of it, but the sight of a man taking the songs' volleys of fire right into the chest and into his body, with the yellowish brown veins on the hands, shriveled like old pomegranate skin, pulsing up and dancing, the chest beating like a bass drum and the useless eyes moving around like mad beneath the closed lids, it all froze him in place and took away his speech, he knew what this was like from other songs, big-time meltdown, it happened to him, too.

Was he envious of him? Did he feel sorry for him? Who the hell was this Litsa, whose memory seemed to flare up every so often like a mine sunk into the undergrowth of the aged mind and could make, like it did tonight, a half-crazed and despicable tyrant look like a hallowed relic in his armchair?

He remembered his girlfriend, a two-year relationship which they'd finished off three months ago, just before he'd decided to enlist with the Pirates of Penzance. He'd had his fill of her penchant for analyzing, psychologizing and criticizing everyone and everything, her grandmother, her mother, her aunt, his mother, his drums, his verses, Ian Curtis, John Bonham, his books, his carbonara, his souvlaki, his build, you walk upside down for the following reasons, yesterday the reason we didn't fuck was, tomorrow you'll tell me this and that but it'll mean such and such. A torturess who only breathed in order to minutely examine and judge, who waited for life to happen not so she could live it but only so she could analyze it.

Litsa Tsichli? Guileless eyes? Body like a flame torch? And her soul a half pound of buckwheat scattered through her house? Where was this house? Where can creatures like that be found?

He took one of the lemon leaves from the tray and squeezed it so the fragrance permeated the cabin. He returned it to its glass, your food is cold, was all he managed to say, he bid a goodnight and left, though not empty-handed because even though in that twenty minutes, he didn't strip down to his true identity, his old man, for reasons unknown, did show him a card he'd been keeping secret.

He wanted to run straight to his cabin, lie flat and think of nothing, though think he would. Stefania, Flora, Litsa. A thought of female gender was also going to be twirling around for some time in the old man's head, were he to give his son the exact words, he'd flabbergast him even more because, next to the guileless wheat and all of that, there were some additional wiles of his unfairly aged siren, that he might have mentioned, her sweet arms and her jubilant breasts, her merciful buttocks and her festive thighs.

***

Good morning. My name is Dimitrios Avgoustis, captain of the Merchant Marine. I've been away at sea for a long time. I came off the ship yesterday. What am I looking for at this hour of the morning in a ladies' hairdressing salon? I just visited my mother who passed away two years ago and I saw white tufts of hair growing out of the grave. Her hair keeps growing, still. I am serious, miss. I made no mention to the priests, I want nothing to do with their lot.

He asked me if there was something I could do straight away, he lived far and, naturally, he carried no scissors with him. I was doubly intrigued. He was such a handsome man that, at that very moment, I believed in God and in Mitsos equally. We were exactly of the same height and we first looked at each other on a level. At work I stretched to 5 feet 8 inches, at home, minus the heels, I went down to 5 feet 5, once I pulled down the perpendicular, two-story bun there was a good, clean 5 feet 2 left, a loss in stature of 6 inches, meaning that when we connected, he may well have been a head taller than me. We both welcomed that difference of one head.

So, then, I turn off the gas flame and remove the long-handled coffee pot. I put the implements I need in my bag and also have the inspiration to grab a handful of quick-lime from the john, and I follow him to St. Lazarus, two blocks away.

That was the beginning of the idyll. I was hired to give the marble slab a haircut. Your grandmother was all dead except for her hair. I looked after that. Her soul needed a complete rest.

St. Constantine's had been closed down, St. Lazarus, a treeless plot, was the new cemetery. It was inaugurated by a city barber, a colleague, done in by his liver, whom we buried in 1957. Our dead, still few and far between then, lay in dirt graves. The only luxury, a thin row of plinths around each one, placed at an angle. Being a captain's mother, your grandma was among the five or six who had a thin slice of marble over them.

I've never burnt a living woman's hair, never lost a client to accidents or carelessness, zero losses in the two hundred heads I've overseen. First of all, naturally, I respectfully passed the scissors flush against the joints of the marble slab and then packed the quicklime good and hard all along the perimeter. Then, I collected the hairs in a scarf and buried it next to the maiden fern that encircled her cross.

That was that, the dead woman never needed my services again. I found out afterwards that the fern had come to Greece in 1912, a memento from the homeland, a plant one and a quarter inches tall, deep in her bosom, when the Turks supplanted them from their homes, in Adzanos. It has no flower, only these tiny reddish balls, like chickpeas. After a week, Mitsos brought me a handful as well. I saw in his eyes how important this was to him and I set up six pots with the plant from Asia Minor, all of them in the hair salon, which turned into a thick, soft jungle.

My first name was another thing that was important to him. His father Triandafilos, his girl Triandafilia, Triandafilitsa, Litsa. It does mean something, you don't just walk past a coincidence like that.

When, years ago, his letters stopped coming, I thought myself forgotten. May my memory live on. And completely lost my zest for work. I took leave of my head. I opened up late in the mornings. I let half the season go by before I ushered in the latest trends. I was turning away weddings. I was saying no to money.

Eventually, I turned the shop over to a poor, hard-working and sweet faggot, a tried-and-true faggot, into lace embroidery already from first grade at school. It suits Argyris perfectly not being a male, such a perfect creature, *a pure and brave leftist. A magician with the scissors, he respects our art form and fondly takes care of all our old customers and my old flower pots.*

Sugarcane is for Cuba. Palm trees sit in Africa. Greece is the living place of olive groves and Elefsina, in particular, is the kingdom of yellow daisies. On my own home ground, maiden fern is at a premium. The kitchen is its headquarters, that's where it's built its green tunnel, spreading over all four walls and the ceiling. The maiden Litsa, however, hasn't managed to entrap anyone in her web.

Nor are his footprints preserved any longer in the pelt of the carpet for me to bend down and study, while picking up the tiny red squashed fern nuggets. Such a great thing, his footprints.

August last year was overly African and December was overly Russian. This year June is going excellently, so far. But, nearby, in the neighborhood square that's chockablock with people, the municipal gardeners are wasting time with strikes and the flower beds are falling way behind schedule.

Us, we bloomed in our time. The pansies adore me. With my swollen knees I didn't give them extra fertilizer this year, nor do I turn their dirt over, but they are turning out twice the size, all by themselves. And the basil smells twice as strong. The celery and the parsley persist, though a bit downcast because they no longer come into the kitchen to contribute to delectable dishes.

Everything in the garden loves me. The whole house loves Litsa. Good old house, three rooms, does not face the sea, nor is there a river Thames passing in front of it.

Seeing as I mentioned Europe, let me tell you about Beethoven, too. It's been twenty-odd years now. It was the holy week before Easter and I was doing the hair of the girl at university who I mentioned before, the one with the novels. The radio was playing a rich music, with no words, with no scenario, that made me go weak at the knees.

The girl, who had an education, a jack of all trades you might say, pointed out what it was, Beethoven's seventh symphony. She explained to me about him, bought me his record, too, and when I get fed up with all the limericks about love and dejection, I put that one on the record player.

Anna. A law student then, now in London, married to a Cypriot news reporter. She loved me with a vengeance. She took photographs of me exactly how I asked her to so I could send one to Mitsos Litsa with an all white face and a geisha outfit that he'd brought me, Litsa right underneath the balcony that didn't exist but which he and I had decided we were going to need, along with the second story we'd add for the family we'd have.

Photograph sessions upon photograph sessions. With eyes open and the dedication, for you to keep my eternally brown eyes and my eternally pleasant smile. With eyes closed and the dedication, as I'm dreaming of you. Seated at the table before a plate and the dedication, as I eat a fried egg. Next to the rosemary bush, Litsa stew. And with a batch of mint in my lap, Litsa meatball.

As soon as the kid realized that the mystery lover was married, she started poking fun, calling me Ms. Silly-Twit. After two or three love wrecks of her own, she started showing respect and being on my side.

There was another degree holder, by the name of Poulopoulou, who also told me off, head manager at the Tax office, a divorcee who had her hair cut like a man's.

You need to see a psychiatrist, she'd say. I need Mitsos, I would silently answer and kept doing her hair, all nervous, till I found out she liked to get spanked by her boyfriend, a right-wing party member.

And the customer who tried to set me up with someone she, too, was at the university in her time, now a retired teacher. A heart of gold, a child with children, an adult with adults, conservative hairdos, the same head of hair for thirty years running. Only on her husband's name day did she ask for something a little more artistic.

I often wonder what educated women might think about. And how they think about it. In what words.

You haven't had it with me, have you? But, listen, you need to learn to allow boredom into your life as well. Those of us who have, didn't piss in the well, you know.

Seeing as you've come, you mustn't leave so early. And don't stand right by the door, or you'll have me thinking you're in a hurry to make your getaway.

You haven't even touched your coffee or your fruit. I don't mind your not talking. Don't talk. You just peel your orange and let me listen to its fragrance.

Silly Litsa, I was dreaming of him coming back for good.

Living together and, on account of old age, him not being able to get it up much. Me thinking, oh-oh!, Litsa dear, you've had him at his best, laying you down and machinegunning you with his automatic, you must love him twice as much now that the fighting and the shooting have died down. My thing has known glorious times with your father. But I won't be graced with having to call a doctor in the middle of night to do his cardiogram.

Youth is done, I am over it. What I'm missing has to do with old age. I'm missing out on the normal things people have when they grow old together. Struggling to love his baggy eyes, his cheeks roughening like stale bread, his false teeth when he laughs, his wounded memory, the gaps in his speech when he can't find a word, his walking slow, his hands that won't linger on my backside and my thighs like they used to.

Last time I saw him, he must have kissed me around eight thirty. He must have disappeared around the street corner at something to nine. I must have sat like a log at the doorstep till eleven thirty. It must have been after midnight that I found some of his apple peel, squashed, under the left back leg of his chair.

I had it in the palm of my hand till it rotted, three full days and nights.

***

–Flora, you know you can't have both a fork and a spoon in your mouth at the same time. Choose. I've been waiting seven years.

It was the only piece of adult talk, his mother and the neighbor's, that he'd caught from the living room, he was six and this had sounded terribly ominous, he went to the kitchen on tiptoe, got a spoon and a fork, shoved both in his mouth along with half a cookie and all that metal didn't allow him to chew or swallow or breathe, it made him so nauseous he thought he was about to spew his guts out.

His sisters were out at a birthday party and he'd been playing by himself in the sitting room since early afternoon, but he couldn't concentrate on the puzzle or the firemen cause his mother was looking through cardboard boxes, opening and closing cupboards, slamming closet doors, walking up and down, wrapping and unwrapping herself at, one time in a weird, very long, shiny piece of cloth with silver dots, don't want to turn myself into a spectacle, next, in a brown, fluffy fabric, I'm going to end up looking like a bear, she huffed irritably.

In the end, she saw her visitor in her regular clothes, after first sending off the son to his room to re-rewrite the spelling exercise and redraw the cow, though there was definitely something fishy going on in their living room, he could sense it because the television was turned off and because he heard something break. He half opened the door of his room, their neighbor said that thing about the spoon and the fork and when, after a while, he was gone and before the girls came home, his mother swept up some gold bits and pieces that were strewn on the parquet.

The weird Mr. Limoyannis, with the paint-spattered hands and bug-eyes like saucers, had been to their home two or three times, at least that's as many as the kid had cottoned onto, to see if the brown kitchen cupboards might be painted a brighter color, which they weren't, or to take measurements out on the balcony for a pergola, that he did, eventually, put in, but not then and not in the years that followed did his mother ever plant whatever it was that was supposed to wrap itself around it.

As he grew up a bit, he had brought those scenes to mind several times and relived them in vivid detail, live, with everything that went on before, his mother disappearing for three hours at the hairdresser's and coming back with two dried up curls hanging like worms from her ears down to her shoulders, and everything that followed, the broken teapot, the half-finished bottle of whisky, her red eyes, her tantrums.

For a long time he watched her walk in and out of rooms like a robot, with a coffee and a cigarette all day long, not saying a word, and him, seven, eight and nine years old, thinking that some people have received orders to spend their life with furrowed brow and tightened lips, like for instance his mum, who would break out unexpectedly and scream, never at his sisters who, at all events, paid her no mind whatsoever, only at him, why, for Christ's sake, do you have to eat your spaghetti one strand at a time?

He ate his spaghetti one strand at a time, his peas speared in twos on the fork tines, his lentils measured out on the spoon in threes, a devotee of the arithmetic of food, just a little kid, weighed down by the confusion that thundered inside his head.

–We're going to the beach. Take the umbrella and the mats down to the car.

At Voula beach his sisters, bikinis, dark glasses and suntan lotion, were flirting with a bunch of certified jerks and he would go in the water, pinch his nostrils with his fingers, close his eyes, do a long dive in the shallows and then wait in vain for his mother's approval. Second dive, third, backwards flip, he splashed and frolicked like a duckling, no response from her, sitting on the beach in her bathing suit, another coffee, another cigarette, you come in, too, mum, you come in, too, mum, at first he was calling out to her longingly, then beseechingly, ten, fifteen times, as if that was the only phrase he knew, in the end he was almost whispering it, barely audibly, and kept on even after he had put on the dry T-shirt and the sandals and was following her to the car, you come in, too, mum, even at the house, not at the table with the women but by himself at the kitchen balcony, facing the plate with his beefburger, no longer with a sense of disappointment or anger but, rather, with fear about the indescribable, but serious, stuff that was going on.

No matter that it was a long time ago, his mother wanted someone else, his father, too, they did not divorce and everyone else paid the price.

That neighbor grew bent and stiff-assed all by himself, he saw him sometimes washing down his tiny verandah or shopping at the bakery for fritters and refreshments and that Litsa, if she was alive, would be, chances are, a lost cause, another entry in his father's victims' list. He wondered, did his old man know about the hardware-shop owner and his mother about Litsa? And why had his father spoken to him of this woman?

The captain's arrogance towards the ship's underlings is law and his reputation is his shield, was how the despicable Flirtakis had pointedly put it in his half-hour induction course. Most of them shared meals with their crew only at Christmas and Easter and many brutes, today's captains aged thirty-eight and forty, didn't even stoop to well-wishing. Avgoustis junior had been apprised of this by those at the receiving end, the Russians, the Romanians and, naturally, by the cook, his father's unwavering and hearty fan.

–Ever heard of a Litsa Tsichli? he'd baited, at an unsuspecting moment.

–A new singer? the chef's innocent retort.

–And a very good one.

–So, then, the cook, his father's bosom pal, didn't know of her existence, which might mean she was a flame of the way distant past and that those two spoke to each other about the ones that turned up afterwards, here and there, losing track in the process.

–Why did the old man say something so personal to a rookie? Had he had some piece of bad news recently about the poor soul? Was it easier to confide to an outsider? Or, did he get an impulse to show himself off as fatherly? If she's a rotten apple let her go, if she's worth-while, don't, had been his words in their first short talk, when he gave the old man his tall tale about the non-existent graphic-artist girlfriend.

The actual Litsa must have been a special case, in order to be still floating around intact in mid-ocean.

In the end, distance is only a thing of the mind. The sea separates those who would be separated on land anyway, and connects those who'd stay together no matter what, whether out of love or hatred.

At one in the morning in his cabin, Andonis Avgoustis, who all this time kept the beat to his retrospection with palms drumming on his belly, did a finale à la Lars Ulrich from *Metallica* and brought to a standstill his contemplation of the middle-aged exterminators of their own lives.

He thought of Maritsa, what a circumstance, his father worked, ate, conversed and slept with a cat whose face he hadn't seen. From Maritsa he went on to Laura, it was for her he was taking all those pictures of the cat, the seagulls, the cormorants, for his niece, whose arrival five years ago had tamed his mother and overcome her resistance to touching. By now, the kid would surely have decimated his drum kit, shredded his issues of *Metal Hammer*, the notebooks with the cursed verses and the shelf with nothing but accursed poets, all of his homemade doom and gloom.

Outside, the sea was swelling and *Ocean-routes* was predicting north-western gales of seven Beaufort and fifteen foot waves. He, thankfully, fell asleep straight away. Because Palm Sunday was bearing with it wind and rain.

Waves with wings.

***

Thirty-three percent of naval accidents are due to the weather, fourteen percent to running aground, twelve percent to collisions, twenty percent to fire, two percent to mechanical malfunction and nineteen percent to miscellaneous causes.

His workmate, the vile weather, showed up right on time and Avgoustis welcomed it, imagining that he was on the peninsula of Mount Athos, gazing across the distance at the lambent, pure-white summit of Olympus and that, inspired by the snow's superbness, he was offering a sumptuous libation-prayer to both the ancient gods and to his Mistress.

The Greek spring made him start the supplication with the fragrant blooms of the waves and the autumn of the southern hemisphere obliged him to proceed with the damned rains that were launching their long assault, to finish with a vow that had never yet failed, of still another golden ring for the sacred digits of his jewel-bearing Virgin.

On Holy Monday, April 21, they docked at Colombo in bad weather, loaded and left on Ash Wednesday with the bad weather still holding, and everyone praying full tilt. Ash Wednesday afternoon, the downpour and the low visibility continuing, with everyone on alert and the captain in the chartroom next to the sailor manning the steering. They were sailing at 14.5 knots and were discussing the cloning of Lenin, a news item by some professor, a Valery Biroff, from Russia where mummification cost three hundred and fifty thousand dollars per corpse, with a two-hundred-year guarantee.

Siakandaris, worn out from the menu of the Easter fast, was getting ready to display his virtuosity with a knockout kokoretsi, followed by lamb roasted on a spit and a sweet, syrupy galaktompoureko to finish them off, and he, too, was praying for good weather so they could celebrate Easter on a dry and sunny deck, which they all badly needed.

Like every year on this day, he'd painted three cartons of eggs red, polished each one with an oiled piece of cloth and used them to decorate the two messes, one platter in each, reminiscing back to days like these at his village when his mother would make him wash the dried bird droppings off the eggs one by one and he, a bit of a smartass and on the lazy side, at eight and at ten, would get grossed out and declare kitchen chores fit only for women, only to be silenced by her slap.

This was his tale to Kazas while inspecting his sparkling and impatient oven trays and his battle-ready spits and waiting for the water to boil for the captain's sparse dinner, olives, hard-baked bread, tea and apple compote. He would take it in himself, he'd every intention of force-feeding him if need be because, recently, the scoundrel captain was totally absorbed by his worrying and had been eating like a sparrow, his trousers and shirts way too loose, small wonder with twelve pounds lost. He found him with the second mate who was checking the electronic maps, and the chief mate who, after jotting some things in the engines diary, including calculations of their needs in turbine oil, axle oil, cylinder oil, said that he'd spotted a hump in the water that morning, also seen by the sailors on deck, the lot of them unbelieving and indifferent to the superstitions and old wives' tales of the land, but somewhat susceptible to those of the sea, where a sea turtle equals bad luck.

–Dactylas, we've seen another hundred of those and there's never been anything untoward, Birbilis said coaxingly.

Dactylas, I wish you'd keep your trap shut, thought the cook, who was himself amenable to every possible ill-starred omen, if only so as to be on the safe side, and, here it was, the wrench thrown in the works of his vision of choir songs, fireworks and a glorious resurrection feast.

On Good Friday the turbocharger broke down and stopped ventilating the engine to get rid of the exhaust fumes.

They stopped, poured several barrels of oil into the sea to calm the waters, the chief mate, agile and a diver, went down in person, found two of the turbine clogs broken. With the second and third mechanic, they spliced together some iron rods, proving necessity the mother of invention, the damage was somewhat restored, they could proceed to their destination at low speed, up to seven naughts, looking to arrive with a two-day delay.

On Good Friday evening, at the time of Christ's Epitaph procession all and sundry on the freight carrier were smoking cigarettes of relief.

On Holy Saturday afternoon, the two electric engines failed one after the other, they started up the emergency one, they had scarcely any light, barely the main functions, there was just enough time for the cross-buns to finish baking, the Easter offal soup was put off. On this day of their crucifixion, they set up outside oil-lanterns for the electricians, as they wordlessly got to working against the ill effects of the jinx.

Avgoustis couldn't avoid communication with the company's head captain at Pireas, whom he nearly missed at the office, it was still early in Greece and, besides, Salamina, where he had his country house, was virtually next door.

–You mustn't have serviced the generators properly.

–You watch your mouth, you good-for-nothing. Pass the word about the delay due to unforeseeable circumstances and make sure I find in Singapore the spare parts I need to fix the turbine properly.

–The old goat will hit the roof. He'll order me to do you in.

–Is he there now?

–In Mykonos. Celebrating the European Basketball Cup of Olympiakos. Without his missus. In distinguished company. A young crowd.

–That's some way to mourn a parent.

Flirtakis had put up every resistance he could, Chadzimanolis would throw them both out on their ear and he couldn't afford to lose his job, he was feeding five and had just put in the foundation for the duplex that was the dowry for his two engaged daughters. After procuring a promise for another fifteen thousand dollars, Avgoustis' contribution to the cost of the German window frames of the two-story house, he gave his word about the spare parts but also asked for Avgoustis' word, this silver ore would be the last, he pleaded, load up every stray cat in Asia if you like and head back full steam ahead to our lovely Pireas, before I have a heart attack.

Avgoustis had no sympathy for him.

–Happy Easter, you scum. As for my resurrection, I'll see to it myself.

He made it, too, and two hours later the celebratory telex was sent, *we have received the divine light.*

But no sooner had they fixed one malfunction that another turned up, someone must have surely jinxed them because, just as the electricity was restored and Siakandaris was able to at

least prepare a fast-food resurrection dinner, spaghetti bolognaise, a mother of a problem turned up, the cogs of the front
drive broke and the propeller was put out of action. They lowered the two anchors and were kept up all night, wallowing
powerless in torrential rain and a seven Beaufort wind, with the
emergency lights on, thank God, and the telegraph steadily signaling on channel 10, at 500 KHZ, 2182 KHZ and 156.8 MHZ
to the vessels nearby and the stations on the surrounding
shores, advising them of the damage.

They were four days and nights away from Singapore and
all the officers were expecting the captain to send the company an emergency request for tug boats but he was putting it of,
piqued after the conversation with the chief captain and
Chadzimanolis' right hand, and when he felt pressured by his
two subordinate officers, one of whom he recognized from the
white uniform as they were approaching before even the man
could open his mouth, he put it to them differently, this year
alone you've each pinched ten videos and twenty silk carpets.

Mitsos Avgoustis spent whole hours conferring with them
and thinking things through by himself, there were no reefs or
sandbanks in that area but the damage was beyond repair.

In his fifty-eight years at sea this was a first, with a problem
like this the right thing to do would be to say I give up, to ask
for tug boats, and accept a replacement and to have everything
end smoothly without risk to the crew's lives and to the ship
itself. But to end it all so lamely and take his leave with his tail
between his legs? He was chain-smoking furiously. He was
cursing his useless eyes. He was pacing the walkways and the
decks. He brought to mind the day, twelve years ago, when,
authorized by the now-dead Chadzimanolis, he made a bid for
ATHOS III, aka SCANDINAVIAN STAR at that point and
five years of age, in a Rotterdam auction. The princely Norwe-
gian vessel was being repossessed by court order and he, the
last bidder, secured an excellent price and then took care of all

the rest, the dry docking, the hull inspection, the painting, the change of name, the change of flag, the documents of the ship's new affiliation.

The ATHOS was his home and his shop, he'd been around the world in it, it had provided a living to dozens of families, it was his very life.

At dawn he came across the crew at their morning tea, coffees, red eggs and the darkest anxiety.

At something past six, the unseeing Avgoustis gave an order that left the sailors flummoxed, the experienced seamen and the inexperienced alike.

–I'm going to steer the ship backwards.

They lifted the anchors, the old trickster took hold of the wheel himself and started maneuvering, the engine's cogs were intact, there were no other ships nearby to crash into, so he might as well give it a go.

No one had ever attempted anything like this. But within half an hour, the crazy ATHOS was sailing the waters ass first. Two vessels in the wider vicinity, a Russian and an Israeli one scattered and, then, sent a questioning signal. Avgoustis answered the first with *Happy Easter, our fellow brothers in Christ*, and the second with *Alleluia, Alleluia, Alleluia*.

At something to seven, his sleepless, red-eyed son, in the role and uniform of ship-steward, found him astern with Maritsa in his arms, whispering in his ear, courage, friend, and asking him put out a prayer, you, too, who have no sins, for the domino of bad luck to end here.

For Andonis Avgoustis the night was a proper disaster, all kinds of difficult emotions at full tilt. Fear. Responsibility. Surprise. Admiration. They were far from any shore and the cell phones weren't any help, but even if they worked, there wasn't a girl for him and he was over and done with all his peer groups, nor could he trouble his sisters or give his mother a

fright. Flora, especially, at times like these, he could do without. In her last phone call, some days ago, she'd called him a
jerk for taking so long to set things right and she'd said it was
for that same reason that other jerk, Flirtakis, had also called
him a jerk.

Pitch black, rain, a hefty swell, no maneuverability, shout-
ing, hard times, a horrid headache. He walked upside down,
on his hands, along a deserted side walkway, the coins and two
sweets from his pockets fell onto the wet deck, in a distance of
less than ten yards he, too, was done in by the ship's roll.

He wished he could be on any cracked and filthy pavement, anywhere, so long as he was on dry land. We'll drown,
he thought, I'll drown. I came to discover the old man, but
I'm not cut out to be a Columbus. If only he could get out
right this minute, since he hadn't had the sense to split during the very first week. He stood upright and went looking
for company and solace but the circumstances didn't brook
any time wasting, most of the men, in their plastic raincoats,
were in the thick of action and the rest were strangely numb
and preoccupied with their destiny. For about five minutes,
he assailed one of the Russians who was mumbling non-stop,
as if hypnotized, about a poor unfed tiger at the Nikolayev
zoo, in the Ukraine, seven years ago, starving. He moved
away, went up to the other Russian and sank with him into
the sea of Barents, listening about the submarine's equipment, the pink light on the sonar panel warning them about
warships, the blue about merchant ships, the green about
fishing ships. Again he took off, attaching himself for about
ten minutes to a Rumanian, a perfect case of fatalism, wrung
dry at age thirty-seven from paying back installment loans
and more than willing to die just to get out of them. Finally,
just before dawn, he went down to the kitchen and glued
himself to Siakandaris who, it seemed, trusted the blind man
blindly and was fending off evil by washing down two lambs

with wine, and took up telling the rookie how you get the piss smell out of the meat. Talk about inappropriate subject matter.

He helped him dry them, impale them on the spits and tie them with wire at the neck and around the thighs, quite a lot of trouble, in truth, in the middle of their greater ones. After that, he washed, put on a clean jacket and took up the tray for the captain. The cook, haughty and determined, was following the example of Avgoustis, the kind of man who'd go into church on horseback, and had every intention of setting up coal fires in two sawn-off barrels on the prow, which would be windless for the first time ever, and hold there the outdoor feast on the backwards-moving ship.

–Sir, I've brought you coffee and a cross-bun, said the son and stood next to his old man who hadn't combed his hair and had neglected his personal grooming to an unprecedented extent.

Avgoustis bent and gently set the cat down, stood up, dusted off his clothing and took the coffee hand to hand.

–Thanks, my boy, he said and took two sips.

The son then, deciding that the truth couldn't be put off any more, took a deep breath, I am your son, what else had to happen to them, their lives and those of everyone on board were at risk, they still had more Stations to carry their Cross through, it was high time they knew who was who, so he said it in a whisper, forming every syllable perfectly, in a steady voice, his own voice, but with slightly changed words.

–I'll be your eyes. Till we get there, I'm going to be your eyes.

***

The danger signal, seven long whistles, the captain on the bridge. The men hurried to put on life buoys and hats, they assembled by the two lifeboats, half on the left and half on the right, the stewards brought blankets and food supplies.

With speed, accuracy and coordination, everyone at their appointed place and task, one man at the rope, another at the hinges, a third at the boat hooks and the boatswain handling the breaks of the lifeboat, all together hanging in midair and, then, being lowered down, lower still . . . onto the deck.

The lifeboat drill lasted for one hour and everything went like clockwork, a hopefully unnecessary but indispensable drill, to cover all possibilities.

If only they knew I can't see to save my own life, thought Avgoustis, whose self-composure was strictly for the crew's benefit, as internally he was facing fear, for the first time ever, from two standpoints: one that knew and was respectful of the risks of the job and another one, worse by far, that grew from being responsible for telling a lie which could promptly cost the lives of nineteen others, including that of his son.

Two hours before the drill, at Siakandaris Easter gala, the well-roasted skin was devoured greedily though in silence, without the tape-deck playing Christ Has Risen From the Dead at full blast, without the circular dances of previous years, without jokes or well-wishing or nostalgia or relaxing small-talk about Kyriaki and all the rest of the villages in each man's place of origin, which at this day, in this season, were being resurrected en mass from winter's hibernation and changing into feral beasts by the anticipation of summer and tourists.

Mitsos Avgoustis had no eyes to see their eyes, but felt them on him, alongside the unknown eyes of his son, continually as of last night, nineteen sets of eyes searching his own two sunk holes of blue, which he himself hadn't seen in the mirror for years, in order to test the truthfulness of his composure and fathom what was in store for them.

The moment the damage was announced, he'd thought it was about time he called Birbilis, who had a sense of the sea and knew well what a ship meant, told him something's wrong and I'm seeing things double, then gather the rest of the officers and assign them the rest.

Would they make it? Always, until then, he'd taken every responsibility on himself. What if they thought him panicky and they panicked themselves? The rest would sense it, the lot of them would get the heebie-jeebies and then they wouldn't stand a chance. Besides, there was his own will, his need to prove that in extreme hardship, he could still pull through.

He was racking his brains for a solution, breaking his prayer record, too, he'd asked one hundred times the Mother of God, who must have surely been rejoicing over her only son's resurrection, to give her pal some practical and timely support, asking, too, for a bit of an amend, as she'd been rather vengeful, punishing and partly to blame for his eyes, then, with the midday thunderbolts in her Garden at Athos.

Parts from the church service, *Look upon me thy sinful and humble servant*, phrases from psalms, fragments of hymns, bits and pieces from liturgies, both relevant and irrelevant, all crowded on his lips, let us pray to our Lady, and, *Provide for us, o Lady*, because, after all, she is the number one ally.

Next in turn was the weather. In the past, he used to read it in the countenance of the sky, in the movement of the clouds, in the wind's rotation, in the direction of the barometric pressure, in the visibility, in the height of the swell. Now, the equipment read it. In the insecurity of his affliction, he'd ask for the weather report at half hour intervals and, in the meanwhile, he would test himself by running through every manner of snowstorm and wind, in every longitude and latitude, the monsoons of the Persian Gulf that are the source of the yearly meltemi winds in the Aegean, the summer typhoons, the Portuguese northerly wind which turns into a storm when reinforced by the anticyclones in the Azores, the ship-endangering Santa Anna of southern California, the tropical and extra-tropical

cyclones and the many types of storm, cyclonic and anticy-
clonic, mobile or stationary, rotating or with a steady direction,
until, at long last, he felt the crashing of the sea diminish, the
ship's tremors die down, and the second mate showed him the
latest radio chart, announcing with relief an end to fins and
winged darts, the weather's good throughout the circle.

–So I see, Avgoustis answered.

–We're shining through and through. Both the sea and my
bald pate, the boatswain reconfirmed the calm three hours
later.

–So I see, the unseeing captain answered again, they
cracked the red eggs and sent off the signal.

Christ has risen. Cloudless sky, no wind. Propeller finished.
ATHOS III continues its course backwards. In the absence of
other emergencies due arrival to port of destination Friday after-
noon. Arrange without fail for repairs.

So then, the mercy of the Holy Mother, not just the one
from Mount Athos but also the one from Asia Minor, the
Vourliotissa with the white flowers, as well as Her helping
Grace of Tinos, the boatswain's island, and the equally compassionate Virgin of the Hundred Gates from Paros, the
mechanic's island, a heavy-duty quartet of the Orthodoxy of
the Aegean and surrounding lands, manifested initially with a
mere four in the Beaufort scale, a wind velocity of sixteen
knots, waves of barely three feet, followed by the inspiration to
travel backwards and, finally, as the cherry that topped the
cake of her solicitude, came the conscript's disclosure.

The son, in the guise of the orphaned Stelios Kazas, had
said he was twenty-four years old, two years older than he
actually was, had told a tall tale about Macedonia, about a
photocopying business, poverty and the wrong soccer team,
and had evidently made that bitter phone call from his cell
phone, while he was already on board the ship, where no one
knew his face.

The family of conspirators had set up a whole web of intrigue and had pulled his leg quite effectively, at least at the beginning. Because Avgoustis had noted that the new recruit Kazas, inexperienced and, therefore, unsuitable as a saboteur or as a spy for the Pireas crowd, would volunteer to the captain information in a manner unconvincingly haphazard and indifferent, at one point Sasha has shaved off his moustache, at another, Papalexakis is wearing pink pajamas, and, there are three steps down here, and, that door is open, and, Sorin's cheek is swollen, and, Maritsa is limping slightly today. He was puzzled that the youngster wouldn't get off at the ports, not even to take the odd photo for his girlfriend, that he'd found the expired pasta and hadn't peeped a word, that, when his cell phone rang in the presence of others, he turned it off without answering, that he couldn't hold back and two or three times either inquired or commented on the captain's personal affairs, that he was circling him like live bait, that he kept looking for excuses to offer his services, here is a cold soda, here's a clean ashtray I brought you.

Flora, when you go down to see him at his army unit in Tripoli, call me from there so I can talk to him. Flora, won't you give me the number of his barracks, hell, I can see enough to dial the numbers.

Mitso, can you hear me? I went to Tripoli and found him sick, feverish with diarrhea, calling anyone was the last thing on my mind. He says thanks for the three hundred bucks. I don't have the barracks' number handy, Laura has mixed up everything in here, I'll give it to you next time.

Mistos Avgoustis had gotten wind that something weird was going on, maybe nature itself was warning him. Once or twice he attempted to blow the boy's cover, but he kept wondering if it was all in his head, and if it was, did that indicate some unexpected, unacknowledged desire for the son, now he was in his damned dotage, far too late, and what, indeed, would happen if he accosted him, grabbed him by the scruff and said you are Andonis, I figured you out, drop the act and he had figured wrong and Stelios Kazas was no other than Stelios Kazas. Tongues would be set wagging, that was it, they'd say, the old man's lost his marbles, Alzheimer's is setting in. So, he backed off, though he kept dropping hints about the wastefulness of his family members, kept allowing himself, sometimes intentionally and others out of need, to open his heart about the guileless Litsa.

What might his brown eyes look like, now that he's grown to be a man? Do they sometimes brim with tears? And when they brim, do they come up like Greek coffee, as they used to say about his grandfather's eyes? And his gaze? Is it warm like his fingers when they pass him the tea and the bread and cheese, hand to hand?

His son, spurned by him, a wounded and enraged but harmless youth, according to his mother's description when the lady turned up out of the blue in Japan, had volunteered for the navy, while being under no such obligation, and was now serving his term on the ship that might never make it to blasted Singapore.

**

It was getting dark at last. Mid-stern, the white center light and to either side, the red on the left and the green on the right, were signaling the backward progress of ATHOS III.

A strange, unprecedented feeling for the stern to lead, the helm to be at the ship's tail, for the prow to be in the ship's wake. The crew were dumbfounded, they started to go do their shift, then turned about face, a couple got seasick, another couple were put out of action because of the nervous tension, and only Maritsa, who'd stuffed himself full with offal galore, was fast asleep in the cabin he shared with the captain. Avgoustis wouldn't be going to bed, he would perambulate like a ghost along the bridge, with coffees and cigarettes. He gave the order, they let down the anchors, they'd bring them back up at dawn, to continue the journey at the slowest possible speed.

Though the sea sprawled as meek as a lamb, he would still much rather the ship was undamaged even if it was scheduled to travel through the three hundred and thirty miles of the Straits of Magellan at eleven Beaufort, with a wind speed of sixty knots and fifty-foot high waves.

Now the swell was a mere whisper to his pricked ears which caught the son's scraping footsteps at fifteen yards and sent out an alarm.

–You need to get a bit of sleep. Everyone depends on you. Go and I'll make sure to rouse you in a couple of hours.

–You go yourself.

–Not a chance.

–Fine.

Mitsos Avgoustis leant against the rail and felt next to him the touch of his son's arm.

–Who else knows?

–Only Flirtakis.

–He's got one over me.

–He helped us, though. He had my papers issued. He took a risk.

–The girls?

–Mother told them after I was gone. They're ranting and raving.

They stayed together for three minutes in all, that's as long as serious discussions lasted in the Avgoustis clan, and this was ample time for all the basics. Almost apologetically, the old man repeated the familiar alibi, the swell has planted trouble in my mind, the sea won't give me back and I have no will for the land, but those very lines were what had worked on the son when his mother had passed them on as the delirium of a man completely out of his senses, these had fired his far-fetched decision and in the last two months, living in close quarters with his father, he had realized that they did make sense and did, indeed, fit him like a glove.

He looked at their arms side by side, he turned his mind to this weird notion of the old guy, the swell that comes in through the body and claims possession of the mind.

–The cook was beat and went to bed early, he said, but he's made something, I'll go get it for you.

–Bring me a cigar, too. Take the keys to the drawer.

Birbilis and Dactylas appeared, walking towards them, the only two from the whole crew in white uniforms, Birbilis first and the chief behind, he forewarned in a low voice, you should be fine, he added, he took his leave in a loud voice, yes sir, as you wish, he also greeted the two officers and set out for the kitchen.

–Kazas, make those cigars three, he heard the order at his back.

***

A poem is a bunch of weird things I feel that can't be said in the normal words that we know.

Mitso. I want to write one poem only and a teeny-weeny one, at that.

I'm telling you so you don't think anything worse.

I'm positive there are plenty of nice poems, some evenings, late, they are on the radio, too, about blond hair and the ancients, the night's hardships and everyone's homeland, I had me a hard time with Souvadivadol. I don't know where it is or how it is, but it exists. He mentioned it.

In the afternoons, when the playground is full of people and the little ones are strewn like sesame seeds on the seesaws and the swings, I would ask the Filipino women, the foreigners that looked after two little rich kids from time to time, is Souvadivadol in your country, maybe? Nothing. And sometimes, in the summer, I would pop over to the beaches, St. Theodore's and Kineta, just to ask the tourists. They'd shrug.

I put Souvadivadol in my poem as the place that has everything I wanted to see in my life and didn't. Imagine, I'm about to turn sixty and I have never been inside a tunnel. That, especially, seems to me terribly unfair.

Thank God, the time of inkpots is past, which means an end to blots seeping through half the page. Now all you get is the gray dust of the eraser and the shavings of the pencil getting into the notebook's binding. And when I copy from the rough draft, I always get me a longlife pen, same as me.

You'll be hearing about the hairdresser's poem and you'll be cracking up to yourself, how on earth, I'm not even a private secretary. But instead of putting me to sleep, loneliness has woken me up. It's put me onto the big picture.

Mitso, I wrote to him, I hereby testify that your Litsa is reading the paper on a daily basis. And is taking an interest in Education. The Ministry is tormenting the kids and the Minister's callousness is making me sick. All the neighborhood kids study and study and they don't get home till late from the all the auxiliary lessons. Themistocles' Anastasia's Aliki is failing in three courses. If she was my daughter, I would take action.

I wanted to have a son that would be University educated. I had even bought him a golden Parker pen, here, in the beige leather case, here it is. I'm letting you have it. Don't be embarrassed, my boy. Take it, just in case, don't want that torment with the poems getting to me again, never again, no way, poetry turns all your life upside down,

from scratch. I attempted two verses about that Souvadivadol with the queer name and there on the paper, like a
black spinning top, came even my father himself, dressed
in the chaps of that oil-resistant fabric they used to wear
to work. A laborer wherever he could find employ, whenever he could find it, for however long. Many hands are
blessed, many mouths are cursed, he'd say, though that
isn't the reason I was an only daughter and an only child.
They killed my mother when she was very young because
she gave our chicken to the civil-war guerillas.

I was brought and raised here, in our Elefsina, by her
sister who was so frightened of rebellions and armed strug-
gles that she brought me up on a sweet diet of necessary
lies and mollycoddled me with plastic bracelets and penny
hair bows from the neighborhood newsstand.

Litsa, sweetheart, you must cut your toenails so they
don't poke holes in your socks. My pride and joy, you,
spaghetti needs three slices of bread with it to do its job
properly.

At Tzanio hospital where she died, I had a nice time
here, she told the nurses, a whole bunch of frightened
neighbors all over her, shedding tears, shelling out bribes.
After that, off goes dad, out of perplexity, he could not
explain the onslaught of calamities. Many people popped
off then from the same cause. I was left on my own at
fifteen. I quit in the fourth year of high school. Listen to
all this as if it was the history of Greece. Everyone lived
through such things. Every house has something of the
story of the house next door.

I rarely watch TV series, they never drew me in. I was
looking for programs to do with tragedies and refugees,
in order to enter the mood he gave off, since, every time,
he came to me a refugee. And because a couple of times,
when I'd sent him handmade anchor-shaped chocolates

and ship-shaped cookies, all of my own inspiration, he'd quite liked them, one October I made about thirty Greek-flag lollipops and mailed them with a postcard from the boy scouts, so they could celebrate on the ship the anniversary of our historic "NO" to Mussolini's request to occupy Greece.

For me, a boundless love sneaks even into national holidays. It parades all the way to the other side of the world.

He couldn't set down roots anywhere. It might be because his true country turned out to be a maiden fern, he might have grown distracted with all those places he met and Greece might have grown lesser in his mind, it might've become like Paraguay and Uruguay, which are not very well-advertised places, though I bet that, in their own way, they are just fine, too. Day before yesterday I was moved on account of Albania. An Albanian neighbor from a few blocks down the street, in mourning over her father-in-law, told me that for forty days following a death, their customs forbid a woman to roll out filo pastry for making a pie.

Mitsos must have lost his bearings with all those nice homelands.

I had to wait for this final decision of his. He always took care to be inexplicable. He made acrobats out of cats that did backward flips on the rails and unfurled on the mast.

I, myself, in the early days had Jenny, a cat more lady-like than her mistress. he'd walk in with his suitcase through one door and she'd walk out the other and wouldn't return before three or four days were out, so it could just be the two of us again.

I never much wanted animals in the house but, during the Mitsos regime, I bowed to his whim and so I had Jenny come through here, then a Cathryn, then a Martha. The last cat, Vicky, who mewed even more hoarsely than me

and was philandering with gay abandon in the garden, disappeared last week. Someone must have stolen her. They
must have craved her blue tail. If they have a garden, their
flowers are going to know about it. Mine were spared.

They say that the evil eye works on cats, horses, beautiful stones and trees. Lots of people offer up a silver likeness
to the Mother of God so that she keeps watch over them.
A customer who came back from Melbourne with a plant
then unheard of, ordered its image made out of silver and
made it a votive offering to Saint Paraskevi. It worked, the
plant did well, it turned into a tree with bright-red hairy flowers, its Australian name was bottlebrush. At the salon, we
made lists of the beautiful plants with ugly names. The blue
evil mothers-in-law, the red stinky-sardines, the red tongue-
waggers, the tall cock-trees, as they are called in Patra. Pray
to the Mother of God to look after your cock-tree.

One old customer made a votive offering out of her
bathing suit. Not enough being widowed, not enough losing my mate, am I to miss out on my swimming, too? At
sixty years of age to have all the idlers of Salamina gos-
siping about me behind my back, was her constant lament.

I'd snip off her split ends, give her invigorating root
massages for the hair loss of widowhood, and was tempted myself to make a votive offering of a sailor's cap. How
I would have liked to have gone on his ship just once.
Even just to give the men of the crew a haircut.

All of this stuff I'm serving you about the anchor-shaped
chocolates and the Mitso-I-love-your-arm business, you
haven't read it in my letters, have you? You didn't find them
in his cabin and pinch my address from there, did you?

If that's the case, don't you admit it. It does me no
harm believing that he found the time to tell you a couple of things about me, no details, just that I'm on the
face of this earth.

He must have kept the latest, unanswered ones, all
modest, thank God, full of anxiety regarding his silence.
Write to me that you're well and never write to me again.

***

–The first customer was old Prasianakis, the wireless operator on your first ship. I put on some Kazandzides, the Wild-
flower. We listened to it, we cried. He took the chicken, I took
the money, three lucky five-hundred-drachma bills, a lucky
start for the business.

This was Stamatis Vekrelis getting in touch by phone with
his uncle the boatswain, with news from the opening of the
chicken shop. Everything he'd learnt on the ship came handy,
he fixed everything up himself, working as carpenter and electrician and plumber and painter and window framer, just as if
he were in mid-sea, he didn't come out of the shop for a month
and a half, until he sold the first chicken and praised the Lord.
He sent wishes and greetings to all, they'd be more than welcome by the faithful wife Zoitsa and by himself, all twenty in
one go if ever ATHOS docked in Pireas, otherwise one at a
time, during their shore leave.

They ought to have been glad and they were, but at the
same time they envied the privileges of ownership and drooled
over the security of solid ground, the lot of them and in particular the cook, who should've also been a tavern owner in his
Kyriaki but, instead, turned shogun, up and at it at three A.M.
sharpening his knives. He was consumed with worry about
things present and things pending. What was wrong with the
ship and why did it keep breaking down? What was wrong
with the captain and why was the captain avoiding him? On
Easter Sunday, and on Easter Monday and Tuesday, he
watched him nailed to the poop, in the same position, with a
pillow and a blanket near at hand, for stealing a nap here and

there, grabbing half a bite on the spot, pissing in the sea from where he stood and, all the while, muttering to himself under his breath. Maritsa, close by for the most part, wove circles around him. Gerassimos Siakandaris would have liked to be that cat and wear on his hand the ring that the animal bore as a bracelet on the front left leg, to stave off nature's rage.

It is beyond me to fix this crooked vessel, but within my powers to fetch you a bowl of delectable pistachio nuts, he'd offered, send it over with the boy, the initial response, I, too, see you as my daddy, he'd persisted, For the love of God, mind your pots and pans and look after the others, the second response, What have I done to you? the third, unanswered attempt to earn a seat by his mate, parent, boss, master and companion, to show his trust and support through his attentiveness and his well-chosen words and to find out what his admiral was planning because, whatever that was, it concerned him, too.

–Sound him out discretely, was his instruction to his competitor, the steward, as he meticulously laid in the bowl an invigorating compilation of nuts garnered from the supplies for the memorial services.

–Sound him out about what? To tell me if we'll get there? That, only God knows.

–I know it, too. We will get there. Avgoustis is Avgoustis. Best captain ever. You find out something else. You only met him yesterday, you don't ache for him, you don't know him like I do after spending twenty-five years by his side him and being able to read his eyes. It's not just the engine trouble, there's other stuff going on with him. Maybe he's got chest pains, maybe he's setting us up for a nice heart attack. Maybe he's thinking that events are now forcing him to quit the sea. Can he survive without a ship? Without the swell? And how would he get back home? How to make up with his children? How to face his son? The kid will be the first patricide to be unanimously acquitted. And you should have seen his wife, separate lives, frozen hearts. She came to Japan to kidnap him and her gaze shot to smithereens both ship and crew. She even looked at the rain with suspicion. It was as if the CIA had barged in for interrogations, as if the Army Investigations Bureau had set up headquarters in my kitchen for three days.

The young Avgoustis filled in yet another question that the cook didn't voice, though, surely, it was burning him up, what would he ever do at sea without his captain.

Gerassimos Siakandaris, short and green-eyed, though with no resemblance to Tom Cruise, gray-haired, though with no resemblance to Richard Gere, with the cheeks and belly of an old-fashioned restaurateur, unburdened by family, needed a solid relationship for his tender heart to thrive and his father had come in handy as the object and recipient of that love.

He received the bowl, looked at it, raisins, hazelnuts and peeled pistachios, his old man had wound up in good hands. While mounting the stairs, he wondered whether this whole thing wasn't a fantasy comic of adventures in running episodes, whether maybe he wasn't living it but, rather, reading it, a different issue each day. Still, he'd never been the kind of guy to get all excited about exotic escapades and explorations, in two months he'd been through five Asian countries without a backward glance. He only had eyes for what was happening on the ship, which was dragging across the seas a small portion of Russia, a small portion of Rumania which, when he was there himself, he hadn't woken up to, and a double helping of Greece, delicious to the palate but a fireball once it reached the gut, like the cook often used to say. As for the spring of 1997, he felt it had started thawing out his childhood and adolescence from the soiled snowfall of the Avgoustis clan.

Outside, fresh air, green waters unfurling, two men painting the winch, another three cleaning out the chain pit and the chains.

The telex by Maritime confirmed dryly that they'd find a repair crew and spare parts in Singapore, there were no congratulations for the unheard-of feat of backwards navigation, there wasn't a single thank you from those ingrates, for saving them the expense of towing.

Mitsos Avgoustis was picking at hazelnuts and pistachios, his teeth, still fine, would have liked to take a chunk out of the drones laying about in Pireas, but now, with his only son as audience, they were churning out a different kind of tough statement.

–I took down a black man in Africa. On the Ivory Coast.

He chewed on two hazelnuts, regained some strength, revved up.

–To say no, you need a long neck and I didn't have one, I wrecked lives, I pushed you aside, I burnt women up, I was the one who turned your mother into a two-horned viper, and it feels lousy to no longer want someone that you can't blame any more than you can yourself.

A raisin, an inhale, another raisin and the rest followed.

–Only Litsa's thing never dripped a single drop of poison on me, the pain would have given her permission for vitriol but all she ever held up was balminess and sunny weather.

***

I heard you. I don't like the news one bit. It doesn't suit him. You are not leaving straight away. You're going to stay until I set my breath right.

He wore his eyes out. He took them here, he took them there, they had more than their fill of the world, right side up and otherwise. Mitsos is paying for his greediness to see it all, life's beauty and filth, everywhere.

But can't he see at all? Is everything black? If someone next to him is wearing a red hat, if the sailors are holding things in bright colors? Will a red bucket go unseen as well?

There's no way that gaze could have dried up, that cherished and ached for every small thing, that let nothing pass unnoticed. He must see something, somehow. Maybe out of the one eye.

His law was the life of sailors. And to keep the ship and the cargo safe. Since he made it with no eyes, he must be superhuman and he must be blessed.

The same respect he showed the sea, never a single oil-spill, that same respect he received in return. His mind bloomed in its presence. But he overdid it. That's always been his way, fanciful and excessive.

With the years all things rust, ironworks and brains, hands and eyes. Why didn't he get pensioned off on time? To make a point against the shipowners and the Minister? Or, maybe, so as not to have to face everyone still waiting for him, down here? Because, that is, you see, how my CV ends.

Litsa Tsichli, the dead woman's bald hairdresser who loved a deaf musician and a blind captain.

And why did you, young man, cough all this up on the seventh visit? Why did you, up till now, make do with good evening and goodnight and thank you for the nice coffee? You certainly didn't haul yourself over here for my cake and my tartlets.

I spoke to you openly because someone should know how Litsa grew to be old and what became of her. I want my story to stay standing. The feat of my devotion and my obsession with one man. Penning his name on my belly so I wouldn't have to go to the tax office alone. Sewing by force of will the word enthusiasm in my life, so as to relieve him of guilt.

In 1964, Mitso, the miniskirt became the formal trend everywhere and I'm too enthused for words.

In 1966, Mitso, I'm full of enthusiasm over having joined the National Health Fund.

In 1971 I enthusiastically took on loans so I could buy the hairdressing salon.

In 1974, because the Communist Party was legalized and I voted for them in memory of my parents. And afterwards I wrote to him, I'm standing at the corner of the fence where the sunflowers are and I've ten golden fists held high above my head and the palm-cactuses have bloomed, they've sprouted magenta fingernails at the ends of their fingertips and I'm full of admiration and enthusiasm. After I got a color television I would enthuse over the storms of lilac shrimps that swept across the haystacks on the sea floor and the groupings of pretty dotted fish that strolled in the deep. And, naturally, I always emphasized my enthusiasm for all the overtime in bed. Silly me, sitting here and telling you about his ravishings of me.

You weren't tape-recording me to take proof to her, were you? She must surely want a divorce at his expense. You are aiming to blackmail him in order to strip him bare. Throw him out in the street now that he's blind. That's why he isn't coming back, so as to not give you the satisfaction.

He used to say that overseas the large cities are silent like villages and the villages are silent like graves. What would he do in Australia? He had no family there to stand by him.

He wouldn't be here, would he? You wouldn't be lying to me? I want you to give me his address. If your mother doesn't want a bar of him, I'll take him in. In this world we live in, I've put up a fight to keep from being seduced by self-interest. I need my humanity. Mitsos will not end up alone.

We are no longer young, for him to be my monument and for me to be his statuette. I'll stand by him with no demands whatsoever. And I'll invent a thousand ways for us to laugh again about all the embarrassing things, the memories and his blindness itself.

Mitsos at home will be my best old-age pension.

But act your age, will you? Keep coming. Keep coming back. Nestle in the chair at ease. Work me up with your nice smile so you can fool me. Your father's son. The same wiles at my expense.

You aren't seriously all teary eyed now, are you? Oh, dear, here he goes.

What do you suppose your tears can mean to me? That you are sorry for me or that there is no guile? An Avgoustis is crying over me. I do deserve it. Go on, cry some more.

Alright, that's enough. Have some water. And air your-self with the fan, palm leaves from Sumatra. I make use of them late at night.

Why you useless whippersnapper, see how much I love him, you see how much he's filled my life and you still couldn't tell me straight out.

On top of everything, I'd made that confession about his eyes and it made you put the brakes on.

It was on account of my terrible need to speak without qualms, to say it all without interruption. I was yelling on the inside, tell him everything, remember everything, in case he doesn't show up again and, if he does, tell it him again.

This is the first time you've come to me on a Sunday. The streets empty, the cranes unmoving. No building con-struction today, no stories being raised. And Litsa isn't cooking. If you stay I'll cut up a salad. With bread from the day before yesterday.

I didn't expect you today, my precious. Three days since I last swept in here. In the past, I used to rub the floors with potash and turn them shiny as coins. They say the sink and the washing trough are whores because they work day and night. I shut my brothel down years ago.

The heat is up and I didn't water the plants yesterday, nor the day before. My legs aren't holding me up, they've

*swollen even more. The veins are like garbled twine, green
snakes wound around the calves.*

*No matter. It's not as if he could see the dust and the
wilted flowers, or my thighs, for that matter.*

*He'd still feel them, though. As I was always wide-hipped
and on the chubby side, ten, even twenty-five pounds over,
my legs would rub as I walked and you could hear the
rustling of my nylon stockings in the bedroom.*

*He liked that. I would sit down and he'd make me get
up again.*

Gnash your thighs at me some more, my dear.

***

Sea traffic. On Friday morning the tankerers of the KORE-
AN SUN and the TOKYO STAR, the bananamen of the
GOLDEN JEWEL, the sugarmen of GREEN ISLAND and
the merry makers of the cruise ship PRETTY LADY, seeing
the backward-sailing freighter, sent signals of puzzlement and
queries about search-and-rescue, to receive in turn, like a
dozen ships before them, the formulaic answer, all's well.

Friday at noon, twenty miles off the coast, relief at long last.
All the cell phones had good reception, most spoke with their
families at home where a gaudy spring reigned and a heaven-
sent optimism. Those especially that came from tourist islands,
started daydreaming about feasts under grapevines, carousing
with their little ones in their car, tanned bodies on beaches, full
tills in the shops, backgammon and ouzo-sculling, Greek summer, the season that deletes several of the ignominies of the
day-to-day and making do, that tricks poverty and, for the
duration of three months, makes the country delectable and
loveable. The Rumanians and the Russians, similarly galva-
nized their craving for their native place and their people's
embrace.

–Say what? The propeller broke and you didn't start hol-
lering, blind, the man is blind? How come? How could you
not? He said you did the wage list for him, with the overtime
and the contributions to the pension fund. Why, good for you!
We spoke to him in turn, your sisters and I, Laura sang to him
on top of everything. Now, you pressure him to get out of
there, so this thing is over, so we can calm down.

Andonis Avgoustis wasn't going to pressure his father,
though he didn't say so to Flora, he wanted no quarrel, he
could no longer abide the familiar terseness of the hostile dia-
logues.

When he first went on board, it was the easiest thing to
change his speech slightly by dragging the *l* along the palate
and making the *b* bump a bit on the lips, the torment was in
speaking politely, in his turn, in trying on some courtesy for
size here and there, in not dressing down all adults en mass, till
then he'd only shown respect to his sixty-year-old souvlaki-
shop owner and a down-and-out piano player, a second rate
talent as far as his playing went, but skillful in gentle words.
he'd lost him since the year before last when, at fifty-some-
thing, he'd gone back to Rethymno, back to his olive trees.

The two months on the ship with his old man, with other
men, commerce, waves, being run off his feet, had changed him,
the shifts of contemplation in rhythm with the swell had made
him grow up, had baptized him in the responsibilities and
decision-making of adult life.

Land. At first, darkish blue and deep green. Then, in the
colors of every port, multi-colored ships, buildings, cranes and
hundreds of white gulls, the air-born convoy of fishing boats.

The port of Singapore, a major redistribution center, collected the goods of Australasia and sent them off to Europe
and America, brought theirs in and parceled them out to the
nations of the region.

Arrangements with the port authorities, dry dock in the offing, and surveying of the ATHOS III by the surrounding vessels that were docked, that were arriving, were leaving, were pulled up on the docks for repairs.

A launch brought three local folks from port authority, only one had some elementary English but they all went cross-eyed with surprise and admiration and broke up in a tittering chorus in the local tongue when they set eyes on the long-haired, now bathed, perfumed and groomed codger who'd crossed two hundred nautical miles, leading with the ass, an Act of God.

The cook ravished them with a spicy meat-roll from Smyrna and, by order of Avgoustis, finished them off with two cartons of Marlboro, two flasks of ouzo and two bottles of Metaxas cognac apiece. Avgoustis' son, as assistant butler, stayed by the captain's side during dinner and everything that followed, too, discretely whispering to him whatever was needed.

Papers, documents, signatures, all things were taken care of in a spirit of collaborative goodwill amongst colleagues, the three officials turned a blind eye not just because of being given a grand time and generous gifts, more than welcome in their state of poverty, but out of respect for the inventive seaman, with the proven ability to safeguard the ship and crew under any circumstances. They were photographed with him, with his officers, his cat, asked for the photos to be delivered to them, since the ship would be staying a few days, wished them that Athens would get the 2004 Olympics and at nine, they said goodnight.

In the days that followed, ATHOS III unloaded the rubber balls and the cinnamon, was taken into dry dock, mounted onto a launching cradle and the first mechanics came on along with the specialized technicians and got to work, the whole place resounding with hammering and drilling, running up and down and shouted instructions.

A telex singing his praises from Pireas, a temporary truce,

given that no replacement could possibly know better than Avgoustis how to handle the repairs of a boat on which he'd spent four and a half thousand days and nights, or the exacting checks of the shipping registry. Sure enough, in fourteen days all was in order, the turbocharger, the propeller ring and the new certificates of sea worthiness, along with warm congratulations by the inspectors to Avgoustis on his far-reaching knowledge, his astute comments and, especially, his unwavering supervision of all stages of the repairs.

On May 17, the ATHOS was brought down off its cradle, was taken to its docking spot, the chief had the lubricants delivered and oversaw the siphoning of oil, the fridges and storerooms were filled with supplies. In the middle of it all, the sailors stepped off on land, inhaled the scent of women, shopped for silly souvenirs, found some time for their much beloved fishing, picked up their mail, small parcels and two or three letters each, at last one for the cook, too, a marriage invitation from a second cousin around his age in Lamia, who would be tying the knot with a twenty-year-old Bulgarian girl. Siakandaris blanched and went into a dark mood. Having himself been deceived more than once, while fanning himself with the invitation, he bemoaned the rings he'd given away out of romanticism, generosity and haste on three occasions, one per country, Bulgaria, Rumania and the Ukraine.

On the same day, there was reference made to a fourth ring, the one that the captain had vowed as an offering and which he fished out of a yellow fabric pouch from among little boxes with pieces of jewelry, trinkets and fancy thimbles, and gave to his son to go and send by post to the monastery of Megistis Lavras on Mount Athos.

Andonis Avgoustis crossed at a run the arena of the containers, turned left at the blue ones, right at the orange, went past the red and past the brown and the yellow and the white and the mixed ones, mailed the ring, developed and delivered the photos to the port officials, took a quick photograph of a guy selling pilaf on banana leaves, a monkey in a pleated skirt, bought, too, a pink silk elephant, all for Laura, and came back post haste to be at his voluntary shift by the side of the old man who was walking up and down receiving reports on this and that.

On Sunday, May 18, they weighed anchor and moved ponderously away from the mooring buoy.

–Have you any idea how much you've just cost me?

That's how Chadzimanolis started his phone call, after the ship had already entered the dark.

–You are being unfair. Because you don't know what the sea means, what a ship means. Nor will you ever find out. So, when you open your mouth to criticize a seaman, you'd better keep in mind the off-chance that you might be talking about things you don't understand.

The phone conversation was left at that. The silver was waiting, a three-day journey away.

On the morning of Wednesday, May 21, feast of St. Constantine and St. Helen, after the coffee and the mutual well wishing over relatives who were celebrating their name day, the shore became visible, though for the three devotees of malcontent it was more of the same, a landscape of monotony, beginning and ending with palm trees.

The relatively small port of Martaban dealt in the goods of Burma, timber, rice and precious artifacts from the small, gold—and silver-smithing factories.

For three days, the Athonites worked as if their immortal souls depended on it, no breaks at all, everything, thankfully, happened within the appointed dates and on Saturday evening they took off and set on their course for Australia.

–For Avgoustis, the days of the long alert were over, the reports were going off as scheduled, the crew had picked up their normal pace and the bell rang out four-times-two for the shift change, one crowd getting straight to work, another heading straight to their cabins.

Despite all that, he didn't want to go get some rest, he patrolled the bridge with hands held behind his back, alone, softly mumbling to himself, rehearsing the words of the next conversation—one minute at most this time round—with his son who made his presence known on approach by dragging his feet from time to time and, as an additional signal, broke up the nightly quiet by calling out, again and again, to the cat. Maritsa was perambulating purring, having dined well on fresh fish and Andonis Avgoustis was quietly playing with him and looking at the lights of distant ships, the moon and the stars, patiently waiting for the hour when the old man would seek him out of his own accord.

–Kazas, he heard him quite some time later, it must have been getting on to eleven. He went over to him.

–We'll be in Perth in twelve days and I'll need another two days there. Book me a plane ticket to Greece.

Straight afterwards, he turned about and walked off with his silver hair billowing in the air. The matter did not need extrapolation, besides, the old man suddenly felt the need and the obligation to mentally make, for his own sake, a last recapitulation of the hundreds of thousands of tons of all the different kinds of cargo he'd loaded and carried for almost six decades, furs from Archangel, timber and cannabis from Riga, televisions from Rotterdam, coal from Cardiff, paper from Edinburgh, dark grained rice from Halifax, chemicals from Bilbao, glass from Barcelona, sugar beets from Tel Aviv, copper from Lima, cocoa from Abidjan, processed timber from Lagos, produce from Vancouver, cotton from Recife, soy from Mason, rubber from Mandras, silk from Da Dang, fake label jeans from Bombay, animal feed from Adelaide, sugar from Fiji, industrial equipment from Kawasaki, Kioto, Osaka, Kouang Tso, Hong Kong, and, now, Burmese silver,

the last cargo in the last departure of the last sea journey of
his life.

***

Mineral ores, the bread and butter of sea freighters, would
be better suited as the farewell cargo of Avgoustis and for his
farewell weather, a sideways swell would do nicely, with strong
side swipes.

Nevertheless, dear ATHOS was sploshing around for the
fourth day in a run very placid waters, a yawning ocean, and
carrying a pricey dowry, silver, in which Australian opal would
be worked to make necklaces, key chairs and cufflinks. Be that
as it may.

*Delivering the cargo in Perth, see to my replacement, captain
Dimitrios Avgoustis*, was the first telex sent to Pireas, straight
after sailing off from Martaban. At noon the next day a second
one was sent, more people would be leaving.

Mitsos Avgoustis had gone down to the kitchen before daybreak, the assistant cook was boiling eggs and spooning mar-
malade and butter onto plates for the crew's breakfast and the
cook was skinning a defrosted blue swordfish and waxing lyri-
cal about choice anchovies, deluxe sardines and frisses, the
musical fish that abound in the Aegean in the spring.

Straight away the coffee went on the stove, the spoonful of
tequila for the rheumatism came first and then, the coffee, the
piece of hard bread, the feta cheese, all together they loosened
the captain's tongue for a total of two phrases and five words, the
viper's nest of Pireas is calling me and that's that for Avgoustis.

The assistant cook quit his chore for a few minutes, as long
as it took for the eggs to boil over and the shells to crack, and
the cook took up pensively slicing up the swordfish till he was
done, then soaped up his hands, picked up the captain's empty
coffee cup and stated decisively, that's that for Siakandaris, too.

No need to talk things over; first off, he agreed with the decision and second, it went without saying that he'd get rid of all expired foodstuffs that were still around, just some tinned tomatoes, and would accompany his mate on the return trip to look after him, keeping an ear out for his heartbeat, as it soon would have to be wound to a different tune, that of the withdrawal from active service and entry into a home on land, and what a home it was, full of tremors and earthquakes and more tremors, and little else.

A short while later, in the sailors' mess, the steward was declaiming certain statements, he couldn't sleep at night, he wasn't cut out to be a sailor. He'd never forget his three months on the ship, he'd learnt heaps of useful things, too, making the officers' beds, mopping their bathrooms, respectfully serving his superiors plus a lot of pretty useless, though enjoyable things, that in Hawaii there are certain horses and oxen that drink no water, they never get thirsty because of a special grass they feed on, that in Haiti, the numerous local sorcerers give alkali and camphor to people deep in hypnosis in order to wake them up, and a whole lot of strange things from around the world that he heard on his shifts and would share with friends for all of the rest of his life.

The two Russians patted him amiably on the back and recited successively in his honor, Sasha the poem Storm, about a maiden out to sea dressed all in white and Andrei The Cloud, the storm's last remnant surrounded by fiery arrows with thunder spilling out of its viscera, in improvised mime and a cursory translation into English. One Rumanian told him to think it over, the sea surely doesn't get mellower, but the seaman does, he gets used to things. A second Rumanian told him, I envy you. A couple of others, bent over their coffee and well used to the departures of the newly-embarked, merely cast a glance his way with no accompanying word. Only the ardent trade unionist Michaloutsos pointed out to him that by leaving before the six month period, he'd be losing his sea service papers and the money for the return fare.

At around ten, the steward took some cake to the bridge, a special treat by Siakandaris and, in the presence of Birbilis and Dachtylas, apprised the captain of his wish to be getting off the ship.

–Why, weren't you the one who was scared of my being old? Now, just when a captain at the peak of youth is coming in, now, you've made up your mind to leave? Avgoustis asked, convincingly surprised and ironic. The other two smiled, Birbilis advised him to be patient a while longer in case he changed his mind, I've thought it through in the past few days, I have no bone with you, I just can't do this any more, I'm not cut out for extreme sports.

Thus, the three tickets were booked.

The following days were taken up with frantic sprucing up, painting, every manner of small repair and the facelift turned out a ship that was youthful and sparkling, food storage, freezers, kitchen utensils, bunk covers, implements, everything spic and span for the inspection and the handover to the new guys.

The crew felt strange to be going on without Avgoustis and they knew he, too, felt strange, to be getting on with his life without them, without the boat and, especially, without the sea.

Daily routines assumed a ritual formality, every task, every word, every bite of food and drink and cigarette had a note of farewell.

Avgoustis junior was relieved that his father didn't want too much talking, once the decisions had been made, the ensuing actions were happening of their own accord.

He saw him every so often burrow down into the ship's innards touching the engines, the cables, the panels, the doorknobs, going up and down stairs, Don't go down into the hold, dad, he'd asked in a whisper, but he insisted on checking through touching, listening, smelling every nook of the ship, so that the s.o.b. who takes my place finds nothing to complain about, he kept saying through clenched teeth.

Still, his son knew that was only half the truth, the other half was he was saying goodbye to his ship and was taking his last strolls which usually ended up in the smoking room, to pass out cigarettes and say, we've all turned out swell.

At nights he shut himself up in the cabin, listened to songs and tidied things up, sorted through any number of trivial things, folded the shirts and just a while earlier his son had come upon him while he was ironing his twenty silk ties, I don't need help, he'd sent him away only to change his mind straight afterwards and ask him to go with him into the ship owner's locked apartment.

Things were about to change for his old man, his mother, his sisters, he had played a part in that himself, and they would change for him, too, at twenty-two, for the first time, inside of him sparked that courage that reigns anger in and gives birth to decisions.

He was sick and tired of marriage quarrels, listening to his mother and father as a young kid, just to his mother later on, a matrimonial tearing asunder with one member of the couple absent, Flora on her own, suddenly catching alight and saying out loud a sentence from a conversation she'd obviously been carrying on internally and then launching herself like a hyena at the old man, thousands of miles away.

He, too, was having quarrels over any number of things until he'd had enough of the same old same old, cut it out and discovered that when everything goes quiet, whoever has wronged someone else, realizes it of his own accord and doesn't need to make amends on hands and knees, and poor Flora was the living proof, cursing at him of a Monday, as an idler and a good-for-nothing and a money waster and by Thursday, Friday at most, sitting next to him as he was munching his toast in front of the TV and briefly caressing the back of his neck. He felt sorry for her. Anger drains. His mother needed a good push, to run out of people to blame and relax her clenched fists.

We need to train our hands and our eyes, he thought, the touch and the gaze show emotions with greater precision and safety than words which, if said awkwardly or out of sync, can send things spinning out of control and get people all churned up.

His father's empty gaze was wordlessly asking for forgiveness and was receiving it wordlessly, not from the eyes of his boy, which he couldn't see, but from the palms of his hands. The Avgoustis pair had gone into the bosses' apartment to carefully gather from the safe all of the captain's personal possessions, packs as thick as double bricks with photographs and letters from the family and other kinds, too, the son stole a glance at the names and addresses on two or three envelopes and then, took his father's hands and held them for a few minutes saying, if you like, I'll look for Litsa.

It was already midnight.

A low-roofed cabin, the floor and walls in lettuce-green, the sink with a mirror whose light came on automatically, a small table attached to the bulkhead and the porthole right on sea level, accommodation right by the sea like it says on the pamphlets of the tourist resorts, this had been the room of Avgoustis junior, where he had thought through the whole of his life up till then and had started seriously thinking about the part that was to come.

Sometimes it does happen like that, the space helps, it draws in both the past and the future, so close, right next to you and they are palpable, a breath away from your breath, both of them visible and transparent.

He had a glass of water, threw off his shoes and lay down. He had a nice five-hour sleep, lulled by the swell which he was going to hanker for in the rooms on dry land and, first thing in the morning, before the whole ship was up, he followed Maritsa in her strolling, the cat on the rails, he by its side, hands walking on the side decks, feet dangling in the air, an Upside-downer who didn't really feel himself so out of kilter any more.

***

Goodbye to sun-bathing in boxer shorts.

Saturday 7, Sunday 8 and Monday 9 of June, a continuous drizzle and the first of the winter chill.

Perth, a large port, paperwork, unloading, payments of port taxes and other expenses, cleaning out the holds, washing down the deck, sending of telexes, checking the books and bringing them up-to-date, one last detailed inspection, the lids on the toilet seats sparkling, the coolers ejecting perfect arches of cold water, the videotapes and the church recordings turned right back to the beginning, the men with fresh haircuts and groomed, a shop-front ship, all set for the big day tomorrow. On Monday afternoon, Avgoustis visited Birbilis in his cabin.

–I'm confused, he told him. I don't know if it was the sea I loved or just the ship. I give you my blessing.

Early that night, the whole crew in the officers' mess, in honor of the occasion, for a farewell dinner.

Some of Avgoustis' favorite CDs, Moscholiou, Sinatra, Kanellidou, at low volume, created an atmosphere that took off with the song I'll Break the Cups beautifully sung by the assistant cook who dedicated it to the captain from Asia Minor and to all of his ilk. The level of music slipped several notches down with a Russian rock piece by the irreverent artsy-fartsy twins, and then, perfectly timed with the rounds of general laughter, the delectable menu came on.

Siakandaris had done the cooking with tissues stuffed in the pockets of his shirt, trousers and apron, wiping his eyes and blowing his nose at two minute intervals while fretting over his expensive materials. Australian oysters and large prawns to start with, steamed barramundi and fried mushrooms for the main dish, an aristocratic choice paid for by the chef personally in honor of the grand seigneur who was so overtaken with emotion that he didn't have a taste of anything at all.

And how could he have seen the oysters or taken the bones out of the barramundi, I should have fed you good old macaroni, Siakandaris complained to him distraught and inconsolable despite everyone else's loud acclamations, despite the spread's being videotaped by Birbilis.

The dinner rolled on with plenty of wine and the group accompaniment of several songs, till Mitsos Avgoustis stood up and signaled for the noise of the revelry to quiet down.

–I'll tell it like a swell. I never meant to be a seaman but I stayed at sea for fifty-eight years. Now, I don't want the land but the dirt is ordering for me to put in an appearance. It is my time. Some of my peers are still alive because we don't realize what's best for us. Damn you, men, I am a flaking sea rope coiled alongside you and without you I'll be in trouble. You are good seamen, you owe me this much. Make sure you don't drown, so you can remember me. Kazas? He then asked for the steward, who was already nearby holding a big cardboard box, here it is, captain, he reported, and started handing him various articles, one by one.

Mitsos Avgoustis called up his men according to rank, one at a time, hugged them, kissed them on both cheeks and gave them as souvenirs the scarves he'd knitted himself, there were more than enough, his ties, cosmetics, cigars and biographies, the old copies dog-eared, those of the last decade, sent by the second daughter, untouched.

Please, no tears, the brimming Siakandaris called out, disappearing into the kitchen to leave the scarf and the Stalin, to reemerge in half a minute with an enormous blue cake. He'd made the whipped cream sea-blue with food coloring, had lain it out in waves and had propped on top a red ship made of sugar, loaded with silver bonbons from the kolliva, it raised a storm of clapping even by the blind man, who neither saw the cake nor had a chance of having it discreetly described by his son.

Gerassimos Siakandaris thanked the captain and the entire crew, the idea for the wavy cake came from remembering some anchor-shaped chocolates and lollipop-flags sent once to the ship by a gay sailor, an expert in sweet-making and sweet talk, an old wireless operator of Avgoustis. That's what he knew, that's what he said and wished them all mellow voyaging with our holy Christ and Saint Mary by your side.

Just in time, a bald, sixty-year-old came into the dining room, wearing a tuxedo and white gloves, the son hurriedly whispered to the father.

Captain Mitso, it's me Theodosis, no wonder you don't know me, dressed up to the nines like this.

That was Theodosis Papadopoulos, an old seaman who'd stayed back in Australia from the time of the junta and that other Papadopoulos, the time of the big strikes in the ports of Sydney and Melbourne as a gesture of support for the Greeks, according to Siakandaris' report to the revelers regarding his old acquaintance and colleague from way back, when they were both assistant cooks.

The tuxedo man must have kissed Avgoustis up to ten times, My precious friend, he called him at least another ten and yet another as many admiring, in his incorrigible Tripoli accent, the captain's rich, silver hair. He hadn't seen him for thirteen years, that was how long it'd been since the ship had docked in Perth. He warmly greeted the cook as well with the code words vineyard and vine leaves and sallied forth with his own concerns. He regularly passed by the port, went out of his way to check out the commercial ships and whenever he spotted a Greek one, he would wave hello from the dock, and would sometimes ask to go up.

–You aren't on your way to your wedding, with that tux on a Monday, are you? asked Avgoustis.

–No, I'm tying the knot for others.

–Best man?

Theodosis Papadopoulos explained he was still working as a private eye, Greek-Australian stakeouts, infidelities and family dramas, but he'd opened a second office, too, for wedding ceremonies.

With a limousine and a camera, he escorted brides to the church or the registry and videotaped the event, the festivities, too, later on, only for Greek and Cypriot weddings, mind you, where the whole extended family gets together and makes some serious music, the foreigners don't have the largesse, what they mean by a wedding is two signatures side by side on a piece of paper.

He also gave out cards to those present, with the photograph of the white thirty-foot limo, looking like a yacht and the firm, *Teo Poulos, luxurious weddings.*

–You never know, we might get lucky in Perth, said Birbilis waving his gifts, the life of Karaiskakis and a pair of knitting needles.

Within a short quarter of an hour, after a glass of wine and a sweet blue ripple on the plate for the visitor, after yet another wave of hugs sprinkled with warm wishes, a bunch of ten seamen with yellow and red scarves, followed the master of ceremonies out, for a guided tour in the wedding limo of the local drinking holes plus whatever else turned up.

Andonis Avgoustis hung back, yet again, as his father's guard. It isn't just the sea you're afraid of, it's the land as well, the cook told him.

Yes, indeed, every single person till then had figured Avgoustis junior to be timid, pretty useless and off with the fairies, but, when it had come down to brass tacks, he'd proven them wrong. His gain wasn't that he'd got his own back, but that he had jump-started a loving relationship with his father, having learned in the bargain that nothing and no one ever falls by the wayside, justice keeps slowly burning out of sight and works itself out, all in good time.

Quiet on the ship and down in the port, night-time, lights spread out near and far. He went to his captain's cabin in case he needed his steward or his son.

But the old man wanted to be on his own. He packed in his suitcase the gifts from the crew, silver worry beads, good-luck charms, a Russian Jesus, an embroidered Rumanian heart, his magnifying glasses, some underwear, a few pieces of clothing and stayed up, uncertain about the footsteps leading away from the ship, footsteps onto a forgotten and changed land, footsteps into a life which he could no longer pussyfoot around.

Dawn saw the ship hung all round with flags like on national celebration days, an initiative of Birbilis which Avgoustis didn't see and a good thing it was that, in all the hurly burly of the last moments, the son forgot to tell him, because he'd have had them take the festoons down on the spot. Siakandaris was all set and waiting for the high pitched bellow, I'm neither Admiral Koundouriotis nor the Queen Mother of England, take those down, didn't hear it and was puzzled with the captain's tolerance, knowing full well that formal festivities weren't his cup of tea. The whole thing, nevertheless, had started informally, in honor of Maritsa. Almost the entire crew turned out, in dribs and drabs, forming an honorary regiment that escorted the cat's last walk along the rails, he'd spent the entire morning going from one man's arms to the next, and listening to their sweet talk, what will daybreak be without you, you princely thing, make sure you write us.

At nine, the telex arrived regarding the next freight, fifteen thousand tons of fish paste and the same amount of mineral ore headed for hilly Mororan, under the new captain.

We're going to have a hard time getting used to him, no matter who he is, the chief kept saying over and over again.

The guy turned up at about ten. Sakis Karayannopoulos, with tankers, cruise ships, Panamax, five flags, four shipping companies and three marriages under his belt. Forty-five or so, fit and trim, with stylish sunglasses, an expensive leather jacket, expensive watch, a show-off and a cold fish into the bargain. Dry greetings, frigid glances, even colder handshakes, a few okays, barely a single thank you, no smiling whatsoever.

His enthronement on ATHOS III had the crew comparing the one going out with the current one and they were drenched in cold sweat, got an ache in their gut and a shiver of sorrow over the old man's departure.

A new cook and a new steward, a completely different kettle of fish, the pair of them. The thirty-year-old Filipino Alfonso Boudeng, the replacement of Siakandaris was given a tour down in the kitchens of the elements on the electric stove, the ovens, the freezers and the cupboards, asked timidly about the dietary whims of the officers and how he might please the crew, heard in awe the epic narratives about pissed lambs and rice-stuffed vine leaves, thanked with a slight bow for the hand-written recipes for tomato salad, stuffed eggplant and honeyed dumplings, a two-page text in broken English, the only kind that a mind can pick up which is boiling all day long in the kitchen's hundred-degree temperatures, and he promised his fretting colleague to pay heed to his advice and honor the profession.

As for the other one, the willowy twenty-year old steward, also from the Philippines, by the name of Marvin Malaouan, he was openly overjoyed at finally getting some work, he had one child and a second one was on the way.

The arrival of the two Filipinos signaled the upcoming

replacement, whether gradual or massive, of the Greek crew with inexpensive Asian seamen, at half the monthly wage. A sense of transience on the ship and of impending layoffs, with the new captain aiding and abetting the greedy ship-owner spread instantly over everyone, darkening their gaze, numbing their tongue, weighing down their step.

Everyone's thoughts turned to Greece, to the sparse prospects of fitting in at some relative's business, of gaining a foothold in the tourist market on their islands or borrowing over their head in order to set up maybe a garage or some other makeshift small business as it was out of the question that they, too, might set up as detectives and drive thirty-foot-long limousines ferrying brides and bridegrooms.

–The gangway has twenty-two stairs.
–I know.
–I'll take Maritsa's cage.
–Be careful.
–I'll first take down all the luggage and put it in the limousine.
–Is it here?
–It's waiting for us downstairs.
–Tux again?
–Regular clothes.

Avgoustis junior went up and down three times to carry the luggage to the bridal car, last handshakes, have a good trip, from those staying to those taking their leave, photographs and departure with the flag-touting freighter blowing its horn many times successively in farewell, the whole crew standing by the rails and, likewise, sailors in the adjacent ships waving goodbye.

Mitsos Avgoustis went down first, Siakandaris second and further back, with baited breath, came Andonis Avgoustis who stumbled like a blind man, lost his footing and came down the steps three at a time, clumsy as anything with Maritsa mewling in alarm.

Teo Poulios sat the friend dear to his heart in the passenger seat. The other two and the white tom settled at the car's elongated interior, covered in cream-colored leather, amongst basketfuls of tulle-wrapped bonbons that filled the space with their fragrance.

The limousine started out for the airport honking rhythmically.

Through the entire trip, the driver expounded to the unseeing man on the beauty spots and progress of the impeccably organized city of Perth and, though a detective, did not suspect the captain's blindness, nor was he puzzled by his silence as, on the contrary, it suited him just fine to go on and on by himself, enumerating his firm's successes, recommending Australia, its parrots, its penguins, its kangaroos, feeling sorry for its koalas getting stoned on their diet of eucalyptus leaves and not rousing themselves in time to beat it during the big forest fires, and in this fashion, not letting them get a word in about Greece, he hadn't seen his mother since 1973.

***

It seems I only saw what the boss wanted me to see. My eyes didn't have the know-how to go after anything more than that, anything suspect. I would point out to him a moon, round and apple-red, winking at him meaningfully, and he wouldn't turn to take a look. I would show him the parcels that slovenly assistant cook was filling up to bursting point for Soledad, winking again, and again he wouldn't turn to take a look. He must be thinking now, I guessed, certain that his eye had latched on to all those things before mine. That's how Siakandaris was making amends to himself, though he still was downcast, not because Avgoustis didn't trust him enough to tell him about his injured eyes but because he, too, went blind and didn't notice it, so as to become a more than willing accomplice and co-conspirator in the set up, so as not to let him go through all those anxious years alone. He brought to mind the decade's Beaufort chart, three killer North Atlantics, the entrapments of the icebergs, three homicidal Patagonias, the thick fogs, two North Pacifics, seventeen and nineteen days and nights respectively, zero visibility, the radar out of action, the deck bell ringing non-stop.

He now admired him a whole lot more, reading the weather, sailing backwards without leading the ship to harm, without a single mishap, and all of it with no eyes.

A fine joke, too, him asking to borrow Birbilis's eye-drops or his order, on a couple of occasions, to boil up some sage for compresses for the captain to give his eyes a rest after five, seven or seventeen days of being continually on call.

No, he didn't mind that Avgoustis hadn't confided in him; if in all those years, there hadn't been a dark moment to make him succumb and pry open his lips, he had to admire him for that as well, on top of everything else. Nor did he mind that when the captain found out the rookie steward was his son— and a sly player the kid was, too—he didn't take him aside to tell him, for how could such a thing be said, My heart never knew my own kin whose photograph I keep facedown in the drawer, he just couldn't come up and just blurt out the things he'd been hiding with such conscientious egoism, with such finely-spun fear.

Everything came to the fore at Perth airport. It was there that Siakandaris noticed the captain wasn't taking a single step without the steward, was literally hanging on the youngster's arm with his gaze lowered and unfocused. When they got in line for passport control, Gerassimos, I'm blind and this young man here is my one and only son, Andonis, he said straight out and didn't speak again, didn't need to answer questions, there

weren't any. The cook, flummoxed, only exchanged silent looks
with Andonis and only later, on the flight from Perth to Sydney,
in between half-hour silences and catnaps, whether real or
feigned by the three sitting in the same line of seats, were some
things mentioned superficially, not any words of surprise or
complaint, mainly practical considerations, can the problem be
medically fixed, what do the folks at Pireas know, what does
the family know, what's Andonis's real job, along with a couple
of amends for going over the top, don't know what put it in my
head to call Mrs. Flora a CIA agent and what demon prompt-
ed me to come up with that business about your father having
three dark-skinned beauties for lunch.

At Sydney airport the son, not just a good looker but with
selfless service as part of his makeup, went off to shop for some
gifts, Siakandaris-Avgoustis were left face-to-face and the cook
started on a speech about the courtyard of his family home in
Kyriaki and the fir tree that had seen ten Siakandaris genera-
tions grow in its shade. He didn't pressure his friend, he did-
n't ask for his dues, just so the other didn't think he was being
demanding, or worse, expressing pity, both of which would be
beside the point.

Nevertheless, the old man wished at all costs to make one
thing clear.

–It's on account of Andonis I'm leaving. I didn't want him
to go back to the jackals at Pireas a loser. I owed him that.

And, surely, none of that was of much importance now,
after takeoff from the impressive city of Sydney, full speed
ahead into the boundless sky, when in the plane seats right in
front of him, the miracle was happening of the father and the
son, at long last, being side by side.

He was listening to the tock-tock of the old man's wedding
ring on the metal arm of the seat and the sound brought to
mind Flora Avgoustis, a sourpuss, full of criticism and interrogations, just the ticket for her husband to stop loving her, on

time, many years ago, as many as the years of her punishment. No detective measured up to the lady, all she needed was a total of two days in Japan to see through what all the others hadn't cottoned onto for ages, not even the cook from Viotia, no savvy to the man, as it turned out, the very soul of naiveté.

When the voluble man abruptly clams up, it never does him good. Gerassimos Siakandaris, who had it in his making to rejoice or, at least, to get relief by singing the praises for hours on end of the beneficial effects of food well cooked and well served, had been made to go for a whole day without his saving device, good in all weather and for any and all emergencies, of the spicy clove and the egg-and-lemon sauce, the curtain screening off his own loneliness. The cat, trapped in the bamboo cage next to him, was not any suitable match for a heart-to-heart, even just to air his grievances, for instance, Maritsa I envy you your being in Greece with our boss, unlike myself, and, as a result, he wasn't spared the dark thoughts about the choppy waters awaiting the captain at his home next to a woman who was dynamic and unhappy, the perfect combination for a nuclear-strength bomb, now that the missus would have the upper hand.

The wedding ring's tock-tocking against the seat was as deafening to him as the rounds of verbal ammunition, smelling of gun-powder, which Flora Avgoustis had spent years collecting in her cartridge belt.

The gorgeous dark-haired flight attendant served him tasteless meals in plastic wrappings, it was nevertheless nice to be served by delicate womanly hands with nails painted a light pink, a golden ring with small shiny stones and, around the right wrist, a gold chain with small amber snails hanging off tiny links, seven in number, a full serving.

He, himself, hadn't been worthy of earning a pair of kissable female hands, hands that might have been waiting for him at Kyriaki, softly getting hold of a bunch of drained spaghetti and shaking it exultantly in view of the bolognaise coming up for dinner.

He drank his beer without eating and closed his eyes.

But the Gibson desert wasn't wasted. In the front seat, Avgoustis junior buttered his father's bread rolls and when, after a couple of bites, he gave himself over to sleep, exhausted by everything, the youth glued his face to the window with his gaze trained on the red, uninhabited desert. He was awed by its grandeur and felt infused with something of its raw power because, however well he'd done so far, he was still going to need more courage and more clear-headedness for what was ahead.

Inside his white limousine, Teo Poulios had told them that the Aborigines believe the world was created out of dreams. You dream of a river, you wake up and it is flowing before you. You dream of a tree and it really grows. You dream of a bunch of wild yellow-tomato plants, you open your eyes and there they are. You dream of the clouds and they gather up and bob in the sky. He had videotaped the marriage of a strange, somewhat drunk, English explorer to a native woman and the happy groom had spoken in front of the camera about the desert tribes' dreams. Andonis Avgoustis would have liked to be an Aboriginal in order to dream up the verve that would be required to clean up the mess at Pireas.

He was determined to size things up at Pireas, to time the truces, to gather up the cartridges from the expected massive rounds of fire and to not leave the future in his hands or in hers, both of them had their record stained.

Up until twenty-two, he'd been the odd man out in the gynecocracy of his home, with Flora, the two sisters and little Laura, and no father, no grandfathers, grandmothers, uncles or cousins—a lopsided clan. Kinship is molded in a crowd and needs all ages, distributed among several men and women so that the ties can be tried and those that really are worth it can take root. Otherwise, it all gets lopsided.

It took five hours for the biblical red dirt that covered all of Central Australia to be over and for the sea to be inserted under them again, he wasn't a bit afraid on the plane this time, nor did he give the flight attendants a hard time, even smiling at one of them who was slowly strolling down the aisle and looking thoughtfully at the old man's body having completely fallen to one side with his head resting on the son's chest.

At thirty thousand feet, Andonis Avgoustis, listening to the old man's breath over his heart and seeing his long hair spread like a white flag over his shoulder, even had a cry, naturally and quietly, at long last it happened to him again, and while snores and silence reigned all around, the minority were asleep, most, with headphones in place, were watching a third-rate flick, he, a revived sky rider, felt the adrenaline sharply rising, a nice rush, not like in the two protest marches, one when he was sixteen, the other at seventeen, when he'd marched along with the roughest bloc and, then, discharged his rage by bringing down store-front windows and setting trash cans on fire.

It's because so few things ever cross your mind that you don't have a grasp of even the basics, he had said that very night to Flora who'd gotten cross over the singed sleeve of his jacket and had concluded, high school anti-authority pranks, parroting the mottoes of Lily's big-mouthed fiancé.

From thirteen, fourteen, everything he'd looked to for redemption had sent him back within a week, at most, to his room and his drumming kit. The list of all the things he couldn't stand was getting longer and longer in his mind, and at the top, as prince of darkness, featured the man now napping on his chest like he was nursing on his heartbeat. I didn't really resist him all that much, he thought. All these years of war and, in the end, all they needed was for their breathing to mix, a bit in the ocean, a bit in the sky, and for their bodies to barely touch, in order to turn the page. Reconciliation wasn't their invention, thousands of years-old hatreds hang on a single gesture, lying in wait for a caress.

Sydney-Singapore, Singapore-Bahrain, Bahrain-Athens, a long but good trip, with no turbulence, with an end-of-season feeling to it.

For his old man, an end to the sea, an end to the bachelor life, for himself, an end to being orphaned, an end to the mongrel years of youth.

***

In the Churchill area there is a large population of polar bears. They feed on fish and seaweed. The male weighs half a ton, the female from five hundred fifty to six hundred fifty pounds. In December she gives birth to up to three cubs. The male is very savage with the mother and the babies, except during mating season.

Hermes Flirtakis delivered the lesson to Laura while picking on slices of crunchy capsicums, with the occasional roar to underline his fondness of the wild and the powerful dynamics between the sexes in the animal kingdom.

Here, Thursday, June 12, another spread of food was in progress, for the welcoming. In the somewhat narrow balcony of the Pireas apartment, revelers were squashed around the hors d'oeuvres and the crisp piglet just delivered by the Albanian hand from the restaurant at the square at two in the afternoon, with Flora's stove having gone out of action the night before.

Honestly, what could they discuss with directness and truthfulness after such a prolonged, virtually inexplicable, absence? The television would ask Avgoustis how he felt being blind, and his wife, how deeply moved she was after the return of her Odysseus.

Thankfully, the granddaughter's presence at the table was the perfect alibi and competition was fierce for who would first educate five-year-old Laura ecologically, politically and historically. Already the poor child had initially become the target of grandmother Diamanta's memories, at your age I was fighting on the mountains of Epiros against the German and Italian fascists, and after that, of Flirtakis' pantomime, who was punching the air with his fists pretending to be the enraged male bear. The head captain had to his right his unspeaking wife Tasoula, her face lined by subservience, shame and boredom and to his left Kassandra Chadzimanolis, his old love and wife of the shipowner while he gambled with others of his ilk in mini cruises to Hydra and Spetses. Next to her, the in-laws of the first born Avgoustis daughter, country farmers, then the daughter herself, her mother, her brother, her sister, her husband, her little daughter, her father and Gerassimos Siakandaris, the thirteenth guest and virtually an infiltrator, not eating, not drinking, only listening and being saddened.

After being introduced to the captain for the first time, his son-in-law, a member of the leading socialist party and comfortably appointed to a post with three job descriptions, complained they'd neglected to bring him a statuette of Mao for his office, then delivered a fiery speech. The USA lay claim to the former socialist countries, enjoying the privileges given up by the defeated and disgraced opponent, he said, shifted Laura off his thigh, emptied her onto the father-in-law's thigh and skipped off without further ado, he was late for a meeting, with whom, where, how, not even his wife made the effort to inquire, Lily was silently smoking her cigarillo and communing with her worry beads.

Ever since her harsh phone call to the old man, the eldest had grown cold towards him, her heart had had more than its fill of conjugal bickering, in her parents' marriage and in her own as well, she just couldn't care less. So, when she gripped her father's hand, she barely held back from speaking the phrase, a good thing you can't see us, your young daughter grown fat and your older one grown broken, but when he pulled her close and held her briefly in his arms, her mood shifted slightly and she whispered to him, in all this mess there's two saving graces, the first that you came back safe and the second that you made up with Andonis.

Her brother had come back a changed man. Twenty hours since his return and he hadn't let loose on his damned percussion set, hadn't sworn at anyone nor had he plunged into the melancholy that affected them all the same way. At noon, he'd gone and fetched the kid from kindergarten to then bring her over to her grandma's, to spread out her gifts for her, to leaf together through the Australian *Gorge, the Worms' Dreaming Place,* to coax her into playing with Maritsa and with the drums, even to mediate in the Laura-Mitsos kiss, as the little girl wasn't exactly enthusiastic about a grandfather so completely different from the normal kind, unshaven even on the day of a festive gathering, and he, in turn, couldn't see where to lay down her stuffed koala and her richly textured dreamtrap or where to place a caressing hand on her hair without poking her in the eye.

Regarding Andonis, Vassia was of the same mind, that this brother of theirs no longer resembled the unnerving geek, whose knee-jerk reactionary, had been to retreat in his room for days at a time, just so he wouldn't have to agree with Flora that Sunday comes after Saturday and February follows January.

The Old Man and the Sea did him good, she conceded, let us now also read in the coffee dregs *For Whom the Bell Tolls.*

Her own heart hadn't skipped a beat, her skin hadn't crawled, her eyes hadn't brimmed to gaze upon Robinson Crusoe with his man Friday, fine, her father was now a blind old man, but she wasn't about to bestow upon him her tears of joy. In fact, she got mad as all get out listening to her mother's monologue, while she was toiling away at the frying pan—seeing that the daughters were allergic to cooking—Whether we like it or not we take things as they come, and, this is how life turned out, a convenient and risk-free way to gloss over your mistakes, to take pity on and absolve yourself.

At coffee, the unity of those seated around the table surely merited a prize and the rapport among them was spectacular. Several of them spoke, for a short spell, in a very contained way, very politely giving up their turn to the next person, without, however, actually addressing anyone else, at least, not anyone among those present.

Tasoula Flirtakis mumbled something about thimbles, I've brought them up to four hundred, she trailed off in a whisper. Hermes Flirtakis answered her that, for fear of pirates, it was a good idea to stick close to Russian ships that had arms and a medical officer. Gerassimos Siakandaris answered him that those that fate never favored, end up in their homes trailing their loneliness like eventide stars. The father-in-law picked up with a tale of a village neighbor who was a snitch for the police during the junta and whom nobody dared confront about not cooping up his chickens which wandered everywhere, stinking up the place. His wife recalled the radical inflation of the currency during the German occupation, the grown-ups had given her and her girlfriends two sacks of bills to play at being princesses.

Avgoustis, aware, by now, that everyone knew about his eyes said, bitterly ironic, how the city has grown, nice view.

Their children simply listened to the adults' foolish effort not to devour each other along with the baked pig, not to bring up each other's dirty laundry during the ice cream and espresso, and privately wondered, each one separately, if the compromise was quite worth it.

Everyone needs a moving encounter every so often and all families need a moving get-together. They once again failed at it.

Laura had fallen asleep in Andonis' arms, her little feet resting on Flora. As her impetuousness around the table had been stymied by the unpleasantness of the adult world, she had disappeared for quite some while to sink her paws into her grandma's jewelry box, and, naturally, she'd put everything on, besides, it all belonged to her, Flora had told her so several times. Unspeaking, she caressed her granddaughter's naked feet and gazed at the pearly beads, coral, silver and gold that covered the sleeping child's body. When I, too, was a babe, I never expected life to turn out like this, the sixty-plus hostess scoffed inwardly and made no wish, even at the final toast, Italian liqueur, a present by the shipowner's wife. It is despicable for people to grow old in the trap of hopes and wishes.

Mitsos Avgoustis, Mimis to his wife once again, was caught in a different sort of a trap. The four-bedroom apartment had been rearranged and the furniture shifted and he didn't even dare go to the bathroom without the cook's arm, or his son's, he lacked that kind of familiarity with the girls and he wouldn't stoop to making Flora, who hadn't blurted his secret out to Chadzimanolis, thus gaining a certain stature in his eyes, a nurse at his beck and call.

Yesterday, during the first fretful night in the house, he held back with difficulty the deep sighs, coming hard and fast with the sleepless realization that no trespass ever grows old enough to be rendered harmless, because you think about it differently at thirty than at fifty, and differently again at seventy and so on, as a person grows, so does the weight of his deeds.

He rose from the conjugal bed, spent the night on the balcony and in the early dawn, before Flora and Andonis woke up, got Siakandaris up from the couch and they went out without a coffee and hailed a cab.

–The covering stone is granite. The cross is tin. The oil lamp is a small fire burning in the middle of her name and his.

Siakandaris was doing some oral reporting on the cemetery in Kifissia, with all the dead of St. Trifon at the mercy of the marble sculptors and the scissor-handed gardeners, old Chadzitmanolis laid out among them for his eternal siesta next to his Stassa, already laid out years before in gray-green tomb, like a king-sized bed.

Evgenios Chadzimanolis, 1909-1997, Anastasia Chadzimanoli, 1919-1981. Evgenios received the small bunch of violets, Avgoustis' standard gift to all colleagues, whether big shots or lowly, Stassa her beloved Swiss carnations. So that she wouldn't get upset, yet again, with her only son's heroics and start blaming herself for all the ways in which she'd spoiled him rotten, Evgenios and Mitsos had covered up for his untoward behavior in Souvadivadol, generously bribing his chief officer who took all the responsibility on his own shoulders. It had been his fault, for not being on the bridge, that they crashed into the jetty, the captain was burning up with fever, they'd said, while the rascal Chadzimanolis junior was in his cabin jerking off.

Mitsos Avgoustis devoted to the dead compatriot, protector, accomplice, colleague and friend the time for a prayer and a cigarette and, given the opportunity, he had a second one in memory of doctor Sifakakis, from Asia Minor also, breastfed in Smyrna, buried in Buenos Aires, one more for his mother, a cask of bones in Elefsina and one last one for his father, in that same cask with her, just like they had been in life, bones tightly hugging on a shelf in the charnel house of Saint Lazarus.

–His Maritsa went every morning and left on his tombstone throttled mice, he said to the cook.

–Yours will be bringing them for you, too, you'll see.

They laughed a bit, gathering strength for the family table, hopped in another cab, shopped for light-weather sleeveless T- s h i r t s, the cook bought the bus ticket for Kyriaki, he would be leaving that very afternoon.

Afterwards, they went on a coffee binge, in Omonia and Pireas, from one coffee-shop to the next, to pass the time, without too many words, with no swell, listening to the city's furor, hasty heels, cars jammed in the traffic, scooters, a crowd making its way helter-skelter in the disorderly and arrhythmic land.

***

The bachelor cook, first time in her house, found it modern, he liked the two deep-forest paintings, works by Vassia's boyfriend of last year, he liked, too, the blue handmade kitchen glasses, works by the one from the year before, her daughter passed on to her the remnants of her failed relationships, which she didn't care to have around her own apartment. Flora had figured it out by now, whenever the second daughter invaded the house with her arms full, the load meant it's over with Achilles, then over with Michalis, Vaggelis, Telis.

The men were smoking on the balcony, talk could be heard about sea business, interspersed with short digressions about the minor wear and tear of age, high blood pressure, a bloated stomach, dizziness, nothing more ominous. Mimis was probably sitting in the swinging couch next to Laura's toys. Yesterday, the first night at home after years, he deserted their bed almost straight away, I slept on the trip and can't go to sleep he'd told her, I'm going to the balcony for some fresh air.

It was two in the morning when Flora got up to look for him, worried that something might have happened to him, found him asleep in the swing with the velveteen elephant as a pillow and holding the key ring tight in his hands, he who had never in the past paid any attention to keys.

She stayed out for a cigarette with her gaze scanning from Mimis to the moon and everything in between, including Limoyannis, across the street, at the white plastic table, evidently doing crossword puzzles again, in the yellow light of his verandah. For some years now he had made his face-to-face appearances scarce and she rarely paid him any persistent attention, though tonight, having grown old suddenly and dramatically, he was at his post as if he had been waiting for Mimis's return.

It's probably a myth that old people forget, it doesn't seem like memory is much help in their getting rid of those wounds that go way deep.

Flora Avgoustis wasn't sad that she had lost him nor was she glad that she had finally regained her marriage, what would be the point of starting to add up the goods in her life, she was no longer the grocer's daughter, nor a part-time grocer, the scales had gone rusty with the produce, local and imported, of her youth.

It was late afternoon and all she was interested in by this time was doing the washing up and putting away the evidence of the family spread of warm dishes and frigid atmosphere. She treated Maritsa to a generous slice of meat, put on the apron and gloves to save her fingernails, freshly manicured the day before, turned on the hot tap and concentrated on the grease.

The women, settled in the living room, young and old, were talking about speed diets, their beach time in the offing, though without meaning it, desultorily, the leftover subjects of a meal they had been wishing over and done with for some time.

Earlier, the mother-in-law having just discovered that Flora's two little trips, last year and the year before, one week in China and one in India, supposedly to meet her husband, were lies, had told her, a good thing your husband's safely back, my girl, so you can have a break from fretting, we're at an age that needs company and calm waters.

—Let me be done with this sink, get it out of the way, and I'll join you for a second cup of coffee, she'd answered curtly and tight-lipped, she urgently needed to be left alone, not to have them in her hair anymore.

One of the sea's gifts to men is it makes them stoic, or insensitive, or something in between, and there isn't enough left over for their women on the land. Against her will, with a sense of disillusionment, with fear almost, she felt her mouth turning into a pestle and mortar, all set to crush her life into a pulp and everyone else along with it.

Before she'd taken off her apron, she'd broken two of the wine glasses from the dinner set and an ice-cream bowl, at every breakage there was a moment's silence out on the balcony and in the living room, though no one dared come into the kitchen, they all had guessed from her expression and her behavior that the Flora Avgoustis who was on the phone to all and sundry ten days ago, waxing triumphant to her daughters, the Company, her neighbors and acquaintances that, at long last, her husband had capitulated, who had emptied the wardrobes and drawers from his, now, old-fashioned clothing and parted with one hundred thousand drachmas in order to present him to the world as she saw fit, who had bought him a walking stick, had dismantled his small office in the hall, useless in every way, had at the final hour gotten cold feet as if she realized that her previous troubles had said goodbye and appointed replacements. Practical matters were the least of it and she knew from experience that people can't hide behind those indefinitely, especially at their age, when neither is away at their business but they muddle daily through a joint existence, assessing the costs of their pact.

So, then, Mimis at home with them, with her, every day from now on, from morning till night, permanently.

How did he feel about it? she wondered. And how did their son?

In order to see his top-secret mission through, Andonis had trained himself to serve the ship officers and scrub out their shitty toilets but, in the course of the three-month journey, he, too, had been initiated to the trials of connecting face-to-face, to the breath of other men right up against you, to the straight-forward silences, the straightforward words, even those few and far between, the well-aimed emotions that carry the smell, taste and sound of presence rather than the echoes of distance.

Now, he wasn't on the balcony with the men, soon as the meal was over, he got hold of a yellow canvas bag and split, to who knows where.

Flora Avgoustis tied up the rubbish bag with a piece of string and had a look in her cupboards and her overflowing fridge. For now, the only decision she could bear making was about dinner, something light, maybe white rice and yogurt, though some feta cheese and a bit of fruit might be better, as something was holding her back from reentering the married-woman-slaving-over-the-stove scenario. The first watermelons were in season, not giving a hoot about long term marriage blunders or any kind of deep-frozen disasters, day by day, they would infiltrate everywhere and take every house by storm, the glorious Greece of summer would again wear its diadem and jewels, watermelon rind and watermelon seeds.

And now a cigarette, urgently.

***

Mitso Avgoustis, I will always love your arm, if you'll let me remind you of my funny letters.

I'm leaving large spaces and using a felt tip pen, so you can see the letters with the magnifying glass.

If you change your mind and come back, whenever you come back, I'll be a devoted fan of your old age and your guide, the blind man's flagship.

I'll take you by car to Parnitha, so that that the mountain tops can breathe down on you, and to the fields around Megara, so that the cicadas, of which you've been so deprived, can sing their hymns for you.

I will leaf through your postcards and describe to you your trips and everything you saw, from the giant Christ with the thirty-foot-long arms in Rio, to Nairobi's beautiful Parliament House in Kenya. And I will believe your every word when you're pulling my leg saying that, in Canada, the birds of prey catch river trout, have their meal and throw the leftovers on the treetops so that the forests, too, get fed.

We will shoot the breeze so that we can get our courage up, together.

We will put on some Moscholiou when silence is in order.

Don't feel ashamed of me on account of how you've acted. I, myself, cast my own anchor to the bottom of your life. It's beneath me for you to take all the blame. I, myself, made sure I stayed on the shelf.

And don't let your eyes get you down. In the past, you've seen a lot of the perfect Litsa, and I, too, have had my fill of you when you were strong and sound. It's more than enough for us.

I'll now describe for you, in my own way, your son, whom you haven't seen since he was ten. You've touched him, you've hugged him, you've smelled him. You will know that he turned out very tall and ever so thin and you'll have heard his voice on the ship, a word here and a word there. His dear eyes, tearful or not, are worth a great deal, eyes of the Avgoustis clan, same with his gentle smile that quiets the nerves. He's turned out into a terrific lad and he struggled all by himself. You incommunicado and the misses busy percolating. I've watched him closely and I've taken his measure. Your guileless boy, when he hears about orgies, blushes.

He paid me several visits, we had us a nice time. He

spotted *Souvadivadol* for me, where your last boss, in his youth, crashed the ship and within three months, the corals had eaten half of it up. It's in the Maldives, he said, further out that I figured in my poem. He promised to show me the song verses he wrote when he was younger, once he translates them into Greek, because I do, every so often, like to chew on half-page poems, swallowing one down like a candy or a pill.

He's going on an excursion, to a village up in the mountains. He doesn't know when he'll be coming back, don't know if I'll see him again.

He came today to get the letter. He truly cares for you, he's forgotten how you'd forgotten all about him, his spleen has fizzled out, although that's more than you deserve.

He brought two dripper hoses, eighty plastic drippers, pliers, and a screwdriver and installed an automatic watering system for me, much needed.

While I'm finishing the letter, he's in the garden, walking on his hands with his feet up in the air. He's doing the rounds of the flower bed, checking to see if the drippers are dripping and he's calling things out to me. That the cactuses need to be tied up and that mice have gotten into the strawberries.

I love you, means I count you in.

Whether you come or not, I'm going to be fine.

You, too, keep well, whether you return or not.

***

Main hall with a balcony that looks out onto the fir trees. Small kitchen balcony that looks out onto the vineyards. White walls, brown casings. Number of rooms three, plus a kitchenette, fully equipped, plus a bathroom, small but with its own heating system. The house was done up, though not resurrected.

That particular armchair, the bulky purple thing to your right, has buried four old women and the camping bed in front of the window's heard three death rattles. Have no fear, you'll be sleeping in the next room, in the double bed I bought that five years ago and nobody's died in it yet.

Kyriaki village, in Viotia.

Everyone in the neighborhood was expecting him to bring them a bride, Siakandaris brought them his captain. He feasted him on embroidered tablecloths, laid him to sleep upon his dowry sheets, and the villagers looked upon the washing put out to dry and, inadvertently, searched the old man's fingers for the heirloom ring of the deceased mother of the cook, who was at long last rendered free and motherless, seven years ago.

A very, very long time ago, in his rare shore leaves, the good fellow had brought a lass or two back to the village, his mother had thought the Korean girl was like a sickly newborn kitten trying in vain to open its eyes, and the girl from Crete was way too shifty-eyed to be a proper match for her poor boy. The poor boy had gone to sea straight after the army, so as to extend his service away from his base for as long as possible and get as far away as he could from the heavy-handed Despina. After completing his term in the army's artillery division he went job hunting, going wherever he was sent by this person and that, to Kolonaki for a position as a doorman, to Nea Smirni as a gardener, to Faliro as a waiter.

About then, worn down by the interminable rounds and the dead-ends, while eating at a Pireas tavern the daily souvlaki of youth, bachelorhood and a meager wallet, he overheard two loudmouths at the next table talking about the cooking on ship, and that was that.

He may have been unhappy on his first ships, but he was recompensed with Avgoustis. Inseparable, consequently, on the shore as well. Andonis had driven them to Kyriaki in the

Fiat Punto that very afternoon after the pig roast. At Pireas, his father hadn't even emptied his suitcase, he couldn't find anything to do in the house, the shadow of a husband, father and grandfather, by the time he put pressure on the reluctant cook and made the deal with him, none of the household's females put up a resistance and it wasn't because they were looking forward to being rid of him. They assumed the old man went AWOL on account of his shock at docking on the truths of dry land, he was justified in part, legal at sea, an outlaw on the shore.

He needed a few days to make up his mind and come back to surrender himself and his cat.

The few days, though, turned into a great number of days, then weeks and Mitsos Avgoustis stayed put in Kyriaki, at peace. At peace, in a manner of speaking because, though he no longer heard the thud-thudding of the ship's engine, or the ear-splitting sound of the mineral ore's crashing into the holds, he did hear dozens of electric saws from down below, cutting into firewood the aged almond trees and the firs that had been done in by the snowstorms and, moreover, the joyous braying of the adolescent boys on scooters and the machine-gun calls of girls' names in the cafeterias: Evas, Lenas, Annas, Chryssas.

Gerassimos Siakandaris nudged him into frequent outings to the cafeterias, where he located the subject matter for his sallies into many a picturesque description.

–The land has its rewards, too, not a day goes by without catching sight on the sidewalk of two pretty calves leading you along and of waist-long wavy hair bobbing around a short, tight-fitting sweater.

It was pleasant for Mitsos Avgoustis to no longer be hearing about the rattails of the beetroot, the glass antennae of the snails and the Christian thorns of the artichoke, to see in his fifty-five year old friend a dreamer renewed, who, despite his long record of failures, was courageously exploring the substance of a couple of matchmakings, without insisting, no matter what, on a Marianthi, the name of his dreams.

—I'm after a widow with letters of recommendation from at least two ex-husbands and medical certificates by cardiologists and neurologists about the state of her health, he'd say to the matchmakers, who enjoyed his company because he was witty and the captain's company as well, even though he hardly spoke: *few words are sugar, none are honey*, was his motto.

At all events, if the unusual-looking, longhaired grandpa wanted to, and if he wasn't paying up his captain's pension elsewhere, an Albanian woman, or girl, could be found for him, too, their village drew a lot of foreigners in need, human beings are prone to despair and to having dreams no matter where they are, old seamen, who've been on well-worn trails far and wide, have a lot of evidence to this effect stashed away in the books of their lives.

Mitsos Avgoustis knew this well, the guileless Kyriaki in Viotia wasn't to blame, his footsteps followed trustingly those of Gerassimos along the narrow streets, he was almost getting used to trotting with a walking stick, and in taverns and fetes he would lick his chops over the sweetness in the simple words of some villager who hadn't been burdened by the anger of the cities and the vehemence of the new times. Still, his very own despair wouldn't be long in coming.

Day by day, the more Siakandaris felt weary and blocked by the responsibility, the more he demonstrated an excess of zeal in his hospitality, all day long on standby, a one-man public relations committee for the captain to the local upper class, narrating his miraculous feats at sea, inviting to the house group after group of local teachers and their prize students to meet the unsinkable man, despotically overseeing Maritsa, who was liaising with the neighborhood cats for the sake of begetting pumpkin-colored heirs, taking the blind man to behold the mountain sides, the mountain tops, the brooks, the vineyards.

No rain in May, the grapes are on their way, the local sages used to say, the mid-June rainfall didn't bother them, on the contrary, as soon as the sun was out again after the rain, their native parts showed up all the prettier with misty gardens and misty hills.

The day was getting fuller, the night was emptying out.

The two men would get back to the house, a boiled egg and a slice of watermelon in their belly, a couple of words about their fathers, the one dear departed had come back from Asia Minor half drunk, along with twenty-seven cats, because all they had to eat were the dark grapes used for the making of dry, brusco wine, the other dear departed, worn to the bone by the fields; on cold nights, they would stare at the sparks in the fireplace, one by one, and blame the couple of lemon—or damson-tree logs for burning too quickly.

And after that, the dialogue halted abruptly, time for the news report, three Palestinians dead in the Gaza Strip, a rise in the price of petrol in international markets, then silence and, finally, just before going to bed, they again dived back into the same old same old, brought back to their nostrils every ship's distinctive smell, started on the shoal of pigfish, catfish and angelfish of each crew, and for about half an hour, were full of murmurs and exhalations, like godforsaken bachelors braiding their sighs into ropes.

Seventeen years ago and fifteen years ago, the cook had invited Avgoustis, bring the wife, too, and the whole family, to put them up and show them each and every beautiful spot around the village and up in the mountains. Now he had to describe those without getting in return the laudatory exclamations which his homeland's natural beauty deserved and, partly because he'd imagined his soulmate's visit to Kyriaki in a completely different light, partly because he was still over-wrought by the condition of his friend's eyes, all these years imprisoned in darkness and what lay in the future, how do we move on from here, he put the issue on the table.

—So that I'm able to say to you, just look at that monument they put up, the traffic, the shops, look at those swallow nests, look at them handsome lasses, make up your mind about it and go see a doctor, no miracle's going to happen but at least you'll be able to make out the photographs.

The night before, on the veranda of the house, again to the sound of a Greek movie on television, since Mitsos couldn't see to read the subtitles of foreign films and Gerassimos couldn't read them a-loud in time, during the add break, the old man gave the cook a photograph.

Andonis, with an almost incomprehensible generosity had gone back time and again to Litsa's house, seven or eight times in all within three weeks, she was alive, she was fine, though alone, and the captain was fit to burst that she'd lost every chance of finally getting her life together, so that he wouldn't have her fate on his head forever, as if at sixty it would be easy to do what he hadn't allowed to happen when she was twenty-five, when Litsa was a wet dream on legs, and he, a genius at self-promotion, had robbed her blind of her youth and beauty.

He'd grown wistful again and wanted to talk of her, her tastiness, the roundness of her form and her loyalty, to adver-tize his everlasting love and defame himself over his dishon-esty, but, first, he had to tell the story to the cook, retrospec-tive explanations once again, did Flora know who the unsur-passable creature was, what she was like, and show him a photo of her.

—What I'm seeing is the statue of a seated young man tak-ing a thorn out of sole of his foot, Siakandaris said disappoint-edly. Some small confusion with the photos, the statue in the park in Sydney was among several others of Litsa in her gar-den, in the middle of fragrant blooms, lilies, cactus or against the background of her pomegranate tree in flower, the source, in times past, of the ship's supplies for the memorial services for the dead.

Gerassimos slowly thumbed through a small pack of photographs, spread them out as if he was playing solitaire, his comments, her hair is dyed, here it's dyed a different color, yellow dahlias, sunflowers, she knows a thing or two about gardens, you're a fool, and, finally, after some consideration and after reading some of the dedications on the back of the pictures, angered and crushed, he ripped his idol to shreds, what happened to you, you scoundrel, to put a woman such as this on ice for thirty-five years?

Life likes a muddle, spills over with lawless trials, with needless tension. Brings two people close, at no mean cost, but doesn't let them stay put. Sometimes, what's more, the appointment cards are switched as if by a hand no one can see which, for the sake of play, shuffles liaisons and, so, the ones that are meant for us, the humble underdogs, end up with others who are unsuitable and they suffer, the poor things, these were Gerassimos' thoughts, half of them voiced, the sender of the pomegranates and of the patriotic lollipops, the faithful Litsa with the orderly yard, the unpretentious smile of devotion, the honeyed cheeks and the wonderful love handles, proof of her delighting in the cooking pot, would be just perfect for him, nevertheless.

–This woman does good just with her eyes, he said, reached out his hand and squeezed the captain's arm in a manly gesture, her eyes, refreshing and delectable, of inestimable value, they are your lucky draw.

Next day at noon, a third place was set at the table with the tiny smelt fish and the wild amaranth, Andonis had come, a messenger from Elefsina, carrying with him Litsa's letter.

The operation took place at the General State hospital twelve days later, summer surgeries had a lighter schedule, the son-in-law from the socialist party was able to secure a connection that helped. All the Avgoustis clan were present, in shifts, without too much excess emotion, but definitely on a different wavelength by order of Andonis, the daughters, in particular, who had turned softhearted, a family that had decided once and for all to clear each other, and themselves, of all blame, to stop revving their wrath.

***

Well, Mitso, I love your arm, for starters, as I do every time you are here. It's been ten days and you haven't strolled down to ancient Elefsina and to ancient Litsa, my boy, you didn't come today either, it's nighttime now and I'm not expecting you, but I'll pretend you're sitting in the chair.

I really like your being at home. Watching your big eyes that overflow with youth. The locks of your hair nearly weightless. Your feet tracing pretty footsteps around the room.

I made you a jar of jam.

The peaches are falling, if you would like, afterwards, I'll get all the ones up in the high branches down for you. And, I was beating for the sake of the beating, I don't play drums that much anymore, I've no talent.

You weren't saying much, I wouldn't give you a chance to say much. Two or three phrases in all, at each visit. I've brought you cakes, on one occasion, better put the box from the pastry shop in the fridge so the ice cream doesn't melt.

I'm looking at you in the photo with your father on the ship, you had your braid cut, you said and then you went and found him longhaired like some rock singer, which makes me wonder how on earth the two of you make sense of one another.

The sea is standing by me, the sea is a calling, the calling turns to an ache, the aching turns to sickness, Mitsos will have no clue, among other things, about how a father talks to his son and about some old words and phrases that will hardly mean anything nowadays to those much younger in age.

Colored photographs don't turn yellow. On Easter day Mitsos and the Atlantic in their formal blue suits and on the back, my beloved Litsa, against forgetfulness.

Mitsos and the cook in a red taxi in Hong Kong and on the back, my beloved Litsa, against forgetfulness.

Mitsos and the calves in the lush green fields of Argentina and, on the back, the same, beloved Litsa, against forgetfulness.

Very few times in my life have I wished for the salvation of a pill that would make me forget him, a little every day. Finally, though, I say thank God they haven't come up with such a pill, and may they never come up with it, even if he doesn't answer this time either, to this, my last letter.

For the first time in years, I spent the afternoon shuffling through his pictures, over one hundred, thrown loose in the drawer. The sinner's images my holy icons, pieces of cardboard on which my faith shone and his forgetfulness shimmered. I never set them out on the furniture, never hung them on the walls, so that strangers wouldn't ask who that is. Only my relatives and my childhood years are framed in the hall. And I like how we have all turned yellow and to see that black-and-white photographs are no longer a stark black-and-white, their black's no longer alive, not scary, in time, the picture frames have faded, too, and all the dark colors on the wall have now sweetly blended with one another, in their extra-faded version.

Large olivegreen-brown frame and gray-brown family.

Gray-black frame and gray-gold couple, the parents.

Oval cinnamon-brown frame and dark brown woman, my aunt.

Gray-yellow little frame and silver-black baby, me.
Ash-green frame and black-green girl, me again.

The necklace I'm wearing is a cut-off golden hand, the
wrist and palm, the five fingers holding a bright-green opal
tear, all together the size of an okra. You'll see it when
you come next, you brought it to me. It was in the yellow canvas bag with the gifts he bought for me in the last
years, but never sent.

I put it on and feel calm. And listen to what I remember.

Sunday morning, fall, 1979. I take a plastic bag and go
out from the house. The streets are almost empty, without
the crowds of workers. I go to the sidewalks where olive
trees are planted. I've noticed from some days ago that
they are loaded, the olives are dropping on the pavement
and going to waste.

So I gather them from the bent branches and slowly
the bag fills, a mix of little ones for crushing and fleshy
ones for cutting. I'll separate them afterwards and prepare
them for the first time, never done it before, the ones from
the supermarket are just fine. As I stand under the last
tree and reach up to pick the last little olive, just the size
of the tear held in the fingers of the necklace, all of a
sudden I feel so full, so pleased, only the week before I've
enjoyed another three-day cruise of your father's in my
sheets and I instantly forget I'm forty years old and have
never walked down a tropical path, and I forget the rest,
too. I recognize what's happening to me at that moment
and it is, beyond any doubt, happiness. At peace and
utterly certain I'm wishing, let me die now, right now, right
this instant, now, God, there is a God, because I don't want
to leave life whining and complaining, but with enthusiasm.

One other time I was blessed to live a moment like this,
twice sentenced to death. At the age of fifty-one, the day

before St. Dimitrios, late noon. I'm tidying up my place for his name day. He, of course, has disappeared from my life. This is the first year without a hairdressing salon. I have no Demeters or wives of Dimitris coming to me to do their hair, while I'm stuffing myself with the cream puffs and chocolate fingers they brought along to celebrate their name day, me, too, in secret celebration and perpetual anticipation of his arrival.

In the yard, I bend down with the pan and sweep up the dry leaves. For the first time, something comes over me, as if I feel sorry for them, as if I am mourning them. Litsa, pull yourself together, I say to myself, think of poor autumn. Every year losing its billions of leaves.

High up, a tiny little sun in its appointed place. The house inside all clean. A few chrysanthemums in the vase. Some killer liqueur chocolates in the bowl. On the radio, as if by request, Mitsias signing the one about my girl in Elefsina, I have the album, a gift from him.

I eat half the chocolates at an even pace, many happy returns, Mr. Invisible, with every new one I pop in my mouth just as the notes of each new song are starting to roll.

I sing along with all the choice personages on radio, no matter if it's Charoula, or Mitropanos or Galani, all on National Radio 2.

The first chilly day, the first day when a person is so lucky as to put down the rugs again and turn the heater on, is a great day. I get strength. I feel filled with home, with fall, with man, with songs.

I am happy and fearless. And at about this time I again say the infamous, come on, let me die now. Before tomorrow dawns and I'm caught again in some delirium of sorrow, roped into some circle of sobs.

The moment and the way of saying goodbye to life are important; I ponder this as I watch on the news the wars, the car accidents, the shipwrecks. I'm certain that even if some-

one's in a deep coma, there is a cog that starts up at the moment of death and makes noise inside the body, so that the person can realize that everything's coming to an end.

We all have the right to be overwhelmed with our death. Some thing must definitely take place, it might be a minute at the most, but what a minute, the last of each and everyone of us. At some point the scientists will surely investigate.

Meanwhile, the years pass normally and I eat and drink and see around me and further away and I listen from a distance and I live.

Let my living go on, I think.

Is it half past ten, already? Listen to a trick, it might come in handy in an hour of need. Before I go to sleep, I choose a pretty dream and take it to bed with me.

***

Lasers and artificial retinas. The cataract was one thing, but the slow detaching due to the post-traumatic glaucoma, a souvenir from being hit by lightening on the last pilgrimage to Mount Athos, had slowly, through the years, worn the optic nerve away.

Vision in the right eye went up from two-tenths to four and in the left, from three to five, just enough to approximately train on Laura's cheeks for two kisses and on the hands of the son-in-law, the doctor and the cook to successively squeeze them with a little, a lot of immeasurable gratitude.

He let them think that the few additional tenths of vision were a great deal and well worth the trial of the operation, didn't let them know that they weren't worth the anxious expectation for some real difference, or the envelope with the enclosed five hundred thousand in bills.

He made do with the little extra summer light, the slightly upgraded vibrancy of colors, the shadow of his son's profile and the shadow of his son's hands on the wheels of the Fiat, as he was starting up the engine.

Siakandaris had gone back to Kyriaki, something was cooking with a well kept and even tempered forty-five-year-old, when it's all said and done, life is to be had one bite at a time. If things bottomed out this time, too, he'd enjoy the golden harvest on a regime of grapes, would drop in for a visit and would sail again with another company for a couple more years.

The news of ATHOS III was as expected, with the exception of Dachtylas and Birbilis, the posts of the Greeks were taken up by cheap Filipinos, and the Greeks were whiling away the time unemployed on land, a couple of them had dropped in at Vekrelis' for lemon chicken, he was happy as a lark and they were down on their luck and agonizing over their lack of prospects.

The Union of Greek Shipowners reappeared with suggestions for a reception in his honor at the Pireas Marine Hall under the auspices of the Ministry of Merchant Marine, an exhibition of seascapes by a shipowning woman artist, a documentary by another shipowner and a retired emeritus professor as a speaker who would expound on the subject, *Dimitrios Avgoustis, the untiring Greek in the service of the naval spirit.* They'd already printed the invitations.

–Shove them up your backside, his answer, he wasn't going to let them chew him up, his own private medal, on the inside of his chest, was the company of the swell.

Flora was away on a group tour in Egypt, calm and probably relieved, and was making her annual plans for two week-long overseas trips with the same troupe of cultured and chivalrous bon vivants in their early sixties. Mimis had left her the two bankbooks with eight-digit deposits, always a gentleman when it came to finances. The marriage had ended with a great deal of delay, because she and her husband had bowed their heads and waited for time to solve their problem.

If only their Lily got the message in time.

The Fiat was speeding towards Elefsina. It was Wednesday, 23 July 1997, thirty-eight years after Mitsos Avgoustis had seen Litsa Tsichli for the first time and twelve since he'd seen her last. In his youth, he had loved her torrentially, without courage, with the passing years he'd grown to love her ever more deeply, each day of his life, with unflagging remembrance and staunch guilt.

Now, his own child was taking him to her, who would have thought it. And who would have expected such courageous forgiveness from the two persons he had harmed.

Andonis was totally anxious while driving, he'd be silent for a ten-minute stretch and then prattle, laughing almost, about how the ocean's silent wave, the swell, had also planted trouble in his mind and he was probably going to look into becoming a sound technician, a Peeping Tom of sound waves, setting up ruses by turning the volume up and down, mixing together three whispers and a bang, the crashing down of the storm as aftermath to hysterical cries of women, and a tambourine accompanying Maritsa's mewling, come what may he was taking the cat with him for company in the bachelor flat he was looking to rent.

–You, I can't deny the cat to, the old man had said to him.

Meanwhile, the sea-worthy cat was continuing its vacation at Kyriaki, spoilt rotten by the local kids and happily compromised with the land, the houses, the cars, the carnal pleasures in the fields. The fragrant expanses of ocean were a thing permanently assigned to his past.

Litsa Tsichli was waiting for them in the middle of the street, a target hard to miss with the canary-yellow wrap and the cockscombs in her hands, unsuitable for a bouquet but the dark purple, the richest color of all the garden's blooms at this time of year, whit white gladiolas and white daisies.

She ushered them in the yard with a welcome, as if she had-n't seen them for a week at most. She showed them in the living room, stood till they were seated, sat herself down as well and took to staring persistently at the furniture, at her pillows and her linen towels, as if she was an indiscreet visitor at some-one else's house.

And how to lift her eyes up to Mitsos, straight away, and face the one who had been missing from that place for all these years and believe, moreover, that he had showed up at last and had lit the first cigarette. The lighter's snap and the smell of the smoke were a good start.

She took him the ashtray and didn't go back to her seat, she sat close to him, a foot and a half away from his desirable arm, which she imagined naked, without the jacket sleeve, stretched across the pillow and, of course, upon it, her head, like old times. Her silence didn't last long.

–Look at your hair! she chastised him and caressed it.

In a flash, she recalled the stupefied twenty-year-old sailor he'd sent her many years ago to dye his hair, so that his mother wouldn't see he'd gone white his very first year at sea.

Her captain had silver wavy folds down to the shoulders, his insurance stamps for the hardship and hazard of fifty-eight years at sea. Tomorrow, in her own good time, she would lay out her implements and spruce his head of hair, straighten a carnation in his buttonhole, take him into the kitchen among the maiden ferns of his youth. I've no family at all left in Trikala, so I, too, come from Asia Minor a little, after the event, on account of you, she'd tell him.

–Are you guys up for a galaktoboureko? Andonis asked in a very low voice, they didn't hear, didn't answer him, he volunteered on his own to play hostess and went off for plates and refreshments.

The two of them were left in the living room and it was now Mitsos's turn to slowly cast his gaze about the room.

–But you can't see, she laughed and took it from there, unstoppable now, this morning as soon as Andonis called to say that Australia is no go and that you'll be sailing home, I went around and put the chairs and tables in their old place so that you wouldn't stumble. Everything's exactly as you left it, except for my good self, overflowing flesh and wrinkles, and lucky for me you can't make out the details.

Avgoustis put his hand on her arm, his wedding ring's gone, she thought and couldn't watch enough as that splendid finger, without the other woman's gold hook, slid along with his whole palm towards her own. As soon as he squeezed her fingers, a moan left his chest, forerunner of the sobs that followed wracking his whole body, which was awkward and unfamiliar with exercises of this sort.

Whether these were tears of apology or powerlessness, Litsa didn't like them one bit. She didn't want him remorseful or beaten down like a dog. She had made her decision to have him after thinking it through, not out of pity but love, she did intend to fight for it tooth and claw, but from the reunion she nevertheless had expectations of enthusiasm and an uplifted spirit. Straight off, she'd sized him up to be melancholy and scared but she was certain that if she handled him gently, Mitsos would locate his know-how for navigating on land and, soon enough, everything would flow along on a wellspring of garden, garlic spaghetti and songs.

She rose, as if on brand-new knees, sauntered over to the record player and put on the old hits, tried-and-true between the sheets and through all the broken promises.

The bouzouki music and the galaktoboureko disarmed him, when times get rough, people look for something to hold onto and plenty of pretexts can always be found.

Mitsias was right in there, leading, a burning question about the tsakma baboons who lay about placidly on the rocks of South Africa all day eating muscles, then a requisite mention of the pension sums, his and hers, a little white alcohol for the hands, because the cockscombs made him itchy, a monologue delivered by Litsa in one long breathless stream of words. Whereas she used to sleep like a log without daring to dream, recently, starting in April, she'd given in to the indulgence of dreaming, at one time wandering on icebergs like a bear, at another, dipping in and out of the tide like a crab, yet another time she was a coral herself in the midst of other corals suckling on multicolored shores, and, lastly, a charming mini-crisis over the burnt smell from the kitchen, she pulled out the forgotten tray with the stuffed tomatoes turned to charcoal, no matter, worse things have happened.

At around nine, when Andonis finished watering the plants outside and looked in through the window, his father had taken off his shoes and was resting his legs on a footstool, a sign that everything was coming along just fine. Litsa by his side, victorious at last, was prompting him, making sure her wayward traveler hadn't forgotten the words to the song, *I took to the streets one night and was asking people I knew, about the girl of mine in Elefsina I once loved.*

The gorgeous bedraggled gal, phosphorescent with love and patience, speaking or fumbling through the language of sweetness, foreign to the Avgoustis men, had won the son over as well, his heart was acclimatizing to pleasant things and synchronizing to the triumphant drumbeat in his chest.

Still, there was something that overshadowed his joy. His father would have time to render justice to the old affairs, but he might not live for very long. He wasn't cut out for the land, inaction and serenity.

He walked out to the car's trunk, brought in the old man's suitcase, left it on the hallway and made a phone call. After that, he took out two plates and napkins to the table on the veranda, it was cool, there were stars, cicadas, the works.

–I ordered you a pizza, he said, and bid them goodnight.

*

It was about midnight, the two had had a bite to eat some while ago, had drunk their beer, had listened to what songs there were to be listened to, enjoyed the jasmine's luscious fragrance, Litsa had freshened her admiration for his eyes and how their blue was shown to advantage by his blue suit, had watched the veins in his neck dancing like seaweed, and made up her mind once and for all that she'd been right to fall for him in her youth, his beauty and princely sadness, may they be blessed, could still bring a woman to her knees.

She saw him feeling on the table for his lighter, almost rushed to light his cigarette, a good thing she didn't. At that same moment she thought she wasn't going to treat him like an invalid nor would she be impatient for those things to get done quickly that he could do more slowly on his own. She wasn't going to glorify him and she wasn't going to pamper him.

The last cigarette of the evening in ten drags, took Mitsos Avgoustis on a round of the millions of nautical miles and the one hundred round-the-world trips, until he arrived at the sheltered bay of the house in Elefsina.

—My good sir, you haven't come here to get out of action and grow rusty, we're not going to turn into piles of useless junk, you are to be my captain forever, Litsa had told him earlier smiling, as if she'd already studied the charts of the seas that lay ahead, already embarked on the new day-to-day.

So, putting out the cigarette, he gave her a set of coordinates for what he was more or less, and rather unavoidably, going to be spouting in the days to come.

—Last night, I spent the whole night at Dar es Salam.

She, at long last admitted into his swell, registered the signal, retired wireless operator, as much as hairdresser, that she was, and twinkled enthusiastically.

—Myself, captain, I spent it in Souvadivadol. She got up, it hasn't been easy learning to correctly pronounce such a tongue twister, she said, cleared the table and chuckling in advance for the guaranteed fiasco, intoned her pathetic little poem, not the whole thing, just half.

My Souvadivadol, distant and sweet
which I'll never get to see
you might be Indian or you might Persian be,
but you're every foreign land to me
all in one, in glorious unity.

Mitsos finally cracked his first smile in the house, he bent looking for her hands to offer congratulations, missed his mark, got his fingers all messy with the leftover pizza.

–When I see you absent minded I'll back off, so you can travel at your own speed as much as you like, with whoever you want, anywhere at all, far away, Litsa took care to mend the situation, slipping a napkin into his hand. I'll keep sailing around Elefsina, she went on, I can navigate it pretty well.

She had found things out by docking, during her walks, at the chimneys, the eucalyptus trees on the seaside road, the bakery, the newsstand, the pharmacist, the supermarket and by riding the car into the surrounding area, Nea Peramo and Pachi Megaron, a world not at all small, it turned out, more than enough, as Litsa calculated with gratitude and confidently took things even further.

And I really like a lot, more than anything else, to be on my way home carrying a cauliflower. To have almost arrived and to see, from twenty yards away, the two acacias standing in their place without fail, thank God and right at the edge of the sidewalk, the squirting cucumber bush also in its appointed place.

About the Author

Ioanna Karystiani was born on the island of Crete and now lives in Athens. She is the author of three novels, including *The Jasmine Isle* (Europa Editions 2006), a collection of short stories, and the screenplay for *Estrella mi vida*, directed by Costa Gavras. She was awarded the Greek state prize and the Athenian Academy prize for her first novel, *The Women of Andros*, and the Diavazo literature prize for *The Jasmine Isle*.

Swell won the Greek National Book Award for best novel in 2007.

Carmine Abate
Between Two Seas
"A moving portrayal of generational continuity."
—*Kirkus*
224 pp • $14.95 • 978-1-933372-40-2

Salwa Al Neimi
The Proof of the Honey
"Al Neimi announces the end of a taboo in the Arab world:
that of *sex!*"
—*Reuters*
144 pp • $15.00 • 978-1-933372-68-6

Alberto Angela
A Day in the Life of Ancient Rome
"Fascinating and accessible."
—*Il Giornale*
392 pp • $16.00 • 978-1-933372-71-6

Muriel Barbery
The Elegance of the Hedgehog
"Gently satirical, exceptionally winning and inevitably bittersweet."
—Michael Dirda, *The Washington Post*
336 pp • $15.00 • 978-1-933372-60-0

Gourmet Rhapsody
"In the pages of this book, Barbery shows off her finest gift: lightness."
—*La Repubblica*
176 pp • $15.00 • 978-1-933372-95-2

Stefano Benni
Margherita Dolce Vita
"A modern fable...hilarious social commentary."—*People*
240 pp • $14.95 • 978-1-933372-20-4

Timeskipper
"Benni again unveils his Italian brand of magical realism."
—*Library Journal*
400 pp • $16.95 • 978-1-933372-44-0

Romano Bilenchi
The Chill
120 pp • $15.00 • 978-1-933372-90-7

Massimo Carlotto
The Goodbye Kiss
"A masterpiece of Italian noir."
—*Globe and Mail*
160 pp • $14.95 • 978-1-933372-05-1

Death's Dark Abyss
"A remarkable study of corruption and redemption."
—*Kirkus* (starred review)
160 pp • $14.95 • 978-1-933372-18-1

The Fugitive
"[Carlotto is] the reigning king of Mediterranean noir."
—*The Boston Phoenix*
176 pp • $14.95 • 978-1-933372-25-9

(with Marco Videtta)
Poisonville
"The business world as described by Carlotto and Videtta
in *Poisonville* is frightening as hell."
—*La Repubblica*
224 pp • $15.00 • 978-1-933372-91-4

Francisco Coloane
Tierra del Fuego
"Coloane is the Jack London of our times."—Alvaro Mutis
192 pp • $14.95 • 978-1-933372-63-1

Giancarlo De Cataldo
The Father and the Foreigner
"A slim but touching noir novel from one of Italy's best writers
in the genre."—*Quaderni Noir*
144 pp • $15.00 • 978-1-933372-72-3

Shashi Deshpande
The Dark Holds No Terrors
"[Deshpande is] an extremely talented storyteller."—*Hindustan Times*
272 pp • $15.00 • 978-1-933372-67-9

Helmut Dubiel
Deep In the Brain: Living with Parkinson's Disease
"A book that begs reflection."—*Die Zeit*
144 pp • $15.00 • 978-1-933372-70-9

Steve Erickson
Zeroville
"A funny, disturbing, daring and demanding novel—Erickson's best."
—*The New York Times Book Review*
352 pp • $14.95 • 978-1-933372-39-6

Elena Ferrante
The Days of Abandonment
"The raging, torrential voice of [this] author is something rare."
—*The New York Times*
192 pp • $14.95 • 978-1-933372-00-6

Troubling Love
"Ferrante's polished language belies the rawness of her imagery."
—*The New Yorker*
144 pp • $14.95 • 978-1-933372-16-7

The Lost Daughter
"So refined, almost translucent."—*The Boston Globe*
144 pp • $14.95 • 978-1-933372-42-6

Jane Gardam
Old Filth
"Old Filth belongs in the Dickensian pantheon of memorable characters."
—*The New York Times Book Review*
304 pp • $14.95 • 978-1-933372-13-6

The Queen of the Tambourine
"A truly superb and moving novel."—*The Boston Globe*
272 pp • $14.95 • 978-1-933372-36-5

The People on Privilege Hill
"Engrossing stories of hilarity and heartbreak."—*Seattle Times*
208 pp • $15.95 • 978-1-933372-56-3

The Man in the Wooden Hat
"Here is a writer who delivers the world we live in…with memorable and moving skill."—*The Boston Globe*
240 pp • $15.00 • 978-1-933372-89-1

Alicia Giménez-Bartlett
Dog Day
"Delicado and Garzón prove to be one of the more engaging sleuth teams
to debut in a long time."—*The Washington Post*
320 pp • $14.95 • 978-1-933372-14-3

Prime Time Suspect
"A gripping police procedural."—*The Washington Post*
320 pp • $14.95 • 978-1-933372-31-0

Death Rites
"Petra is developing into a good cop, and her earnest efforts to assert her
authority...are worth cheering."—*The New York Times*
304 pp • $16.95 • 978-1-933372-54-9

Katharina Hacker
The Have-Nots
"Hacker's prose soars."—*Publishers Weekly*
352 pp • $14.95 • 978-1-933372-41-9

Patrick Hamilton
Hangover Square
"Patrick Hamilton's novels are dark tunnels of misery, loneliness, deceit,
and sexual obsession."—*New York Review of Books*
336 pp • $14.95 • 978-1-933372-06-

James Hamilton-Paterson
Cooking with Fernet Branca
"Irresistible!"—*The Washington Post*
288 pp • $14.95 • 978-1-933372-01-3

Amazing Disgrace
"It's loads of fun, light and dazzling as a peacock feather."
—*New York Magazine*
352 pp • $14.95 • 978-1-933372-19-8

Rancid Pansies
"Campy comic saga about hack writer and self-styled 'culinary genius'
Gerald Samper."—*Seattle Times*
288 pp • $15.95 • 978-1-933372-62-4

Seven-Tenths: The Sea and Its Thresholds
"The kind of book that, were he alive now, Shelley might have written."
—*Charles Spawson*
416 pp • $16.00 • 978-1-933372-69-3

Alfred Hayes
The Girl on the Via Flaminia
"Immensely readable."—*The New York Times*
164 pp • $14.95 • 978-1-933372-24-2

Jean-Claude Izzo
Total Chaos
"Izzo's Marseilles is ravishing."—*Globe and Mail*
256 pp • $14.95 • 978-1-933372-04-4

Chourmo
"A bitter, sad and tender salute to a place equally impossible to love
or leave."—*Kirkus* (starred review)
256 pp • $14.95 • 978-1-933372-17-4

Solea
"[Izzo is] a talented writer who draws from the deep, dark well of noir."
—*The Washington Post*
208 pp • $14.95 • 978-1-933372-30-3

The Lost Sailors
"Izzo digs deep into what makes men weep."—*Time Out New York*
272 pp • $14.95 • 978-1-933372-35-8

A Sun for the Dying
"Beautiful, like a black sun, tragic and desperate."—*Le Point*
224 pp • $15.00 • 978-1-933372-59-4

Gail Jones
Sorry
"Jones's gift for conjuring place and mood rarely falters."
—*Times Literary Supplement*
240 pp • $15.95 • 978-1-933372-55-6

Matthew F. Jones
Boot Tracks
"A gritty action tale."—*The Philadelphia Inquirer*
208 pp • $14.95 • 978-1-933372-11-2

Ioanna Karystiani
The Jasmine Isle
"A modern Greek tragedy about love foredoomed and family life."
—*Kirkus*
288 pp • $14.95 • 978-1-933372-10-5

Swell
"Karystiani movingly pays homage to the sea and those who live from it."
—*La Repubblica*
256 pp • $15.00 • 978-1-933372-98-3

Gene Kerrigan
The Midnight Choir
"The lethal precision of his closing punches leave quite a lasting mark."
—*Entertainment Weekly*
368 pp • $14.95 • 978-1-933372-26-6

Little Criminals
"A great story…relentless and brilliant."—*Roddy Doyle*
352 pp • $16.95 • 978-1-933372-43-3

Peter Kocan
Fresh Fields
"A stark, harrowing, yet deeply courageous work of immense power and magnitude."—*Quadrant*
304 pp • $14.95 • 978-1-933372-29-7

The Treatment and the Cure
"Kocan tells this story with grace and humor."—*Publishers Weekly*
256 pp • $15.95 • 978-1-933372-45-7

Helmut Krausser
Eros
"Helmut Krausser has succeeded in writing a great German
epochal novel."—*Focus*
352 pp • $16.95 • 978-1-933372-58-7

Amara Lakhous
Clash of Civilizations Over an Elevator in Piazza Vittorio
"Do we have an Italian Camus on our hands? Just possibly."
—*The Philadelphia Inquirer*
144 pp • $14.95 • 978-1-933372-61-7

Lia Levi
The Jewish Husband
"An exemplary tale of small lives engulfed in the vortex of history."
—*Il Messaggero*
224 pp • $15.00 • 978-1-933372-93-8

Carlo Lucarelli
Carte Blanche
"Lucarelli proves that the dark and sinister are better evoked when one
opts for unadulterated grit and grime."—*The San Diego Union-Tribune*
128 pp • $14.95 • 978-1-933372-15-0

The Damned Season
"De Luca…is a man both pursuing and pursued. And that makes him one
of the more interesting figures in crime fiction."
—*The Philadelphia Inquirer*
128 pp • $14.95 • 978-1-933372-27-3

Via delle Oche
"Delivers a resolution true to the series' moral relativism."—*Publishers Weekly*
160 pp • $14.95 • 978-1-933372-53-2

Edna Mazya
Love Burns
"Combines the suspense of a murder mystery with
the absurdity of a Woody Allen movie."—*Kirkus*
224 pp • $14.95 • 978-1-933372-08-2

Sélim Nassib
I Loved You for Your Voice
"Nassib spins a rhapsodic narrative out of the indissoluble
connection between two creative souls."—*Kirkus*
272 pp • $14.95 • 978-1-933372-07-5

The Palestinian Lover
"A delicate, passionate novel in which history and life
are inextricably entwined."
—*RAI Books*
192 pp • $14.95 • 978-1-933372-23-5

Amélie Nothomb
Tokyo Fiancée
"Intimate and honest…depicts perfectly a nontraditional romance."
—*Publishers Weekly*
160 pp • $15.00 • 978-1-933372-64-8

Valeria Parrella
For Grace Received
"A voice that is new, original, and decidedly unique."—*Rolling Stone* (Italy)
144 pp • $15.00 • 978-1-933372-94-5

Alessandro Piperno
The Worst Intentions
"A coruscating mixture of satire, family epic, Proustian meditation,
and erotomaniacal farce."—*The New Yorker*
320 pp • $14.95 • 978-1-933372-33-4

Boualem Sansal
The German Mujahid
"Terror, doubt, revolt, guilt, and despair—a surprising range of emotions
is admirably and convincingly depicted in this incredible novel."
—*L'Express* (France)
240 pp • $15.00 • 978-1-933372-92-1

Eric-Emmanuel Schmitt
The Most Beautiful Book in the World
"Eight novellas, parables on the idea of a future, filled with redeeming
optimism."—*Lire Magazine*
192 pp • $15.00 • 978-1-933372-74-7

Domenico Starnone
First Execution
"Starnone's books are small theatres of action,
both physical and psychological."—*L'Espresso* (Italy)
176 pp • $15.00 • 978-1-933372-66-2

Joel Stone
The Jerusalem File
"Joel Stone is a major new talent."—*Cleveland Plain Dealer*
160 pp • $15.00 • 978-1-933372-65-5

Benjamin Tammuz
Minotaur
"A novel about the expectations and compromises that humans create for
themselves."—*The New York Times*
192 pp • $14.95 • 978-1-933372-02-0

Chad Taylor
Departure Lounge
"There's so much pleasure and bafflement to be derived from this thriller."
—*The Chicago Tribune*
176 pp • $14.95 • 978-1-933372-09-9

Roma Tearne
Mosquito
"Vividly rendered...Wholly satisfying."—*Kirkus*
304 pp • $16.95 • 978-1-933372-57-0

Bone China
"Tearne deftly reveals the corrosive effects of civil strife on private lives and
the redemptiveness of art."—*The Guardian*
400 pp • $16.00 • 978-1-933372-75-4

Christa Wolf
One Day a Year: 1960-2000
"Remarkable!"—*The New Yorker*
640 pp • $16.95 • 978-1-933372-22-8

Edwin M. Yoder Jr.
Lions at Lamb House
"Yoder writes with such wonderful manners, learning, and detachment."
—*William F. Buckley, Jr.*
256 pp • $14.95 • 978-1-933372-34-1

Michele Zackheim
Broken Colors
"A beautiful novel."—*Library Journal*
320 pp • $14.95 • 978-1-933372-37-2

Children's Illustrated Fiction

Altan
Here Comes Timpa
48 pp • $14.95 • 978-1-933372-28-0

Timpa Goes to the Sea
48 pp • $14.95 • 978-1-933372-32-7

Fairy Tale Timpa
48 pp • $14.95 • 978-1-933372-38-9

Wolf Erlbruch
The Big Question
48 pp • $14.95 • 978-1-933372-03-7

The Miracle of the Bears
32 pp • $14.95 • 978-1-933372-21-1

(with Gioconda Belli)
The Butterfly Workshop
48 pp • $14.95 • 978-1-933372-12-9